D0953465

FIRESTORM

IRIS

JOHANSEN

FIRESTORM

BANTAM BOOKS

FIRESTORM
A Bantam Book

Published by
Bantam Dell
A Division of Random House, Inc.
New York, New York

This is a work of fiction. Names, characters, places, and incidents either are the product of
the author's imagination or are used fictitiously. Any resemblance to actual persons, living
or dead, events, or locales is entirely coincidental.

Book design by Laurie Jewell

ISBN 0-553-80340-9

Manufactured in the United States of America

FIRESTORM

PROLOGUE

She couldn't breathe!

"Mama!"

"I'm here, baby." Kerry was being gathered in her mother's arms. "I'm going to put this cloth over your nose. Don't fight me."

Mama was coughing and Kerry could barely hear her through the crackling.

Crackling?

Fire! Flames were climbing up the curtains at the window.

"It's okay, Kerry. We'll be out of here in just a few minutes." Mama was moving toward the bedroom door. "Just try not to breathe too deep."

"Daddy!"

"He's not here, remember? But we can make it. We're a team." She opened the door and then took an involuntary step back as black smoke blasted into the room. "Oh, God." She braced herself and then ran into the hall.

Fire everywhere. Crawling up the walls, licking hungrily at the banister going down the steps.

Her mother was crying. Tears running down her soot-stained cheeks as she hurried down the stairs.

Don't cry. Don't cry, Mama.

Her mother had reached the landing when she suddenly lurched and pitched forward.

Falling. Tumbling. Hurting.

Where was Mama?

She couldn't see her in the smoke-filled darkness.

"Mama!"

"Go on, Kerry. The door should be only a few feet away from you. Go outside and find someone to help us."

"No, I won't go." She was sobbing, whimpering. "Where are you?"

"Right behind you. I've hurt my leg a little. But you have to mind me. Run!"

Her voice was so commanding that Kerry instinctively jumped to her feet and ran toward the door.

Fresh cold air.

Find someone. Find someone to help Mama.

She slipped on the icy steps and fell to the sidewalk.

Find someone.

There was a man across the street, standing beneath the streetlight.

She picked herself up and ran toward him. "Help. The fire. Mama . . ."

He was turning and walking away. He must not have heard her.

She ran after him. "Please. Mama said I had to—" He turned and she stared up into his shadowy face only dimly lit by the flickering flames.

She screamed.

"Shh, be quiet. There's nothing you can do." He raised his hand and she saw something glittering, metallic in his grasp. A gun? He brought it down on her head.

The night exploded.

1

This isn't the end of it, Brad." Cameron Devers's lips tightened with irritation. "I've no intention of standing by and watching you waste your potential working with those damn nutcases. You're one of the most brilliant men I know and I have a job for you here."

"Where you can keep an eye on me?" Brad grinned as he leaned lazily back in the chair and stretched his legs out before him. "It wouldn't do you any good. I'm a lost cause."

"Only because you want to be. And it's not good for you. You're burning yourself out. Look at you. You've lost weight since I saw you last."

"A little. I've had a rough four months."

"Then give it up and come to me."

"And do what? If I were anywhere close to you, the media would eventually ferret out our connection. Besides, you can't trust me. I'd get mad and open my mouth at the wrong time and blow your political career." His smile faded. "I've done a hell of a lot of harm to you in these last years, but I won't do that."

"I'd chance it. I've been in the Senate for twelve years and if my reputation can be damaged by just having you around, then maybe it's time I stepped down."

"No!" Brad paused and then tempered his tone. "Look, Cam, don't be an ass. Everything's going fine. We don't need to change anything." He stood up and glanced around the elegant, book-lined library that breathed wealth and solidity. "This isn't my world. You can't squeeze me into your mold because you want me to share the good life." He smiled. "Besides, what would Charlotte say?"

"She'd come around. She just has some weird ideas about you."

Brad looked at him inquiringly.

Cam made a face. "She says you make her uneasy. She thinks you're . . . sinister."

"She used that word? I didn't think anyone could make your wife uneasy. Maybe I'm more intimidating than I thought."

"She doesn't understand you. Like I said, she'll come around."

"There's no reason to force her to make the effort. Things are fine as they are."

Cam was silent a moment. "Did it ever occur to you that I'm being selfish? I've missed you, Brad."

He meant it. Cam was always honest. "Oh, shit. Don't do this to me." Brad shook his head. "I've missed you too. Maybe we can arrange to get together more often."

"That's not good enough. I've been looking at my life since that horror on September eleventh, and when it all comes down to the bottom line, it's friends and family that count. I won't let you walk away again."

"Cam." Charlotte Devers was standing in the doorway, sleek and sophisticated in a black gown. "I didn't want to disturb you, but we're going to be late for the embassy dinner." She smiled at Brad. "You and Cam can talk when we get back."

He shook his head. "I'm just leaving, anyway."

"No, you're not," Cameron said firmly. "I'll only be gone a few hours and I want you here when I get back."

"Perhaps tomorrow?" Charlotte suggested. "I've had a room prepared for you, Brad."

As usual, Charlotte was trying to control the situation with gentle skill, Brad thought. She wanted Cam to leave and she didn't want him to talk to Brad until she could find a discreet way to ease Brad out on his ass. Well, he couldn't blame her. She valued Cam's career more than his brother did and was always on guard to protect it.

"I'm not going anywhere until you make me a promise." Cam stared Brad in the eye. "Will you be here?"

Brad glanced at the faint frown between Charlotte's eyes and then smiled slyly. "You couldn't budge me."

"Great." Cam slapped him on the shoulder before turning away. "Come on, Charlotte. Let's get this thing over with." He strode out of the library.

Charlotte hesitated and started to speak.

"Don't say it," Brad murmured. "We're on the same side." He added, "If you don't piss me off." He followed Cam into the foyer and watched George, the butler, help him into his coat. "Very impressive. I haven't worn a tux in fifteen years. Does that tell you anything?"

"It tells me you're damn lucky." Cam took Charlotte's arm and helped her down the front steps toward the waiting limo. "Make yourself at home, but don't go to bed. You made me a promise."

"Does that mean I can't get drunk on your excellent brandy?"

"No, I want you stone cold sober." He smiled at him over his shoulder. "I have an ace in the hole and need to tell you about a job that may intrigue you enough to lure you here. It's right up your alley."

"Weird and sinister?" he asked, straight-faced.

"I'm going to get my way, Brad."

"Now, don't nag him, Cam," Charlotte said gently. "Brad knows what he wants to do."

"But not what's best for him."

Brad watched them get into the limousine. He'd planned on going back inside, but he couldn't resist standing here and letting Charlotte see him so at home on her front step. Dressed in tennis shoes, worn jeans, and an old sweatshirt, he couldn't have been more of a blot on her fine landscape. His enjoyment was totally immature, but he didn't give a damn. He usually didn't mind Charlotte's attempts at manipulating Cam. She was a good wife to him and that was all that was important to Brad. Tonight she was trying to manipulate Brad as well, and that he couldn't tolerate.

"Would you like me to serve you coffee in the library, sir?" George asked from behind him.

"Why not?" He grinned at him over his shoulder. "Since I've been forbidden the comfort of—"

Whoosh.

"Dear God!" George's eyes were wide with shock.

Brad's head jerked around and followed his gaze to the limo.

"Christ in heaven!"

The interior of the limousine was a sheet of fire. He could see Cam and Charlotte writhing like burning scarecrows in the flames.

"Son of a bitch!"

He flew down the steps toward the car.

———

Kerry carefully touched the blackened timber lying across the bathroom sink. It was still slightly warm from the fire that had destroyed the restaurant two days ago. That wasn't unusual. Sometimes, hidden pockets of embers remained burning for days.

Sam, her Lab, whined and pushed nearer to Kerry. He was easily bored and they'd been here at the burned-out ruins for over an hour.

"Be quiet." She reached beneath the timber and dug. "We'll be out of here soon."

There it was! With an effort she pushed the timber aside.

"Find anything?" Detective Perry asked from behind her. "Bad wiring?"

"No, gasoline," Kerry said. "The fire originated here in the bathroom and spread throughout the restaurant." She nodded at the burned and blackened device she'd found beneath the timber. "And a timing device to set it off."

"Dumb." The police detective shook his head. "I thought Chin Li was brighter than that. If he wanted to collect the insurance, why didn't he set the fire in the kitchen? He'd have had a better shot at convincing everyone the fire was accidental. You're sure?"

"Sam's sure." She reached out and touched the dog's silky black head. "And I usually go along with him. He's not often wrong."

"Yeah, so I've heard." Perry awkwardly patted the dog's nose. "I don't understand how these arson dogs do it, but it makes my job a hell of a lot easier. I guess I'll go talk to Chin Li again. Too bad. He seemed like a nice little guy."

"And not stupid?" Kerry got to her feet and dusted the soot off her palms. "Then maybe someone else set the fire. Someone who didn't have access to the kitchen. Insurance isn't always the right answer. Just the easy one."

His eyes narrowed on her face. "Are you saying that I'm looking for an out?"

She grinned. "I wouldn't presume. I'm just saying that you should ask Chin Li if he had any enemies. Perhaps rivals in business? Or—this is a high-crime area—are there any protection rackets operating that might have decided to make him an example?"

"Possibly," he said slowly. "There are a couple teenage gangs that are stepping up to the plate and trying to control the area."

"Would they know how to set timing devices?"

"Everyone who has Internet has access to practically any information. Want to make an atomic bomb? Go on the Internet."

She'd done all she could. Time to step out of the picture before he got belligerent. "Well, we'll know more once we finish the investigation. Sam and I are just the advance team." She smiled. "And we're finished for now. Have a nice day, Detective."

"Wait." He said awkwardly, "This is a lousy neighborhood. If you'll wait until I finish with Chin Li, I'll give you an escort back to your office."

"That's nice of you, but I'm not going back downtown. It's my day off and I'm going to visit a couple friends at the firehouse on Morningside."

"If it's your day off, why are you here?"

"They needed Sam's nose."

"Then I'll drive you and Sam's nose to this firehouse." He frowned. "Why do they let you go to neighborhoods like this alone, anyway? You're just a little bit of a thing."

She felt a prickle of resentment that she quickly quenched. She was average height, but she knew her slender frame and delicate bones made her appear smaller. He was a nice guy and she was used to having her fragile appearance equated with helplessness. She gave him the answer he was most likely to accept. "I have Sam to protect me."

He gave the Lab a skeptical glance. "He may have a great nose, but he doesn't look very threatening to me."

"It's because he has those crossed eyes. He's really a great guard dog." She waved and carefully picked her way through the rubble toward the door. Sam lunged eagerly forward, almost pulling her from her feet. "Idiot," she grumbled. "Do you want to break both our necks? I'd think you'd learn."

Sam burst out into the street and started barking.

"Oh, God." All she needed was to attract attention in this slum neighborhood. She hurriedly pulled the dog toward her 4Runner. She knew as well as the detective that Sam looked about as dangerous as a cuddly koala. "Why didn't I get a big German shepherd at that pound?"

Because she'd looked at him in that cage and hadn't been able to resist. "Let's go, Sam. And, for Pete's sake, *shut up*."

<hr>

Full house." Kerry grinned as she pulled in the pot from the middle of the table. "That should just about take care of my rent for the month. Another hand?"

"No way." Charlie grimaced as he pushed back his chair. "I'm cleaned out. I'm going to go peel the onions for dinner." He cast a sly look over his shoulder. "Beef stroganoff. Remember? Firehouse Number Ten specialty of the house."

"I'm drooling. May I stay?"

"Hell, no. Go back to your snooty office downtown and eat in that fancy cafeteria."

"Cruel." She looked at Jimmy Swartz and Paul Corbin. "Another hand, guys?"

"Not me." Jimmy stood up. "I've got to have enough money to make sure my wife lets me in the house when my shift is over. Come on, Paul. Let's play a game of pool." He gave Kerry a stern glance. "And, no, you can't play with us. This is for real firemen, not desk jockeys like you."

"You're just scared I'll beat you." She got up and followed Charlie to the kitchen. "You're trying to torture me. You know I love your stroganoff. Come on, let me stay."

"Maybe." Charlie handed her a bag of onions and a knife. "If you do the onions."

She beamed. "I'll chop." She sat down on a stool at the counter. "How's your wife, Charlie?"

"Putting up with me." He grinned. "That's all you can ask after twenty-five years." He put dredged pieces of beef in the hot pan. "Edna told me to give you hell about asking her to take care of Sam while you were on vacation. She and the kids are in love with the mutt. Though how she can like a dumb dog like that Lab of yours is beyond me."

"Everyone loves Sam. Not every dog is an Einstein." She picked up another onion. "And you like him too. He's very lovable."

"But everyone *thinks* he's Einstein." Charlie shook his head in amazement as he glanced at Sam snoozing in the corner of the kitchen. "How he can be so smart on a job in the field and so dumb in every other aspect of life boggles the mind."

"He has a good nose. He has a good heart. You can't expect him to have a good brain too."

"All I can say is that it's good you're the other half of this arson investigating team or Sam would be chasing butterflies in the ashes."

She couldn't deny it so she changed the subject. "I'm going to drive down to Macon to visit my brother, Jason, this weekend. Do you suppose Edna would be willing to take Sam again? You know how carsick he gets."

He nodded. "He threw up all over my new Suburban. And the kids blamed me for yelling at him." He shrugged. "Sure, drop him over. He's no trouble. All he does is sleep and eat and chew on everything in sight. Including my best pair of golf shoes."

"I paid for them." She smiled. "Thanks, Charlie. Jason's wife, Laura, is pregnant, and I really wanted to go down and see her before the baby is born. She won't have time for me then."

"I imagine she'd make time. You're not too bad to have around."

"Thanks . . . I think."

"And I know how boring those last months of pregnancy can be. Edna nearly drove me crazy when she was carrying Kim. Of course, she was over forty and had a right to be a little crabby."

"Laura's thirty-eight, and she's too happy she finally got pregnant to be bad-tempered. But she's definitely nesting." She smiled. "Besides, Edna wasn't really crabby. She was . . . temperamental."

"You didn't have to live with her." He chuckled. "Believe me, she was crabby. Edna's not used to having to sit around with her feet up."

"Well, Laura is definitely not sitting around. Jason said she was building a gazebo in the backyard. So it's okay?"

"Of course it's okay." His smile faded. "You need to get out and see people. What the hell are you doing spending your day off back here at Number Ten playing cards with a bunch of guys?"

"I like playing cards, and I couldn't be happier with anyone than I am with you. Even though you are all sore losers." She put the onions in the pan with the melted butter to sauté and started cleaning the mushrooms. "And you'd all become stodgy and boring if I didn't keep you on your toes."

"Well, you certainly do that." He glanced down at the beef. "But you need to put on a pretty dress and go out and whoop it up. Haven't you got any friends, dammit?"

"I have a few college pals I see now and then, but I'm too busy to keep in touch. Besides, I like being with you guys. I don't need anyone else." She shook her head. "Stop frowning. It's the truth. I'm lucky. It's not as if I sit around my house and brood. I go to plays and baseball games and movies. Hell, you and Edna went to a movie with me last week. People who like their jobs tend to socialize with coworkers. What's different about me?"

"You ought to have someone to take care of you."

"Chauvinist."

"I am not. Everyone should have someone. Edna takes care of me. I take care of her. We both take care of the kids. It's the way life should be."

She smiled. "You bet it should. But sometimes life doesn't cooperate. After Aunt Marguerite died I found out I was something of a loner. Not that I wasn't before. She did her best, but she wasn't the warmest person in the world. The closest I've ever really come to a real family was when I was here at Number Ten." She made a face at him. "So stop trying to kick me out."

"Well, if you feel that way, do something about it. We miss you. I think you miss us. Why the devil don't you give up that job and come back to where you belong? You had the makings of a great firefighter, Kerry."

"That's not what you said on that first day I came here."

"I had a right to be skeptical. How was I to know you weren't some women's lib fanatic who might get one of us killed to prove a point? You didn't look like you could carry a miniature poodle out of a burning building."

"And you found out that I'm stronger than I look. It's all in knowing the technique. I knew I had to pull my weight and I did it."

"Yes, you did. That's why I'm telling you to come back where you belong."

"I'm better off where I am."

He sighed. "With that dumb dog. I hear the department wouldn't even accept him until he found evidence in the Wadsworth fire."

"They didn't understand his potential. I got him from the pound and he had problems adjusting to discipline."

"Butterflies."

She nodded. "He gets distracted." She reached for another mushroom. "But I can focus him on the—"

The alarm bell was blaring.

"Duty calls." Charlie turned off the burner and strode out of the kitchen. "See you, Kerry."

She followed him out of the kitchen and watched them hurry into their gear. "I'll finish the stroganoff. It'll be ready when you get back."

"The hell you will," Paul said. "I remember your cooking. We'll wait for Charlie."

"You're not so good yourself," Kerry said. "Okay, I'll let you starve. Sam and I were going to go to the children's ward at Grady's later, but I might as well go now. I can't do—" She was talking to air. The guys had left the room, and a moment later she heard the fire truck roaring out of the station and down the street.

Jesus, the room felt empty.

And, Jesus, she wished she were on that fire truck with them, every nerve and muscle alive and geared to the job ahead.

Stop wishing for something that was out of reach. She'd made her decision and it was a good one. She'd have ended up a basket case if she hadn't distanced herself after Smitty died. She was still too close, but she could survive.

"Come on, Sam," she called into the kitchen. "Let's go visit the kids."

Sam didn't come.

She went back into the kitchen and found him with his nose under the cabinet trying to scrounge a piece of beef Charlie had dropped on the floor.

"Sam."

He looked up with his head pressed sidewise on the floor. He looked perfectly ridiculous.

She shook her head as she chuckled. "A little dignity, please. Come on, let's go."

He didn't move.

She got a piece of meat from the frying pan and tossed it to him. He lunged upward and caught it. Then he trotted toward her with a doggy smile on his face.

She stooped and leashed him.

"I thought you weren't supposed to give arson dogs treats anytime except when they came up with a scent."

She glanced up warily to see Dave Bellings, the tech repairman, standing in the doorway. He'd been a fireman before he injured his leg and was forced to take disability. Now he was a skilled computer technician focusing on the equipment here and at other firehouses in the county. "You're not supposed to give them extra treats. But Sam's different." And she'd almost been busted. She was lucky it had only been Dave. "It works for him."

"You can't argue with success." Dave patted Sam's black silky head as he went past him to the coffee dispenser. "He deserves a little pampering."

"Where's the fire?"

"Standard Tire warehouse on the south side. Three-alarm."

Smoke. Black, curling smoke.

"Shit."

He nodded. "It's going to be a bad one. I guess we're lucky we're out of it, Kerry."

"Yeah. I guess so."

Overpowering heat. The stench of burning rubber.

Bellings grimaced. "Who are we kidding? We'd both be on that truck if we could. We're junkies. Why else would we hang around here as much as they let us?"

"You're right." She tried to smile. She had to get out of here. "Bye, Dave. See you."

He tilted his head. "You okay? You look a little pale."

"It must be the light in here. I'm fine." She quickly led Sam from the room and out of the firehouse. Brace yourself. It might not come. But she had that damn prickling in the back of her neck. She had gone only a few yards down the street when the blinding pain knifed through her head.

Black smoke curling over the stacked tires. The smell of burning rubber. Sirens.

Her stomach was twisting and she couldn't breathe.

It was going to be all right. She closed her eyes. Just inhale slowly and rhythmically.

Sam whined.

It was better now. The pain in her head was fading to a dull throb. She opened her eyes to see the dog staring up at her with that endearing cross-eyed soberness. "Stop worrying," she murmured. "Just a bad moment."

The hospital. She'd been on her way to the hospital to visit the kids. It was only a few blocks away and she didn't dare drive right now. She turned left and started up the street. "It's going to be okay."

God, she hoped it was going to be okay.

Fire.

Brad Silver's hands tightened on the wheel of his car as he fought to keep the image away.

He couldn't breathe.

He pulled over to the side of the road and switched off the ignition. Ride it out. It was usually over quickly.

Christ, the *smell*.

Then it was gone and he leaned his head on the steering wheel, gasping for breath.

He reached blindly for his phone and dialed. "Dammit, Travis. I almost wrecked the car. Get me *out* of this."

"Easy, Brad." Michael Travis's tone was soothing. "She must be having a bad time. Is it still going on?"

"No, but it may come back. It has before. Why the hell isn't she more controlled?"

"Denial. How close are you to her?"

"A mile or two. She's on her way to some hospital."

"Maybe that's it. Perhaps someone's been hurt."

"No, it's her usual weekly visit to the pediatrics ward. She's not upset. Or she wasn't before this episode. Can you do anything to quiet her down?"

"No, I told you she was a wild card. And dirt stubborn. If she calls and asks for help, I might have a chance. Otherwise, you're on your own."

"Thanks a lot," Silver said sarcastically. "You're the one who told me how much help she was going to be to me. You just neglected to tell me that she might kill me before we were through with each other."

"You knew how she could rock you."

"The hell I did. I've never been this close to her before."

"You can always back out and we'll try to find someone else."

Silver thought about it. It was tempting. Kerry Murphy was a powder keg set to go off. He liked to be in control, and these last few minutes had proved he'd have the devil of a time keeping her in check enough to manipulate her.

"Brad?"

"I've devoted too much time to her to walk away. I know her inside and out."

"Yes, you do. Probably better than she knows herself."

"I'll handle her."

"No force. I know what you're capable of. I don't want her damaged."

"I said, I'll handle her. You just stand by in case I need a backup." He added grimly, "Or an ambulance." He hung up and took a deep breath before pulling out into the traffic again. Only a couple more miles on this freeway. If he concentrated, he could keep his guard up long enough to get to her. After that, he'd play it by ear. He didn't want Kerry damaged either, and he could usually trust his knowledge and experience to overcome his own violent impulses. He'd learned long ago that finesse was better than force. He just hoped this looming battle wouldn't prove the exception.

Or neither one of them would survive.

———

Orange juice?" Melody Vanetti smiled down at Kerry sitting cross-legged on the floor of the hospital lounge. "You've been reading to the kids for the past hour. You must be a little dry."

"Thanks, Melody." She took the orange juice from the nurse. "I seem to be forgotten for the moment. Sam's on center stage." She grinned. "Not that I'm surprised. I don't know any child in the world who'd prefer a grown-up to a dog."

"You're great with the kids." Melody tilted her head. "But you look a little tired today."

"Nah," Kerry said. "I'm good. Even if I wasn't, I wouldn't dare complain. These guys would make me feel ashamed." Her smile faded. "Who's the new kid? The one with his arm around Sam."

"Josh. Came in with burns on his arms. We're stalling until DFACS can make sure they weren't inflicted by his grandmother."

"Sweet." The kid looked to be only four or five and he was hugging Sam, his face buried in his throat. She felt a wrenching pang as she saw the bruises on his face. But he was smiling now, and that was no surprise. Kerry had found that kids responded to Sam no matter how damaged they were. "If I can help, let me know."

"What could you do?"

Kerry shrugged. "Find someone to declare the grandmother's house a fire hazard so she wouldn't have a residence to bring the kid back to? I don't know. Just do me a favor and let me know."

"Sure. It's nice of you to care." She started for the door. "I have meds to give. I'll come back and check on you later."

"We'll be okay. And the kids aren't going to get into any mischief as long as they have Sam to play with." She checked her watch. Everything must be all right at the tire company. She'd been here over an hour and she'd been fine. A dull throbbing headache, but that wasn't unusual. It was a big fire, a dangerous fire. Naturally, she'd be nervous and afraid of—

Backdraft.

An oak door on the third floor.

Smoke. He can't see.

Who couldn't see?

Two men climbing the stairs toward the door.

The burning stairs were crashing behind them.

Go back. Go back, Charlie.

It was Charlie. Oh, God, she'd known it would be Charlie.

They'd reached the third floor.

Don't open the door, Charlie.

Backdraft. Backdraft.

He opened the door.

That deadly whoosh.

Fire. Everywhere. Hurt. He was hurting.

"Kerry." Melody was looking down at her with concern. "Are you okay?"

No. Hurting. Hurting.

She leaped to her feet. "Sick. I have to get to the bathroom." She ran out of the lounge and down the hall.

Hurting. Hurting.

Find a place to hide. Somewhere dark where no one could find her.

Closet.

She opened the door and slammed it behind her. Alone. The closet was dim and small and she'd be safe here. But what about Charlie?

Dear God, she could smell smoke and burning flesh. She sank to her knees and scuttled back against the wall.

Hurting. Hurting. Hurting.

2

For God's sake, shut it out."

Someone was standing silhouetted in the open doorway, she realized dimly. A man. A tall man. A doctor? It didn't matter.

Hurting. Hurting. Hurting.

The door slammed behind the man and he was kneeling beside her. "Listen to me. You've got to shut it out."

"Charlie."

"I know." He took her hands. "But you can't help him by hurting like this."

"He's in pain—backdraft. Down . . . down . . ."

"And you can't shut it out." He drew a deep breath. "But I can. Don't be scared. I'm coming in."

What was he talking about?

"Look at me." His dark eyes were holding her own. "It's going to go away now."

It wouldn't go away. The smoke and the fire were going to go on forever. Charlie . . .

They're coming up the stairs to get you, Charlie.

Too late.

Hurting. Hurt—

The pain was gone. Charlie was gone. No smoke. No fire.

A blue lake. Sunlight. Green grass.

Peace.

"Come on." He was standing, pulling her to her feet. "We have to get out of here. I don't how long I can hold it back."

Two deer were coming to drink at the lake. A soft breeze was blowing the tall grass.

"Come on." He opened the door and pulled her out into the corridor. "We're going to go get Sam and then you're going home."

"Charlie . . ."

"He's not here at the lake now. We'll go back to him later." He was pulling her down the corridor toward the lounge. "I'll explain everything and get us out of here. But when we enter the room, you have to smile at the kids. You don't want them to worry."

No, children shouldn't worry. Their world should always be full of sunlight. How they'd love to be away from the city by this beautiful lake.

And suddenly they were there. She could see the little boy, Josh, laughing as he ran through the grass.

"Are you all right?" It was Melody Vanetti, gazing worriedly at her. "I went to the rest room to check on you, but you weren't there."

"She's a little under the weather," the man holding her arm said. "I ran into her in the hall and took her out to get a little fresh air." He smiled and held out his hand. "You're Nurse Vanetti? She's told me how good you are with the kids. I'm Brad Silver. I work with Kerry."

Melody shook his hand, but she was still frowning as she gazed at Kerry. "Do you think she should see one of the doctors?"

"That's what I suggested, but she just wants to go home. Isn't that right, Kerry?"

Home was the lake. Home was the children playing in the meadow.

"Kerry?"

She nodded. "I want to go home."

"Then I'll just go get Sam." Silver moved across the room toward the children. He squatted beside Josh.

But how could that be when she could see Josh running by the lake? Silver must be talking to some other little boy.

"I have to take your buddy away now," he said gently to the little boy who looked like Josh. "But I promise you'll see him again." He touched the little boy on the shoulder. "Everything's going to be all right." He smiled at the other children as he led Sam toward Kerry. "Kerry will see you next week. She has to leave now." He nodded at Melody. "Thanks for everything. I'll let you know how she's doing once I get her home."

Then he was nudging Kerry out of the lounge and down the hall.

The sky over the lake was getting cloudy. Or was that smoke in the distance?

No smoke. The answer came immediately and firmly.

Sunlight. Children playing. Blue delphiniums growing straight and proud on the hillside. How she loved delphiniums....

They were out of the elevator and he was leading her toward the parking lot. "Only a little longer, Kerry." He opened the door of a black Lexus. "Jump in, Sam." Sam jumped into the car and immediately settled down on the seat. He opened the passenger door for Kerry. "I'll have you home in no time."

He was smiling as he helped her into a boat at the dock on the lake. Then he was rowing, his oar lifting and falling in the glittering blue water.

He pulled into her driveway and stopped the car. He reached for her purse. "I need your keys." He pulled them out, opened the rear door for Sam, and strode up the steps to the front porch.

They had drifted under the overhanging branches of a weeping willow and she could see the reflection of the lacy fronds in the water. He was smiling at her. Warmth. Safety. Joy. "Kerry." He was holding out his hand to help her from the boat. "Come with me."

Where? It didn't matter. She knew wherever he led her would be beautiful. She took his hand.

They were going up the front stairs. Sam was tearing around the porch and Silver let him into the house before he pushed her gently into the foyer. He followed her into the house and closed the door.

He leaned back against it and drew a deep breath. "Thank God."

Clouds again over the lake, she noticed uneasily. She didn't like it. . . .

"Not clouds. Smoke," Silver said. "I can't keep it away from you any longer. It's smoke and it's getting thicker. But it's not going to hurt you anymore. That part's over, Kerry. I'm getting out. I'll try to do it slow and easy, but it's going to be a wrench."

Smoke was swirling about her like fog, obscuring the lake and the willow and the children. And beyond the smoke . . .

Fire.

Charlie!

She screamed.

———

E asy." Silver grasped her shoulders. "You knew it was coming. Accept it."

"He's dead. Charlie's dead."

He nodded. "He died about five minutes ago."

She closed her eyes as she tried to absorb the shock and sorrow. "How do you know that?" Her eyes flicked open and she tore away from him. "And what the hell are you doing in my house?"

"Trying to keep you from blowing your cover. And don't give me any grief." He added roughly, "I'm too pissed to feel sympathetic at the moment. Do you think this was easy for me? I suppose I could have left you in that closet until someone found you. But by that time you'd have probably had to be treated at the local funny farm."

"Get out of here. I don't know who you are and I don't care." She moved toward the telephone. "I have to call the station."

"To find out what you already know? Charlie's dead. The other man on the staircase is on his way to Grady Hospital. He'll probably live." He paused. "And you suspect who I am. Or at least what I am."

"Go away. Maybe Charlie's not dead. It doesn't have to be true." She dialed the station number and Dave picked up. "Dave, I heard there was trouble at—"

"Oh, God, Kerry." His voice was cracking. "Charlie. What a hell of a—I knew him for thirty years. He was thinking about retiring in the spring. Why did it have to happen to—"

She hung up. She couldn't take any more. She leaned her head against the wall, the tears flowing down her cheeks.

"I'll give Sam some water and make a pot of coffee," Silver said quietly. "Come when you're ready. Kitchen's down the hall, right?" He didn't wait for her answer.

She moved into the living room and dropped down on the couch. She should call Edna and see if she wanted her to come over. No, not now. She didn't even know if she'd been notified yet. Kerry dropped her head on the arm of the couch and didn't try to stop the tears from coming. Charlie deserved tears. . . .

She could hear Silver in the kitchen saying something to Sam. This stranger was clearly making himself at home, and yet she felt no sense of threat. Maybe she was too stunned to feel fear.

Or maybe he was making sure she wasn't afraid. That thought was terrifying in itself.

She wouldn't think about it. She was too upset to deal with anything right now. She'd give herself a little time to regain her composure before she had to go and face him. She'd close her eyes for just a moment and escape from all the pain and sorrow. . . .

She was sleeping.

Silver stood in the doorway and looked down at her, curled on the couch. He knew it was a sleep that wouldn't last long. She'd been exposed to too much and had to recoup from the overload. He'd seen it many times before.

She looked almost childlike with her tousled, short, chestnut hair and smooth, satiny complexion. But she wasn't a child. She was tough and stubborn and was going to give him a hell of a bad time.

So stop feeling sorry for her. He'd try to give her something in return, but there was no doubt he was going to use Kerry Murphy.

There was too much in the balance for him to walk away now.

It was over an hour before Kerry woke and another fifteen minutes before she felt steady enough to leave the shelter of the living room and go to the kitchen to face Silver. If that was his name. How could she be sure anything he told her was true? He'd exploded into her life when she was at her most vulnerable and he was still only a shadow figure to her.

She stopped in the doorway. He was sitting at the kitchen table, talking on the phone, and he didn't look in the least shadow-like. He had dark hair and dark eyes, was somewhere in his mid-thirties, and powerfully built. Yes, *power* was the key word to describe him. He exuded authority and confidence. The impression was so dominant that it made no difference that he was dressed in faded jeans and sweatshirt and that his features were less than handsome. Particularly now that he was frowning at something that he was hearing on the phone. He glanced up and saw her and said quickly, "I'll call you back, Gillen." He hung up and rose to his feet. "Sit down. I'll get you a cup of coffee."

"I'll get it myself." She moved toward the cabinet. "After all, it *is* my house."

He shrugged. "Suit yourself." He sat back down. "Just trying to be accommodating. I promised I'd be nice to you." He scowled. "It's been damn hard."

She stared at him in disbelief. "I couldn't care less whether you're nice to me or not. I don't know you and I don't want to know you. I lost a good friend today and I just want you to get out of here and leave me alone."

"Can't do it." He sipped his coffee. "I need you. Believe me, if I thought I could get the same kind of help somewhere else, I'd be out of here. I've had a hard week and you've made it tougher. Sit down and we'll talk."

"I don't want to talk." She poured her coffee and had to steady her hand before she picked up the cup. "I was pretty much out of it, but I believe you were kind to me earlier today. But that doesn't mean you can barge into my life. If you don't get out, I'll have to call the police."

"You don't want to call in the cops. Any questions they ask me may have awkward consequences for you." He added, "And you're not going to get rid of me until you sit down and listen."

She hesitated, staring at him. She was tempted to tell him to go to hell, but there was something she had to know, something that was filling her with fear. She slowly moved across the room and sat down at the table. But she found she couldn't ask that question yet. Instead, she asked, "How did you know I was in that closet?"

"You were sending out a distress call that was nearly blowing my mind." He studied her expression. "You're afraid of me."

"I'm not afraid."

"Not that I'm going to mug you or rape you. You're afraid I'm going to intrude." He shook his head. "No way. It hurts too damn much."

"I don't know what you're talking about."

"The hell you don't." He shook his head wearily. "I was told you were stubborn and preferred to turn a blind eye. I meant to be patient and kind and all that crap, but you blew me out of the water. You must have really liked this Charlie—"

"Of course I liked him. He was a great guy."

"But not too perceptive. He liked you, but he never realized how you were using Sam."

She stiffened. "Sam?"

He sighed. "Okay, let's jump over this hurdle and get things out in the open. Sam's a nice pup, but as an arson dog he's a complete washout. He couldn't sniff out a beefsteak in a butcher shop."

"You're crazy. Everyone knows he's the best arson dog in the Southeast."

"Because that's what you wanted everyone to believe. You didn't want anyone to know the truth." He paused. "You didn't want them to know that the only way you knew where and how the fires were being set was that you saw it being done."

"You're nuts. Do you think I'm some kind of pyromaniac?"

"No, I think you have a special psychic talent triggered by fire.

If you come anywhere near the area a fire was set, you receive vibes; sometimes you actually see it being done. In cases where you have a relationship with the people involved in the fire, you don't have to be close." He was silent a moment. "Like with your friend Charlie. You connected and couldn't get away."

Smoke. The door on the third floor. Backdraft.

"Steady," he said quietly. "It's over now."

She drew a deep breath. "You seem to think you know a good deal about me. Who are you? Some kind of reporter?"

"No, and I have no desire to let everyone know how you're using Sam. That's your business."

"That's good." She tried to smile. "Because it's all ridiculous. No one would ever believe that hocus-pocus."

"I agree. It's a nitty-gritty world with no room for fantasy. I can understand perfectly why you needed to protect yourself. You wanted to make sure the bad guys got what was coming to them, but you knew you'd be laughed out of your job if you didn't have a way to validate what you were seeing." He reached down and patted the Lab's head. "Enter super arson dog Sam. But you could have picked one who had a little more credibility."

"I don't need your understanding. And Sam's just fine." She moistened her lips and looked down into her coffee. "And if you're through making outrageous guesses, maybe you'd like to tell me why you're here."

"I have a job for you."

"What kind of job?"

He studied her for a moment. "You're not ready yet. You'd turn me down." He stood up, reached in his pocket, and threw down his rental-car keys. "Use my Lexus if you need it. I'll arrange to have your SUV towed from the fire station back here. I'll be in touch."

She glared at him. "Don't you dare walk out of here. I want answers."

He smiled faintly. "There's only one answer you really want right now. It's to that question you've been afraid to ask me." His voice lowered to a murmur. "The lake. It was pretty, wasn't it? I worked very hard to make it beautiful for you. And, no, you aren't going bonkers." He threw a card on the table and headed for the door. "That's my cell number. Call me if you need me."

"Wait. Dammit, who sent you?"

He glanced over his shoulder. "Michael Travis." A moment later she heard the door close behind him.

She felt as if she'd been kicked in the stomach. She'd last seen Michael five years ago and she'd sworn she'd never see him again. She'd thought he was out of her life.

Stop panicking. She slammed the door on Michael all those years ago and she could slam it again.

But could she slam it on Brad Silver? She had an idea he was completely different from Michael. Less patient, more ruthless, more direct.

How did she know that about him? she wondered suddenly. He was a stranger.

Oh, God, the lake.

Or it could be just her own judgment of his character. This connection she felt with him didn't have to be anything bizarre.

Yes, it did. *He* was bizarre. If he'd managed to do what she thought he'd done, then he was even more of a freak than she was.

But she wasn't a freak. She'd learned to deal with her problem. And she could still do it. Nothing was changed. She could send Silver on his way and get her life back in order. But first she had to make sure he stayed away from her, and that meant getting Travis to call him off.

She drew a deep breath, reached for her phone, and quickly punched in the number she'd not dialed for over five years.

"What the hell are you doing, Michael?" she asked when Travis answered the phone.

"Kerry?"

"You know damn well it's me. I told you to stay out of my life, and that included turning loose any of your sycophants to make my life miserable."

"I suppose you're talking about Brad Silver? If you knew him better, you'd realize there's no way he's anyone's sycophant. Silver is a law unto himself."

"You sent him. You told him about me."

"Yes. I thought long and hard before I did it, but I decided that it was necessary. He needs you."

"Bullshit. Call him off, Michael. I don't want him anywhere near me."

"That may be difficult." He paused. "You're very upset. What did he do?"

"He's . . . weird."

"But he's not stupid. He wouldn't have tipped his hand if he hadn't had to do it. Did something happen?"

"I'm not talking to you any longer." She tried to keep her voice steady. "Just tell Silver to stay away from me."

"What did he do?"

Blue lake, delphiniums, a child running.

"I think you know what he did. He's like you and Melissa and all those other people you told me about." She bit hard on her lower lip. "No, he's not like them. He's . . . different."

"Yes, he is. He's a controller."

"Controller?" Anger seared through her. "I don't know what the hell you're talking about. Is this one of your stupid mind games? I won't have it, Michael." Panic followed rage and she whispered, "My God, I didn't even know there were people like him."

"Shh, I'm sure he never intended to—"

"I don't want to hear it."

"He frightened you." Michael sighed. "If you'd let me explain, you'd see that he's not as bad as you think."

"He's worse. He's a nightmare. Get him out of my life." She hung up the phone.

Controller. Just the word struck at her sense of independence and individuality. Well, now that she was on guard there would be no chance of a repeat performance if he came on the scene again. Her will was strong enough to make certain that Silver—

Stop thinking about him. She had more important things to worry about than Silver or Michael or any of their wacky friends. She had a life. Get busy. Don't think about him. She dialed Edna's number. It rang six times before she picked up the receiver. "Edna, this is Kerry. If you don't want to talk, just tell me to hang up. But I thought I'd bring Sam over and take care of the kids for you."

"He's dead, Kerry." Edna's voice was numb. "I can't seem to take it in."

"Do you want me to come, Edna?"

"I think so. I haven't told the kids yet. I have to find a way, but what can I say?"

"We'll work it out together. Maybe I could do it."

"No, it's my job. How can I tell them he's not coming home, Kerry? It's not right. He was such a good man."

"I'm on my way." She hung up and got to her feet. It was going to be a hell of a night, but at least she could try to do something to help. She started to fill up Sam's dog-food bowl. There was no telling when she'd be able to feed him if she didn't do it now. "Eat your dinner. You've got a job to do. Charlie's kids are going to need you."

Kerry Murphy was coming out of the house, trying to keep the unruly black Lab from jerking her down the porch steps. It was the first time Trask had gotten a good look at her. He'd been too far across the hospital parking lot when Silver had taken her to his car, and he had to be careful of the bastard. She was slender, like Helen. But Helen had been brunette, with wonderful dark eyes. This woman had blue eyes and chestnut hair that gleamed deep red under the porch light.

Fire red.

His hands tightened on the steering wheel.

She was getting into Silver's Lexus with the dog. Time was running out. He had to make a decision. Should he kill her now?

She must be of value to Silver if he'd come all this way to see her. He might not be right, but it could be best to remove a weapon before it could be used against him.

No, he knew nothing about Kerry Murphy yet except her name, which he'd gotten from the mailbox. It might not be necessary to waste his time on her. He had to get back to Washington and prepare for the next target. Then he could come back and investigate her more thoroughly. And if she became involved with Silver, then he would take care of her death in the usual manner.

Until then he'd wait and watch.

Michael Travis called Silver when he was on his way to check into a hotel. "Kerry just called me yelling to high heaven. I gather you made contact."

"Oh, yes. For all the good it did me."

"What did you do to her?"

"For God's sake, I didn't damage her. What would be the point? I need her."

"You could do it accidentally. You're not patient, and you're walking on the edge right now."

"If you're so worried, why didn't you come with me and give her some tender loving care?"

"Because she told me to stay out of her life."

"That's about what she told me." Silver pulled into the Marriott parking lot. "She lost a good friend in a fire today."

"Shit."

"That's my reaction. I had to escalate my move and now I have to step back and give her breathing room."

"The President called this afternoon. He wants me to call him back with a report. He wants answers."

"No more than I do. You can't have it both ways. If I push her, I risk damage." He paused. "But I'm damn curious about why President Andreas is risking our involvement. If the media found out, they'd tear into him. He's too squeaky clean for them."

"He considers the situation critical."

"And he thinks we can help. Why should he believe that? Does he have a reason to think we'd be effective?"

"Are you going back to Washington?"

It was clear Travis wasn't going to answer any questions about Andreas. He was a secretive bastard and never betrayed a confidence. Well, Silver had no right to complain. Travis had kept plenty of his secrets during the past years. "No, I'm sticking around here until I can find a way to bring her into my camp. She's going to be busy for the next few days comforting the bereaved widow. All I can do is keep an eye on her." He paused. "God, she's powerful, Michael."

"I told you that she was on her way five years ago. And instead of smothering her talent, she's been using it. Not to any great degree, but she must have honed it."

"She can find Trask. Dammit, I *know* she can find him."

"If he doesn't kill her."

"I stand corrected. If he doesn't kill her."

"I'll be very displeased if you let that happen, Silver. I would never have let you have Kerry if you hadn't made me a promise."

"I'll keep it," he said curtly. "Get off my back. I'll call you and keep you posted. If you hear anything valuable from Andreas, let me know." He hung up.

He couldn't blame Michael for doubting him. No one knew better the recklessness of the explosive anger that was driving him. Hell, sometimes he doubted himself. Would he let Kerry Murphy die if it meant getting Trask?

Jesus, he didn't know.

———

Her brother, Jason, called Kerry as she was leaving Charlie's house to go to the funeral. "How's Edna?"

"As good as she can be. Her sister, Donna, arrived last night from Detroit and that's a help. They're pretty close."

"And how are you?"

"Sad." She stiffened. "What do you expect?"

"Don't get uptight. I'm just concerned."

"I'm fine. Just fine. You keep expecting me to go off the tracks again. It's not going to happen."

"I know that. But I think you need a few days' R and R." She heard someone talking in the background and then Jason laughed. "Laura doesn't agree with me. She thinks you should come down and help her finish the gazebo like you promised. She needs you to paint. The fumes make her sick."

"Tell her I'll drive down tomorrow. Now that Donna is here Edna won't need me. Family is always better."

"I agree." He paused. "Dad stopped by last week on his way to Florida. He asked about you."

"Did he?" She changed the subject. "I have to go. Edna is waiting. I'll see you tomorrow, Jason."

"He's your father too, Kerry. You can't blame him forever."

"I don't blame him. I just don't want to see him. Tell Laura not to touch that paintbrush. Together we'll get that gazebo in shape." She hung up and drew a deep breath. Jason never let an opportunity go by to attempt to bring her father and her together. He didn't understand. She had told him the truth: She didn't blame her father, but contact brought back the pain and disturbed the balance that she'd fought so hard to establish. She couldn't permit that to happen.

"Can we take Sam, Kerry?"

She turned to see Gary, Charlie's ten-year-old son, coming down the stairs. He was dressed in a blue suit and tie and his face looked pinched and pale. Poor kid. He had held on tight to his composure after the first night of tears, but this was going to be a rough day for him.

A rough day for all of them.

"I don't think they like dogs to go to funerals, Gary," she said gently. "And Sam isn't always well behaved."

"Dad wouldn't care." Gary swallowed hard. "He liked Sam. He used to complain, but Sam made him laugh. I think Kim would like to have him there. She's only six and she's kind of—Sam sort of makes it easier for her."

And it made things easier for Gary too. Touching a warm and loving animal was always a comfort to children. "I'll ask your mother if I can drive back here and pick him up when we leave the chapel for the cemetery. But you and Kim will have to make sure he doesn't cause a disturbance. Do you promise?"

Gary nodded. "He'll be good. He's smart. He'll know that Dad is—" His eyes filled with tears and he hurried past her out the front door. "Kim will be glad that Sam is coming. She's only a kid. . . ."

Kerry's eyes were also stinging as she followed him out onto the porch. Gary was only a kid too. Two great kids who had lost their father and would have to grow up without the warm, tough man who had been Charlie—

Forget the future. Right now it was her job to help get Edna and the kids through this nightmare of a day.

Good-bye, Charlie.

Kerry tossed the rose she'd been given on top of the casket and stepped back.

Little Kim and Gary were clutching their mother's hands, tears running down their faces as they placed their roses on the coffin. Kim reached down and clutched the fur on Sam's neck. Thank God, the dog was behaving himself, Kerry thought. She was glad the burial was almost over. She couldn't have taken much more without breaking down. She tore her gaze from the coffin. Don't look at it. Think of Charlie the way she had known him. It was better to—

She stiffened.

There was someone standing in the shadow of the giant oak a good distance from the grave site. He was half behind the tree and his attitude was . . . surreptitious.

Imagination. Everyone had loved Charlie and he had no secrets. Why would someone think it necessary to hide behind a tree to keep anyone from knowing he was watching Charlie's interment? Yet she was sure that—

He was gone. First he was there and then he had slipped away into the shrubbery.

"Can I ride back to the house with you and Sam?" Gary was standing beside her.

She nodded. "If your mother doesn't mind."

"I already asked her." Gary slipped his hand into hers. "She and Aunt Donna have enough to do taking care of Kim. She won't miss me."

"She will miss you. She needs both you and Kim. You have to take care of one another now."

He nodded. "I'll take care of her." His hand tightened on Kerry's. "I'll do everything my daddy would want me to do. But not today. Okay?"

She nodded slowly. She had been as guilty as Edna for not being aware of Gary's needs. He had to come to terms with his own grief, and the overpowering sympathy with which he'd been surrounded was keeping him from doing it. "Plenty of time. No one's hurrying you. Go get Sam and we'll get out of here."

She watched him hurry back to his mother before shifting her gaze back to the oak tree.

No one.

Why was it bothering her? There didn't have to be a reasonable explanation. It could be someone who worked for the cemetery, who didn't wish to intrude. Or it could be some sicko who hung out at graveyards to get some kind of macabre thrill.

Silver.

It was possible. She hadn't gotten a clear look at the man. She'd only had an impression of height and tension and a glimpse of a navy windbreaker and baseball cap.

But she couldn't imagine Silver skulking behind a tree. He was too impatient, too bold. But what the hell? Everything connected to Silver was guesswork, and she'd deliberately blocked all thought of him since he'd left her house three days ago.

But that hadn't stopped him from being the first man who sprang to mind when she had that moment of uneasiness.

Because there was no one who made her more uneasy than Brad Silver.

"Let's go, Kerry." Gary was back, leading Sam. "Everybody's

leaving." He glanced at the grave and whispered, "But we're not really leaving him, are we? Mom says he'll always be with us."

"Mom's right." She took his hand and started down the path. "As long as we keep the memory alive. Did I ever tell you about the first day I met your dad? He was mad as the devil because I'd been sent to replace one of his buddies, who'd been transferred to—"

3

Stay away from here." Kerry frowned sternly over her shoulder at Laura. "You brought me here to paint this blasted gazebo because the fumes made you sick. Now I can't keep you away from it."

Laura handed her a glass of lemonade. "I just thought you might be thirsty." She stared critically at the wood banister Kerry was painting. "And to tell you I think you should—"

"Laura."

"Okay. Sorry," Laura said guiltily. "Jason told me not to harass you. But I didn't think a few words of advice were harassing. After all, you're a sensible woman who—"

"Likes to do things my own way." Kerry smiled. "Get back to the house before you throw up. Now, that I'd consider true harassment."

"I'm fine." Laura wrinkled her nose. "I had crackers before I came out to give you the benefit of my advice. They always help settle my stomach. Besides, I was lonesome. You insisted on coming out here and working right away. You could have been sociable and let me tell you how Pete is mistreating me." She patted her round stomach. "Kicks me all night long."

"You asked for it."

"You bet I did." Laura's radiant smile lit her round, freckled face. "For three years. Asked. Prayed. Took every hormone pill under the sun."

"I know you did." Kerry's eyes twinkled. "Gee, and all just to make me an aunt. I really appreciate it."

"There's Jason's car in the driveway." Laura sprinted toward the house, then yelled over her shoulder, "He's back early. I called him and told him you'd driven down this morning."

Kerry smiled affectionately as she heard the screen door slam and Laura calling to Jason as she ran through the house. Even eight months pregnant, Laura was like a whirlwind. A warm, sunny whirlwind . . .

If such a phenomenon existed. But then, Laura was a law unto herself. She'd always been—

"I hear you're ruining my wife's gazebo." Jason was coming out on the back porch. "She wants me to take you in hand."

"For God's sake, you know nothing about painting, Jason." She dipped her brush back in the can. "And Laura knows it."

He came toward her. "Where's Sam?"

"I left him with Edna's kids. They needed him. Now, get out of that fancy business suit and help me with this painting. I'm having a devil of a time with your wife. She keeps coming out and critiquing."

"It annoys her that she can't do it all herself. Sorry I wasn't home when you got here. I had business in Valdosta."

"No big deal."

"How's Charlie's family?"

"Not good. Coping."

"How about you? Are you doing okay?"

"Coping."

"Dad was worried about you. He wanted to help."

She stiffened. "How? Did he want to put me back in that sanitarium?"

Jason frowned. "He thought he was doing what was best for you. You were having hallucinations. You needed a doctor's care."

"And it was so much easier to pawn me off on an institution than to work through it with me. Do you know how many times he visited me in that hospital in the year I was there? Twice. If you hadn't come as often as you did, I'd have felt like an orphan."

"He was uneasy around you. From the time you were a little girl you were antagonistic, and you were fighting mad after he committed you."

"I wasn't crazy. I was just having a few problems. He should have let me work them out on my own."

"He was afraid the hallucinations were a result of that coma you were in when you were a kid. He felt responsible."

"He felt guilty."

"You do blame him."

"Maybe. I don't know. I just don't want to deal with him now." She wished he'd drop the subject. Jason could be a bulldog once he got his teeth into an issue. She sat back on her heels and smiled with an effort. "Now, are you going to go change and help me? The two of us can whip this job in time for supper."

"Right away." He frowned and she knew he wasn't going to let it go yet. "But those doctors did do you some good. After that psychiatrist, Dr. Travis, showed up, you were just fine. Within two months you were out of that place. So maybe Dad did the right thing."

She had been released because Michael Travis had told her what to say to the hospital personnel so they would think they'd cured her. "I agree that Travis got me out of there. About everything else, we'll have to agree to disagree."

He was silent a moment. "I always wondered . . . Do you blame me too?"

"I did for the first couple weeks I was in that place. I felt betrayed. Then I realized that you'd gone along with him because you loved me, and love is too rare for me to jettison it because you made a mistake."

"It wasn't a mistake. You're healthy and normal now. You have to admit that."

"Perfectly normal." As normal as she'd ever be. "Now, can we drop it and just paint Laura's gazebo? I came here because I wanted to be with my family, not to get a lecture."

He nodded and turned away. "Sorry. It's just that Dad's such a great guy. I think you're missing out."

She watched him cross the lawn toward the house. It was natural that Jason would think she was being deprived. He had spent those two years she was in a coma after her mother's death with their father, and Kerry's withdrawal from the world had only brought father and son closer. Then, after she'd regained consciousness, she'd spent time in rehab. Jason was ten years older than Kerry and had been heavily influenced by that time with his father. Later, both Jason and Kerry had been sent to private schools but spent vacations at Aunt Marguerite's place in Macon. She only vaguely remembered the few times her father had come to see them during those years. He'd been charming, charismatic, and amusing when Jason was around. When it was just her father and her, he'd been stilted and uneasy.

Her fault? Maybe. She remembered staring at him as if he were some kind of rare species of mammal. She couldn't be natural with him. Then, when she'd started having the nightmares and then the visions, he'd sent her to Milledgeville, and that had destroyed any possibility of intimacy.

She turned back and started to paint the banister again.

It didn't matter. She had Jason and Laura and all her friends at the fire station. She didn't need a father figure in her life. Certainly not one like Ron Murphy. Let him work out his own guilt feelings about Kerry and her mother and that hideous night in Boston.

Kerry was laughing, joking, and looked more relaxed than Silver had ever seen her. Her brother was standing at the barbecue pit grilling hamburgers, and Laura Murphy, very pregnant, was sitting in a chair at the picnic table, staring with satisfaction at her gazebo.

Silver lowered the binoculars. Was it time to go knock on the door and talk to Kerry? She was calm and almost content. The trauma of the last few days had faded. He should probably take advantage of the moment and step into the picture again.

No, give her tonight.

Once he drew her into the nightmare in which he was living, she wouldn't have any more tension-free periods for the foreseeable future.

The President." Melissa handed Michael Travis the phone and mouthed silently. "Not pleased."

He wasn't surprised. Andreas had been growing increasingly impatient for the last three days. "Hello, Mr. President. I was planning to call you and update you this evening."

"Update me now," Andreas said curtly. "What the hell is happening? Why is Silver spinning his wheels? Doesn't he realize the urgency?"

"He realizes. He's trying to ease her into the offer gently."

"While he's trying to be diplomatic I'm having to deal with the carnage this nut is creating. Tim Pappas's car ran off the road into a tree last night. It exploded and he burned to death before anyone could get him out."

"Shit."

"Exactly. I told Pappas he'd be safe. I don't like to be made a liar. And I hate having a decent man die because we can't find Trask."

"Silver will find him. There's no one with more motivation."

"That's the only reason I'm trusting him." Andreas paused. "This woman is really necessary?"

"Her or someone like her. And I've never run across anyone with that particular specialized talent."

"But she's reluctant to help?"

"She may not be. We just don't know. She didn't want to have anything to do with me or the group five years ago. She's very independent and wanted to live a completely normal life."

"Fat chance."

"She's done pretty well. She's smart and very good at covering her tracks."

"You never gave me a complete background check on her. Talk to me."

"Her mother was killed in a fire in Boston when Kerry was six. Kerry was struck on the head by the arsonist who set the fire, and she was in a coma for two years. Even after she came out of the coma, she couldn't ID the person who had set the fire. Her father, Ron Murphy, and her mother were in the process of getting a divorce at the time of the fire and he'd taken Kerry's brother, Jason, away on a hunting trip to Canada. Murphy is a freelance reporter and never in one place for long. The children were in private schools or with their aunt most of their childhood. When she was twenty, Kerry began having nightmares about fires and the usual visions. Her father clapped her into a sanitarium. That's when I came on the scene. I'd been keeping an eye on her since one of my informants heard about her background. I thought she might be one of ours."

"The comas."

"Yes. I forged documents and showed up as a visiting psychoanalyst. I was able to ease her through the anger and bewilderment, but there was no way she wanted anything else to do with me. She said she didn't need my help and she didn't want to live her life as a kook."

"Understandable."

"I do understand. I felt the same way. That's why I was reluctant to give Silver her name when he came asking for recommendations."

Andreas was silent a moment. "Could he have forced it out of you?"

"I don't know. I don't think even Silver knows what he can do. Maybe he doesn't want to know."

"My reports say he's . . . remarkable."

"And that may just cover the tip of the iceberg." Travis rubbed his temple. "Don't worry. He's not going to go soft on us. He'll get Kerry Murphy."

"Soon," Andreas said. "Damn soon. I don't want to have to go to another funeral."

"I'll convey your displeasure."

"Not that it will mean a damn to him. Evidently he's not someone to be intimidated. Get back to me." Andreas hung up.

F*ire!*

Mama couldn't get away. She was hurt. She had to find someone to help.

The man across the street.

Help Mama. Please, help Mama.

But she knew he wouldn't help.

Time after time. Time after time.

But she had to try. She ran across the street toward him. "Please. She needs help."

She looked up at his face.

No face. No face. No face.

She screamed.

Kerry sat bolt upright in bed, bathed in sweat. Her heart was beating so hard it was painful. It was okay. She wasn't standing on that street in Boston. She was in Jason's guest room in Macon.

Only a dream.

Only? It was the same nightmare she'd had since childhood. But she hadn't had it for months and had hoped she might be finally rid of it. It was probably Charlie's death that had triggered its return.

It didn't matter what had caused it to come back. It was here, and if she went back to sleep it would follow her. The pattern was always the same. The dream repeated time after time the moment she went into deep sleep. Sometimes it continued for days before it stopped, leaving her exhausted and drained.

Well, she couldn't lie here waiting to go back to sleep so it could pounce on her.

She tossed aside the comforter and got out of bed. Go downstairs and get a glass of milk. Sit on the porch and let the night air cool and soothe her. And maybe, just maybe, she would get lucky and the dream would fade so far away it wouldn't attack her when she went back to sleep.

Yeah, sure.

She went to the bathroom, washed her face, and then crept quietly downstairs to the kitchen. All she needed was to wake Jason and have him cross-examine her. She had told him the nightmares that had plagued her childhood were a thing of the past. Wishful thinking.

She got her glass of milk and went outside and sat down on the back-porch steps. The wood was cool against her bare legs, and she drew a deep breath of the honeysuckle-scented air. This was normalcy. This was real. That shadowy figure of her dream was only a monster figment of her imagination.

But it wasn't imagination. He was out there. He'd done that horrible thing and was still free to destroy more lives. Her fault. Her fault.

Forget him. She had to live her own life. She couldn't keep punishing herself. She was no martyr. Her mother wouldn't have wanted her to blame herself. She lifted her glass and took a swallow of milk.

The gazebo gleamed white in the moonlight. She'd have to give it another coat of paint tomorrow, but it looked pretty good right now. Laura had done a good job on the—

"Is there room on that step for me?"

She went rigid, her gaze flying to the man standing a few yards away.

Brad Silver. Anger flared through her. "No, there's no room. Not on this step. Not in my life." Her grip tightened on the glass of milk. "And what the hell are you doing here in the middle of the night? This is private property."

"You woke me up." He sat down on the step beside her. "Entirely your fault. If you weren't so messed up, I'd have a much easier time of it."

"What do you mean, I woke you up?"

"How often do you have dreams like that? I don't remember more than one or two in the last six months."

"Why should you—" She drew a deep breath. "What *are* you, and what have you been doing to me for the last six months?"

"I haven't been doing anything but monitoring. I had to become familiar with you once I decided that you'd be the best choice. Travis told me that you were the one in the beginning, but I like to make my own choices."

"Monitoring?" She moistened her lips. "You've been prying in my mind. You're one of Michael's freak friends, aren't you?"

He made a face. "I think he probably told you that I wasn't exactly normal when you called him. What did he say?"

"Controller. He called you a controller." She tried to keep her voice steady. "You were controlling my thoughts when Charlie was dying. How did you do it?"

"Experience. I wasn't sure that I could shut down your connection and replace it with a false image. You're very strong."

"But you did it, damn you."

"Because you couldn't do it yourself. If you'd let Travis train you, it might not have been necessary for you to huddle in that closet like an animal in pain."

"I don't want to hear this."

She started to get up, but he reached out and jerked her back down. "I don't care if you want to hear it. I've been cooling my heels patiently in the background waiting for you to recover from all this trauma over your friend's death. Now I'm going to have my say and you'll listen."

"The hell I will." She glared at him. "Keep your hands off me."

"I will. I've no desire to touch you." He glared back at her. "But you will listen or I'll wake your brother and discuss both your nightmares and how I know about them. I don't think you want him to worry about having a nutcase for a sister."

"You bastard."

"Actually, I am. But that doesn't alter anything. It should only convince you that I'll do what I say."

He meant it. She glanced away from him. "Talk."

"I want you to do a job for me."

"No."

"Why not?"

She said through her teeth, "Because you're a freak and you want to make me one too. I don't want anything to do with you. I told Michael Travis that five years ago."

"I don't have to make you a freak. You're already one. When you came out of that coma, you brought something back with you. You know it but you don't want to deal with it."

"I did deal with it," she said fiercely. "I *use* it. That doesn't mean I have to join a bunch of weirdos like you and Travis. I want to live a normal life."

"Too bad. You joined a fairly exclusive club when you came back from that coma. Your talent is damn rare, and I need it."

"Screw you."

"Travis let you off the hook. He could have pressed the gratitude button after he told you how to finesse your way out of the sanitarium, but he didn't do it. He let you go your own way. Did he ever try to recruit you?"

"Recruit?"

"Wrong word? What did he say to you?"

"He said that I wasn't a freak, that the visions were telepathic, and that I had to learn to live with them as best I could. He said that I wasn't alone and that there were others who had demonstrated psychic abilities after they'd woken from comas when they were children. He and his wife were trying to search out and find and help them."

"Because both Michael and Melissa went through it themselves."

She nodded. "That's what he told me. He said if I'd come to their place in Virginia, they'd help me control it." Her lips tightened. "I didn't need help. All I needed to know was that I wasn't crazy. I can handle the rest. I've built a good life for myself."

"Even though you're crippled."

"You're crazy. I'm *not* crippled."

"You quit being a firefighter because you were afraid. Fear's a great crippler."

"I'm not afraid."

"Not of the fires. You're afraid to go through the hell you did when Smitty Jones died in that fire two years ago."

"Smitty?"

"You went through school with him and you were both stationed at Firehouse Number Ten. You were very close. Lovers?"

Her lips twisted. "Don't you know?"

"I didn't intrude. I have to have some ethics."

"Bullshit."

"I skimmed deep enough to know it was a relationship that tore you apart when he died. Were you joined with him like you were with Charlie?"

She didn't answer.

"I think you were. But you must have managed to pull away before he died. You were lucky. Without control, he'd probably have taken you with him if you hadn't managed to break free."

"I would have died?" she whispered.

"I think you knew. That was why you instinctively broke free."

She looked away from him. "Maybe."

"But you didn't want to go through that again, so you transferred. You thought if you weren't near the fire that you'd be okay." He shook his head. "But it doesn't work that way, Kerry. Not if you have an emotional connection."

"I had to try," she said unevenly. "Smitty was my friend, my best friend. I think in time we might have been even closer. But we didn't have that time. He died, and I couldn't bear to feel that same..."

"It's hell." His voice harshened. "Do you think you're unique? Do you think none of us has had your special experience? It goes with the territory."

"Well, it's not my territory. I don't want anything to do with it." Her glance shifted back to him. "Or you. Michael told me there were all kinds of talents on both a major and a minor scale, but I never thought there would be anyone like you. You're an abomination."

"That's not an uncommon response. It's sometimes bearable to have someone peek into your thought processes but not to change them." He shrugged. "I've learned to live with it. You'll find this particular abomination can be very useful to you."

"I don't want to use you. I want you to go away."

"But you haven't let me tell you what I could do for you."

"Nothing. There's nothing I'd ever want you to do for me."

"On the contrary. I can give you what you've wanted all your life." He paused. "He does have a face, you know. And somewhere deep in your mind you know what he looks like. You just haven't been able to fight through the horror of that night to bring the memory to the forefront."

"And you're supposed to be able to do that for me?" She shook her head. "After I woke from that coma, the police tried everything including hypnosis to help me remember. It was just gone. The concussion and coma erased it."

"But not permanently. It's just hidden. I can help you bring it out in the open. It won't be easy, but I can do it."

"I don't believe you. If I could have remembered, I would have done it already. Do you think I don't want to see that bastard punished? He killed my mother. He left her in that burning house to die." Her voice was shaking. "They told me later that there were only her bones left to bury when they finally were able to put out the fire."

"You don't want to find him enough to bring back the memory."

"Bullshit." She stood up. "I don't believe you can help me, and even if you could, I wouldn't risk dealing with you."

"Because you're afraid I'd mess with your mind. I promise not to do that. I usually don't barge in without permission."

"Like you did in the closet?"

"That was necessary. I didn't want you to have a breakdown be-fore I could put my proposition in front of you."

She stared at him in amazement. So cool, so hard. "That would have been inconvenient for you."

"Yes." One corner of his lips lifted in a sardonic smile. "I couldn't afford the time to find another talent like you. Sorry if you're disappointed in my lack of the milk of human kindness. I have to move too hard and fast to try to finesse you. And I'd judge you're too honest and straightforward to appreciate a snow job."

"I'm straightforward enough to turn you down and tell you to get out of my life."

"Aren't you even curious what I want from you?"

"No." It was a lie. She was curious. How could she not be?

"I want you to find a monster. A monster who makes the man who killed your mother look angelic in comparison."

"Who?"

He shook his head. "I have to have a commitment. I promised Travis I wouldn't give away the show unless I was sure you'd keep it confidential. Some people would tell you it's your patriotic duty. I don't give a damn about patriotic duty." His expression was flint hard. "I just want you to find him."

"And I don't like having my duty defined by you, the govern-ment, or anyone else." She opened the screen door. "So you've put your proposition to me and I've refused. Now go away."

He shook his head. "This was just the opening foray. I knew you wouldn't cave right away. I'll have to keep after you until you agree."

"If I see you anywhere near here, I'll call the police."

He got to his feet. "Then you won't see me. But I'll be here. Think about it. The son of a bitch who killed your mother is still making you a prisoner. Don't you want to be free? Don't you want to see him burning in hell?"

"I'm not even giving that question the courtesy of an answer."

"Then let me light the match to send him there." His soft voice was coaxing and his expression lit with intensity. "Believe me. I can do it."

She almost did believe him in that moment. Every muscle in his body seemed electrified by purpose. My God, she had recognized his strength of will in their last meeting, but now she realized she had barely skimmed the surface.

All the more reason to avoid any contact with him. Even when he wasn't using that talent she found so repulsive, he was far too persuasive. Yet he didn't try to hide either the ruthlessness or blunt self-interest that seemed integral to his character. He was a stranger who wanted a service from her, and she couldn't trust him or believe him. "You can't help me. Good-bye, Mr. Silver."

He smiled. "I almost had you there for a minute, didn't I?"

"No way."

He nodded. "Yes. You were edging close. You want what I can give you, but you're afraid. That's understandable. But it's not been a bad night's work for me. It's a relief to know I may not have to get radical."

She stiffened. "Radical?"

"Never mind. Have a good night, Kerry." He glanced at the gazebo. "You did a good job of painting that gazebo. But it needs another coat."

"I know that. Tomorrow."

"But you won't be too tired tomorrow. You'll sleep well." His gaze never left the gazebo. "I know you're worried the nightmares will come back, but it's not going to happen."

"What?"

He looked back at her. "A little gift for you. A down payment for future services." He started across the lawn toward the gate. "And a demonstration of how useful I can be."

"What the hell? I don't want any gifts. I want you to stay out of—"

He was gone.

And good riddance, Kerry thought, as she entered the house and locked the kitchen door. She was shivering, she realized. He had disturbed her almost as much as the first time they had met with his talk of the monster he wanted her to find.

She had enough demons of her own. She didn't need to search out any for him. His so-called gifts were definitely suspect. Particularly if he could twist her perception of reality as he'd done before. It still seemed almost impossible that such a talent existed. It frightened her. She wanted to hide her head beneath a blanket as she'd done as a child. The sensible adult alternative was to avoid Silver like the plague, and she had been right not to have been swayed by him.

You're worried the nightmares will come back, but it's not going to happen.

And that frightened her too. Not only that he'd known about the nightmares, but that he said he could prevent them. She felt . . . tampered with.

But it wouldn't happen. He was probably using positive reinforcement on the chance that maybe he'd strike it lucky. But the nightmares always came, and they were so strong she couldn't believe that anything would stop them.

He's still making you a prisoner.

Forget Silver. Go to bed and lie there fighting sleep. Because, in spite of what he said, she knew the nightmares would come.

------

moke.

Hurting her lungs.

If she opened her eyes, she knew that she'd see the flames.

Silver had lied. Why was she feeling this terrible disappointment? It only proved her will was strong enough to resist whatever suggestion he'd tried to implant.

Crackle of flames.

Soon her mother would come in the door and wake her.

Heat.

Mama!

Her eyes flew open.

Flames eating the curtains of the guest room like a hungry gargoyle.

Guest room?

Jason's guest room. No dream.

Fire!

The next instant she was out of bed and running for the door to the hall.

Billowing smoke.

"Jason! Laura! Get out of here."

"I'm on my way." Jason's bedroom door was open and he was half carrying Laura out of the room, wrapped in a blanket. "She's hurt. She tried to put out the fire in the drapes and her nightgown caught—"

"Downstairs. Get her outside." Flames were breaking out all over the house. Random. Crazy. No pattern. No connection. The banisters. Then the table in the hall.

Oh, God, the front door was suddenly an inferno.

"The kitchen door." Kerry nudged them toward the back of the house. "Quick."

Please, God. Not the kitchen door. Let them be able to get through the back door.

The kitchen cabinets were ablaze with a fire so hot it was melting the hardware.

But the kitchen door was still untouched by the flames.

She threw the lock and opened the door. "Out!"

She didn't have to tell Jason. He was already down the steps and halfway across the yard. Kerry flew after him. "Put her down. Let me look at her."

"She's hurting." Tears were running down Jason's face. "She was moaning when I was carrying her down the—"

"But she's alive." She swallowed as she looked at Laura's arms and shoulders. Christ. "Stay with her. Hold her. I'm going to run next door and call 911."

"Hurry. For God's sake, hurry."

She darted across the yard toward the gate. Call 911. Get help.

Pain shot through her temples and she had to clutch the gate to keep from falling.

Monster. Monster. Smiling.

He was sitting at the wheel of a tan SUV over a block away, staring at the flames destroying the house. He loved looking at the fires. They were the proof of his power. No, it was the deaths that were the proof. The fires were just the weapons.

But this fire was not a total success. The small dish still needed work. He couldn't control it from this distance and couldn't be sure that Kerry Murphy had been killed. Well, there was one way to be certain.

He started the SUV and pulled away from the curb. Time to get out of here before the last hurrah. . . .

He pressed the remote control in his hand.

Kerry heard a whoosh that was like the sucking sound of a tornado beside her.

Jason's house was destroyed in the space of seconds.

4

———————

Let go of the damn gate." Silver was prying her clenched hands from the metal. "You have to get out of here. There are sparks flying all over the place."

"Laura," she said numbly. "911."

"I've already called them." He pushed her toward the street. "You go out to the street and guide them while I get Jason and Laura away from these sparks."

She shook her head to clear it of the throbbing pain and then started for the street. Laura. She was the only one who was important. They had to save Laura.

Don't think about the monster.

———————

Silver came into the hospital waiting room and handed Kerry a cup of coffee. "How is she doing?"

"She's going to live." She took a drink of coffee. "But they don't know about the baby. They're trying to save him now."

"I'll think good thoughts." He sat down beside her. "She was almost full term?"

"Eight months. He has a good chance." She stared at the clock. "It's been two hours. You'd think they'd—"

"It's a boy?"

She nodded. "They were going to name him Pete." She drew a deep breath. "They *are* going to name him Pete. I won't be negative. God wouldn't let this happen to Jason and Laura. They want a child so much. They've been trying for the past three years. They were going to adopt if she couldn't conceive, but then the miracle happened. At least it was a miracle to them." She sipped her coffee. "I won't give up hope."

"Hope's a wonderful thing."

She glanced at him. "Do you know what's happening in that operating room? You knew about the fire."

He shook his head. "Only because it was connected to you. It doesn't work the same every time."

"You have limitations?" Her lips twisted. "I'm surprised."

"We all have limitations. We work with what we've got. You'd know about that if you'd cooperated with Travis." He looked down into his cup. "You don't have to be afraid of me, Kerry. I'm not here to hurt you."

"And I suppose that man who set Jason's house on fire didn't want to hurt me either." She moistened her lips. "He was enjoying it. He was . . . hideous. He was sorry he wasn't close enough to smell the burning flesh."

He went still. "You made contact with him?"

She nodded. "He was your monster, wasn't he? You were in the back of his mind all the time he was looking at the fire."

"Yes, I'm sure he set the fire. No one else is capable of that pattern of ignition."

"It was strange." She rubbed her temple. "No connection. Different pieces of furniture seemed to ignite all by themselves."

"Yes."

"And that last explosion . . ." She turned to look at him. "Why? Why did he set fire to Jason's house?"

"He's probably been watching you because he thought you might be persuaded to help me."

"So he tried to kill Jason and Laura as well as me just because he saw me with you?"

"He wouldn't care how many people he killed. You've got to understand that about Trask."

"You *know* who did this? You have a name?"

"I have a name. I don't know where to find him. He's brilliant at covering his tracks. He's very smart, close to genius."

She shook her head. "He's mad. He loves the fire as if it were his child. But he's angry with you . . . angry and afraid."

He was silent. "You picked up a lot from him tonight."

"Not because I was trying. He was bombarding me. He was wide open and spewing venom." She closed her eyes. "It made me sick. Laura . . ."

"You're hurting," he said quietly. "I can help. All you have to do is give me permission."

Her lids flew open. "Don't you dare. My pain belongs to me. It's a sign I'm alive and functioning. If I wanted a sedative to block it out, I'd ask the doctor, not some half-baked—"

"Okay, okay. I just thought I'd offer." He leaned back in his chair. "Sometimes it's hard for me to know how to strike a balance."

"Don't strike any balance. Just act like a normal human being."

"I am a normal human being. Most of the time. May I get you something to eat?"

"No. I don't need or want anything from—"

"We lost him, Kerry." Jason was standing in the doorway, tears running down his cheeks. "He was dead. How am I going to tell Laura?"

"Oh, damn." Kerry jumped to her feet and ran into his arms. "Lord, I'm sorry, Jason. I hoped with my whole heart that—"

"Me too." His arms tightened around her. "I *knew* him, Kerry. We'd talk to him. It was like Pete was already part of the family. Laura...How am I—"

"I'll go with you to her room. We'll talk about it. If you want me there, I'll be there."

He nodded. "You're always there when I need you. But if you could..." He shrugged. "I don't know what you could do. I don't know what anyone could do."

She turned him toward the door. "First, we have to go to Laura. She'll want you there when she wakes up." She brushed the tears on her cheeks away with her fist. "We'll worry about everything else later."

Jason nodded. "Laura first."

"Right." She slipped her arm around his waist and opened the door. She glanced back over her shoulder at Silver. "You stay here," she said fiercely. "No matter how long I'm gone, you be here when I get back."

"I'm not going anywhere." He stared directly in her eyes. "Why should I? I'd bet that bastard Trask has done my job for me."

Kerry didn't return to the waiting room until three hours later.

"Let's go," she said curtly.

He rose to his feet. "May I ask where?"

"I need a shower, food, and something to wear besides these surgical greens the nurse gave me."

"What about your brother?"

"He won't leave Laura. They're letting him stay here at the hospital."

"You don't want to stay with him?"

"He doesn't need anyone but Laura now. I'd be intruding on a private grief." She headed for the door. "Where are you staying?"

"The Marriott." He reached for his phone. "I'll book a room for you and one for your brother for tomorrow night. Okay?"

She nodded. "I don't know if he'll use it, but it's a good idea. Clothes?"

"I'll have them open the gift shop early and buy you a few things to hold you over until we can get yours from Atlanta."

"I'm not even going to ask how you intend to make them do that."

"No hocus-pocus." He took her elbow. "I'll bribe them."

Kerry had showered, washed her hair, and was blow-drying it when Silver knocked on the door two hours later.

He had also showered and changed, and he handed her a plastic bag when she opened the door. "That towel is fetching, but you'll be more comfortable in these. Pants, sweatshirt, and makeup. Sorry, they didn't have underwear. I sent the bellhop to the mall to pick up some."

"You know my size, I suppose."

"Bra thirty-four B, size-five panties." He sat down in the easy chair by the window. "I've ordered room service. Soup, chicken sandwiches, and coffee. Okay?"

She nodded. "Anything." She took the bag into the bathroom and closed the door. A few minutes later she came out of the bathroom in the tan pants and green sweatshirt. "Shoes?"

"They'll arrive with the underwear. Size-seven tennis shoes. New Balance, not Nike."

Her lips tightened. "You know everything about me."

"No, I don't. But details like that are hard not to pick up."

"When you were 'monitoring' me. Do you know how angry that makes me?"

"Of course. I'd be furious too." He smiled faintly. "You look like Little Orphan Annie with your hair curly like that. It's very appealing. I don't know why you struggle so to keep it straight."

"Because I'm not Orphan Annie. I'm an adult, and I want to look like what I am." She sat down opposite him. "I don't like deception and I hate invasion of my privacy."

"You've already made that point."

"Because you intruded in the most intimate and ugly way possible. That stinks."

He nodded, waiting.

"And I'm never going to forgive you for bringing that monster into our lives. Your culpability is only a little behind the man who started that fire."

"I accept that." He met her gaze. "But I think you've decided who's tops on your hit list."

"You come pretty damn close," she said coldly.

"I'm everything you hate. I'm a complete son of a bitch. But you wouldn't be talking to me without a reason. So tell me why I'm here."

"I want answers." Her hands tightened on the arms of the chair. "I want that son of a bitch who killed Jason's son. I want him so bad that I can taste it."

"I thought you'd feel that way. You're a very loving and protective woman and have a strong maternal streak."

"Stop analyzing. You don't really know anything about me."

He shrugged.

She felt a flare of anger. "Damn you. Anything you know is stolen. I feel as if you robbed me." With an effort she smothered the rage. "It's not going to happen again. If I decide to help you find this Trask, you've got to promise me you won't ever do what you did to me when Charlie was dying."

"I promise."

"And you won't . . . intrude."

"Never without your permission."

"And you'll never get that."

"Perhaps. Situations sometimes dictate radical measures." He shook his head as she started to speak. "But I won't trespass again. I don't usually, anyway. Do you think I'm some damn peeping Tom? It's very uncomfortable until I become accustomed to all the nooks and crannies."

"Nooks and crannies?"

"Besides, you've put up barriers against me. It wouldn't be easy to jump over them."

"But not impossible?"

He scowled. "You would have to ask that question when I'm doing my best to reassure you."

"You could do it?"

"Maybe. I'm pretty good." He added, "But like I said, I do have certain ethical standards. When I saw how this thing I have was shaking out, I had to develop a code. Otherwise I could see myself developing into someone pretty unpleasant." He grimaced. "Not that I don't fall from grace more than I'd like to admit. I'm not like Travis. I get angry and I want to strike back with no holds barred."

"If you're trying to reassure me, you're doing a lousy job."

"But I'm letting you get to know me. And the devil you know . . ." He met her gaze. "You've already told me how you hate deceit. I won't be handing you any of that. What you see is what you get. I've given you my promise and I'll keep it."

"If I don't piss you off."

"That's not likely if we're on the same team."

A polite knock on the door.

"Room service." He rose to his feet and moved toward the door. "You'll feel better once you've had something to eat. You're a little hypoglycemic and get edgy without protein."

"I'm not hypo—" She let it go. It was only a pinprick and there were more important things to worry about. "And I'd be edgy regardless of how much protein I'd had. I have the right."

"Yep." He wheeled the service cart into the room and kicked the door shut with his foot. "That you do. But food always helps."

It did help. She hadn't realized she was hungry until she started to eat. She finished the chicken sandwich and the tomato soup in minutes.

"Not so shaky now?" Silver poured her a cup of coffee.

There was no way she was going to admit that she had been shaky before. "I'm perfectly all right." She lifted the cup to her lips. "You didn't eat much."

"I robbed the minibar in my room while I was waiting for you to shower and pull yourself together." He poured his own coffee. "I've got a passion for cashew nuts."

"Really? I wouldn't think you'd have a passion for anything."

"You're wrong. But you have a right to your opinion, and it probably makes you feel safer to imagine me as cold and clinical." He smiled. "I have a passion for all kinds of things. I'm nuts about NASCAR races, baseball, scuba, opera, dogs, and blondes who look like Gwyneth Paltrow. I just don't have much time for them."

"Too busy digging around where you don't belong?"

"Exactly."

"Then why can't you find Trask?"

"Ah, we're back to ground zero." He lifted his cup to his lips. "I can't sense him. I'm blind to him. Besides, it's not my talent."

"I can't believe you didn't try to get one of your psychic buddies who could sense him."

"Oh, I did. No luck. So I've had to try to do old-fashioned detective work, but we've still come up with nothing."

"Then why not call in someone who has more experience, like the police?"

"We did. Police. FBI. ATF. Secret Service. They all batted out."

"And why would any of those government agencies even be interested in trying to catch Trask?"

He didn't speak for a moment. "Do I have a commitment from you?"

"If he's the man who burned Jason's house down."

"I think you know he is."

Yes, she knew. The tendrils of emotion and memory had been unmistakable. She had not been able to decipher or even recognize some of the splinters of consciousness, but the ugliness, the hatred of Silver had been clear. "Why does he hate you?"

"I've come close to catching him a couple times. He likes to think of himself as untouchable. It's important to his ego."

"How do you know?"

"I've studied his profile and I believe I can forecast the way his character would change given the circumstances."

"What circumstances? And why would any government agencies be involved?"

"James Trask was the head of a scientific project funded by the Defense Department. About a year ago the project was scratched and Trask and the other scientists were given their walking papers. He was furious. He packed his bags, slipped away from his CIA tail, and disappeared from view."

"Why would the CIA be tailing him?"

"Because he had information that might be useful to a foreign power. Just because we decided not to pursue the Firestorm project was no sign it wouldn't be attractive to any number of other countries."

"Firestorm?"

"Trask was trying to develop a radio-transmitted method of spontaneous combustion. The method also transformed the molecules, which produced intense heat. He claimed he would be able to target small isolated areas or, with a larger transmitter, an entire city." He added grimly, "Talk about scorched earth."

"He did it, didn't he?" She was remembering the strange way the fire in Jason's house had spread. "He'd completed the project before they stopped it."

He nodded. "He'd done it. He was working on it on his own as well as at the lab. He gave the other scientists just bits and pieces so that he was in sole control. That was why he was considered a security risk. He didn't want his work buried in a locked file cabinet somewhere. He wanted it used and credit given where it was due. After he skipped out, the lab was blown up along with all the data collected from the other team members. The orders from the White House were that the project never see the light of day."

"It was that dangerous?"

"About as dangerous as a mutated form of smallpox set loose in a city. Only quicker. It could destroy a city the size of Atlanta in two hours. The burn would be so intense that it would be impossible to put it out."

"Jesus."

He nodded. "Andreas didn't want to set that kind of firepower loose in the world. It has enough weapons of mass destruction already."

"He should have thought of that before he allowed it to be funded."

"He can't monitor every project. It was the pet project of a group of senators who thought more is always better. They buried the funding in other bills. When Andreas learned about the project, he closed it down. But Trask already had his disks and was out of there. He was enraged, a little crazy, and bent on revenge."

"He's been trying to sell information to a foreign country?"

"There have been leaks from sources overseas to that effect. We have info that he's been dealing with Ki Yong, one of the North Korean government's power figures. But he's not focusing his main attention in that direction at the moment." He paused. "So far he's been targeting fellow coworkers in the project and people in government he feels have victimized him."

"What?"

"Six project scientists have been murdered in the past year. All burned to death."

"Why would he do that?"

"The supposition is that he thought they might be capable of duplicating Firestorm and he wanted it for himself."

"And the government targets?"

"Revenge. Three senators and one member of the House of Representatives brought Firestorm to the attention of Andreas and convinced him it should be scrapped." His lips tightened grimly. "So far two senators and one representative have been murdered."

"Burned to death?"

He nodded. "And he's not been careful about isolating them when he does it. Cameron Devers was with his wife when his car went up in flames. Representative Edwards was on his way to a ball game with his little boy. Both were killed."

"It doesn't surprise me. He didn't care about Jason or Laura." She shivered. "He didn't care about that little baby."

"That's right. It's just as well you get the picture straight. I told you he was a monster."

She nodded. "You have no idea. Ugly . . . So ugly . . ." With an effort she pulled herself away from that memory. "But I don't understand how he could remain free to do that kind of damage with everyone looking for him. He'd have to have a way of stalking or setting up those kills."

He nodded. "I agree. Unless he had help."

"What kind of help?"

"That's one of the things we have to find out. It could be a weak link."

"Why me? He wasn't even sure that I was going to help you. And, even if he thought I was, did he know why you wanted me in particular?"

He shook his head. "The number-one reason is that I wanted to hire you. The second reason is that he must have found out who you are and your success at your profession. That would be a threat enough for him. You put out the fires, and that makes you the enemy."

"Yes, that would make sense. The fire is his child...."

"He really thinks that way?"

She nodded. "I can see now why he might. How long has he been working with spontaneous combustion?"

"Fifteen years."

She shook her head. "It goes back further than that. Maybe... twenty-five years?"

"He's only around forty."

"It's been a long time." She finished her coffee and stood up. "So where do we go from here?"

"Washington. He hasn't finished his death list there. Our chance of snagging him is much better."

"I may not be able to help you, you know. I've never known how this thing works. I can't control or instigate anything."

"You already know more than I do about him. With experience you may learn how to search him out." He paused. "Or maybe I can help you."

"No."

He shrugged. "Whatever you say. I just want you to try."

"And I don't want Jason or Laura endangered. They've been through enough."

"I'll keep them safe."

"I'm supposed to trust you? You have a lousy track record."

"Okay. I'm not perfect. But I've already called Washington, and they'll have round-the-clock guards. I promise they won't be at risk. I don't want them hurt any more than you do."

She couldn't doubt his sincerity. "Thank you."

He shrugged. "I'm damn sorry that Trask was responsible for that baby's death. I had no idea he'd followed me to Atlanta."

"You should have known. He regards you as a threat. He has to destroy threats that might interfere with Firestorm." She turned away. "Now I'm calling the hospital and checking on Laura. You make reservations to Washington out of Atlanta for this evening."

"We could arrange a private plane from here."

She shook her head. "I have a couple things I have to do in Atlanta. And I want to pick up Sam. It's just as well if Trask thinks that I'm only an arson investigator with a very smart dog. I may seem less of a threat."

"Good thinking."

"Does he know about . . . what you are?"

"I doubt it. Besides, I told you that I can't get inside his head."

"Then why does he consider you such a threat?"

"Cameron Devers was my brother." His smile was bitter. "And Trask definitely respects the power of revenge."

She took a deep breath as the door closed behind Silver. What insanity was she getting herself into? But it wasn't insanity. The insanity would have been to let Trask be free to wander the world and inflict that hurt and ugliness on anyone else.

So stop questioning the decision she had already made. The only thing to do was to protect herself as much as possible by finding out as much information as she could. She picked up the phone and dialed Michael Travis.

"I can't tell you how sorry I am about what happened to your brother and his wife," Travis said when he picked up the call. "It was a terrible thing."

"Yes, it was. I suppose Silver called you and told you what happened. Or maybe I shouldn't suppose any such thing. Maybe you had one of your psychic friends in that weird group of yours focusing on me."

"Silver called. He wanted me to be sure and have me contact the authorities and arrange protection for your family. And there's nothing really weird about our group. We're just people trying to survive. No one wanted this talent thrust on them. It just happened. And no one has any desire to exploit it. It's more of a curse than an asset, as you very well know. Some of our people ended up in sanitariums like you. Some committed suicide. And some hid their talent but secretly thought they were insane."

"Until Michael Travis came riding to the rescue."

"I tried to help," Michael said quietly. "I've been there."

She was silent a moment. "You did help me. And I never thanked you for it. I was just so angry and defensive about being shoved back into a sanitarium after spending all those years in a coma that all I wanted was a normal life. I didn't want to think, talk, or hear about anyone who was...like me."

"But I think you're ready to hear about us now." He chuckled. "And I consider it a breakthrough that you're admitting that you're not alone in this."

"Then enjoy it. But I'll never join your little coven. I handle my problems myself."

"So do we. And there isn't any real organization to our group. The cohesiveness is that we know we can reach out and talk to someone who understands. That's a blessing when half the time we're not sure we understand ourselves. We believe in independence and privacy too, and no one would think of violating that premise." He paused. "Except when one of our members goes around the bend and threatens the rest of us."

"Goes around the bend?"

"Some of us are more stable than others, as is true in any group. The balance is always more fragile when subjected to the strain we're under. And it's always possible that, if anyone started to spiral downward, they'd break confidence and subject us all to pain and humiliation." He added ruefully, "The last thing we want is to have *Newsweek* trying to do an exposé on us."

"And what do you do with these exceptions?"

He laughed. "Nothing lethal. God, you sound suspicious. We try to help them. We have one or two of the group make an attempt to help them come to an adjustment." He added, "Most of the time we succeed."

"And when you don't?"

"We ask Silver to come down from Washington and give it a try. If he's not busy on a project, he'll usually agree to help."

"If? I'd think he'd drop everything. Isn't he one of your buddies?"

"No. We respect each other, but you can't call us friends."

"But he belongs to your group."

"No, he's like you. He doesn't want his independence compromised. I didn't find him, he found me. But unlike you, he wanted to explore his full potential. When I first encountered him, he was working in a think tank at Georgetown University, a top-secret privately funded project that was testing psychic abilities. He'd run across one of my less stable people who was turning psychotic. He called me and asked me if I wanted him to straighten him out. I was cautious, but I finally said yes."

"And did he do it?"

"Yes. Jim's not entirely normal—who is?—but he's not going to end up in the loony bin. I'll take you to meet him, if you like."

"Because Silver brainwashed him?"

"No, because Silver flushed out some of the poison and let him see clearer. He was careful not to hurt Jim in any way. That's why I feel okay calling him in occasionally."

"I'd hate it."

"Unless you were going bonkers. Jim has no resentment."

"Maybe he would if Silver hadn't told him not to resent him. How do you know he didn't?"

"I don't. I don't know that much about Silver's talent. But I do know he's been a godsend. That's why I gave him your name when he came looking for someone who might help."

"A return of favor. My head on a silver platter?"

"It seems intact at the moment."

"But Laura's child is dead."

"Yes, but it was Trask, not Silver, who was responsible. And I thought long and hard about giving your name to Silver. But I'm sure he told you about the urgency of catching Trask before he sells information to another power."

"Yes. He also told me his brother was murdered by Trask."

"Half brother. But I believe they were very close. He's been a driven man since Devers's death."

She remembered the cold ferocity of Silver's expression. "I can believe that." She paused. "He made me a promise not to . . . interfere with me. Can I trust him?"

He hesitated. "I think so. He's a wild card, but he's always been straight in our dealings."

"That's not very comforting."

"It's the best I can do." He paused. "Besides, you're an independent lady. You always like to make your own judgments."

"Can I stop him if he doesn't keep his word?"

"Maybe. If you concentrate. If you try to sense any intrusion and repel him. You're very strong. It's possible."

"Thanks a lot," she said sarcastically.

"It's all I can give you. As I said, I'm not that familiar with his talent. He doesn't talk about it. He just goes to work and does it. But it would be more comfortable if you'd try to trust him."

"Like trusting there are no land mines in Afghanistan?"

He chuckled. "You're probably a little safer than that. Do you want me to talk to him?"

"Would it do any good?"

"Probably not."

"Then just be on call in case I find I can't stand Silver and need you to send someone else like him to help me."

"There is no one like him. I've never run across another controller. He's unique."

"In more ways than one. Good-bye, Michael. I wish to hell you'd never given my name to Silver."

"Do you? But then you'd never have known about Trask. All your life you've been hating and fighting those sickos who start the fires and now you've met the king of them all. Isn't there just a little adrenaline rush at the thought of bringing him down?"

Adrenaline? She remembered the feeling of filth and horror she'd experienced when she was hurled into Trask's world. They were emotions she'd never felt before. No, she wasn't eager to go through that again, even though she knew she had to do it.

It wasn't the rush of adrenaline she was feeling.

It was fear.

5

Trask was driving through Atlanta when his phone rang.

"I haven't heard from you in over a week," Ki Yong said when Trask answered. "I believe you're abusing my patience."

"I've been busy."

"So Dickens tells me. He's getting very nervous."

"That's his problem. You promised me a professional and I expect professional behavior."

"He came highly recommended." Ki Yong paused. "I understand you have certain priorities in the United States, and you can't say I'm not cooperating. But I have pressures from my superiors. They want delivery of Firestorm—soon."

"They'll get it."

"Not if you're dead or captured. You're playing a dangerous game. It's not as if I haven't offered to totally take over your agenda there. I'd put all my efforts into winding up those loose ends for you. I want you out of the U.S. and safe."

Safe? Ki Yong wouldn't give a damn about Trask's safety once he got his hands on Firestorm. That's why he'd had to be so careful. "Dickens is enough help. I don't want anyone interfering." And cheating him and the child out of the pleasure they deserved. "It won't be too long now."

"There comes a point when patience gives way and the price becomes too high."

"Not for Firestorm. I showed you what it could do on that island in the Pacific. As I remember, you were very impressed. You told me it would take years for that island to be anything but a burned-out shell." He decided to take the offensive. "So don't try to bluff me. You want it and you want it bad. I'll call you when I'm ready to leave."

The silence vibrated with Ki Yong's displeasure. "Soon. Make it soon." He hung up.

Arrogant bastard. Trask pressed the disconnect button and thrust the phone in his jacket. Ki Yong had been polite and saccharine-sweet when he'd thought he'd be able to manipulate Trask. Well, that hadn't lasted long and he didn't like the idea of Trask running the show. Too bad. Trask was in control, and they could all jump when he snapped his fingers. He had the power.

He had the child.

But the child had not performed well last night, he thought, troubled. He'd thought he had the small dish perfected, but it had behaved erratically at the Murphy house. Obviously there were some serious alterations to be done on it before he entered into negotiations with Ki Yong.

And Kerry Murphy had survived Firestorm. The knowledge was a bitter pill on his tongue. Before, she had been a mere inconvenience, a possible threat, but now she was a symbol of his failure, the child's failure. He could feel his rage begin to sear like acid.

Keep calm. Control the fury as he controlled Firestorm. He

hadn't been able to rectify his mistake at the hospital in Macon. It would have been too dangerous with Silver standing guard every minute. But he would make sure there would be other opportunities.

Until then, he would think about Kerry Murphy and anticipate the marvelous destruction the child would visit on her.

———

Thanks for leaving Sam." Edna gave Kerry a hug. "He was a great comfort to the kids."

"I'm sure he loved it. You probably spoiled him rotten."

"We tried." Edna hesitated. "And thanks for everything else, Kerry. I don't know what I would have done without you."

"Are you doing okay now? Anything else I can do to help?"

She shook her head. "Donna's here, and the kids love her. We'll be fine." She tried to smile. "Well, maybe not fine, but we'll survive. That's what we have to do, isn't it?"

Kerry nodded. "You're pretty wonderful. Charlie would be proud of you." She hesitated. Oh, what the hell. "Come on out on the porch."

"What?"

"Just come." Kerry opened the door and went out ahead of her. "I know it's the wrong time, but maybe it isn't. Not for the kids." She pointed to the large mutt tied to the porch post. "This is Sandy. I called him that because he looks like that dog in *Annie*. I got him at the pound."

"A dog?"

"Underneath all that dirt, he's definitely a dog. He's also definitely friendly, and house-trained—maybe. Think of it this way. It will be a challenge for the kids to—"

"I don't know..." Edna frowned. "I'm not sure—"

"If you don't like him in a few days, call me and I'll find another home for him." She gave Edna a quick kiss on the cheek and led Sam down the steps.

"Everything okay?" Silver asked from the driver's seat of the SUV. "She doesn't look too thrilled."

"He's a sweet dog. Edna's a born mother, and he'll give her something to think about. And I hated taking Sam away from the kids."

"She's petting him," Silver observed. "Cautiously. It may be okay."

"I hope so." She was wiping her eyes as she opened the back passenger door and gestured to Sam to get into the car. "You know, life sucks. Charlie's dead and his family is hurting. They'll always hurt."

"But it will get better."

"I guess so." She got into the passenger seat and closed the door. "I'm trying to think so." Sam had lunged up on the top of the seat and was trying to lick her cheek. "Sit down, silly." But she gave him a hug before turning to Silver. "We can go now."

"No more errands? What did you do when you had me stop at your office?"

"I had to ask a favor of one of the fire inspectors. One of the kids at the hospital is going to be released this week to his grand-mother, and the nurse at the hospital wasn't sure he hadn't been abused. I needed to buy some time until DFACS could investi-gate."

"The little boy, Josh."

She smiled bitterly. "Why am I surprised you knew that? You even included him in the little fairy tale you made for me." She gestured impatiently as he started to speak. "Have you made our travel arrangements?"

"Would I dare do anything else?" He pulled away from the

curb. "A private plane is waiting at Hartsfield. I assumed you'd want your pup in the cabin with you."

She nodded. "He doesn't like crates. I think it reminds him of the pound."

"I can tell he's a sensitive soul." Silver glanced at the dog. "Well, happy is sometimes as good as smart."

"He's smart . . . sometimes. Usually when food is concerned." She took out her phone. "I have to tell my boss I'm taking a few weeks off." She made a face. "He's not going to like it after I spent so much time with Edna and the kids."

"I've already had Travis call Washington and ask them to exert a little muscle to smooth the path for you." He glanced at her. "How are your brother and his wife?"

"As good as could be expected. While you're pulling strings, can you find a decent place for Jason to take Laura when the hospital releases her?"

"No problem. I thought that a full-service hotel would be best for the first week or so, and then we'll move them to a rental property. Okay?"

She nodded. "You've thought it all through."

"I have to make sure you're free of worry." He added, "I'm sure you'd be skeptical if I also said I wanted them to be as happy and comfortable as possible." He smiled sardonically. "After all, I'm an abomination."

"Did that sting?"

"Perhaps." He thought about it. "I think it did. I'm used to it, but sometimes a word or a particularly vicious attack gets past my guard."

She was silent a moment. "You can't blame anyone for hating you for messing around in their minds. There couldn't be an uglier intrusion."

"I don't blame anyone. I'd hate it too," he said wearily. "Do you think it's fun for me? You have no idea what ugliness people hide from the world. Some people's minds are cesspools."

"Then stay out of mine."

He smiled. "Your mind is remarkably clean. Oh, a few sexual repressions and fantasies, but on the whole it's clean and honest and bright. Most of the time it was a pleasure monitoring you. The only problems I had were the nightmares and the barriers you hid behind whenever you thought about your mother's death. That was a cross between riding a tornado and being locked in a coffin." He glanced at her. "I can imagine what it's like for you. You should have let Travis help you to control it."

"I'm not interested in your opinion and I'm not looking for a crutch."

"A little leaning until you learn how to stand on your feet isn't a weakness."

"Are you speaking from experience?"

He grimaced. "Caught. No, I was too mixed up and stubborn to let anyone help me. But you should do what I say and not what I do. It's much healthier. Life would have been a lot simpler for me if I'd had a Michael Travis during those early days."

"He told me you weren't actually part of his group."

He shook his head. "The only thing I had in common with Travis or his friends was that the talent came to me in the same way. I was injured in an automobile accident when I was thirteen and in a coma for almost a year. When I came out of it, everyone thought I was normal for a long while. Everyone but me. I knew I was screwed up, but I had no intention of letting anyone else know I believed I was being sucked into other people's minds. I thought I was going crazy, and I intended to live every minute of my life to the fullest before they shut me in the booby hatch. My parents were too busy pushing my brother Cam's political career to pay much attention, so they let me go my own way. And my way was to indulge in every excess under the sun and invent what I couldn't find available." He shook his head. "Talk about black sheep."

"Michael said that you and your brother were close. I'm surprised he didn't step in."

"He tried. He always tried, but I wasn't having any of it. I finally exhausted myself sowing wild oats locally and took off and started wandering the world. I finally hit bottom in Tangiers and was considering going home and committing myself into the local loony bin."

"What stopped you?"

"Ego. I decided that anyone who was as normal as me in every other way couldn't be nuts just because I was sucked into people's brains. So I gave myself six months to experiment and see if I was really nuts or if it was a true psychic ability. It was an interesting six months. I was lucky I wasn't psychotic after it was over. You'd be surprised how many nasty, twisted minds there are out there, and I dipped into some choice specimens. Sometimes the only way I could survive was to turn their reality into fantasy and alter it so that I could break free."

"Like you did with me."

He nodded. "Only their fantasies needed to be much filthier and more complex. I never knew that was part of my talent, but I got to be an expert from sheer necessity."

"What happened after those six months?"

He didn't answer immediately. "You're very interested. Are you trying to find a gallows to hang me on?"

"I'm trying to find a way to protect myself. I don't want to punish you. It's not worth my while. Besides, I may need you to find Trask."

"I'm relieved." He pulled into the airport parking lot. "I don't mind baring my past if it makes you feel safer. What do you want to know? Oh, yes, you asked about what I did after my six months of learning my craft."

"Craft?"

"Craft, skill, talent. Whatever you want to call it. I decided that I had to develop control and harness the craziness or I'd eventually slip down the path to insanity. I started looking for psychic groups and university projects that could teach me something. It was a very delicate operation to investigate without letting anyone know I was there on the outside looking in. While I was searching I ran across Michael and Melissa Travis. They weren't charlatans and seemed honest, but as far as I could tell there wasn't anyone connected with them with my particular talent, so they'd be no help. I had hopes for the Russian government project, but that didn't pan out either. I couldn't find any group or study that did have anyone like me."

"I can believe that," she said dryly.

"So I decided that I was going to be forced to develop it on my own. I joined a psychic think tank at Georgetown University that seemed to be doing some interesting things and I found my niche."

"What kind of niche?"

He smiled. "Everything from espionage and helping with Homeland Security to doing my bit at local mental-health facilities."

She raised her brows. "My, don't you sound heroic and charitable."

"Heaven forbid. I was just learning and expanding my talent so that I ran it instead of it running me. I never wanted to feel as helpless as I did during those first months after I came out of that coma." He met her gaze. "I think you can identify with that feeling."

She could identify, but she didn't want to admit to any bond with him. "I didn't know what was happening, but I never thought I was going crazy. I just thought I needed to get a handle on what was going on in my head."

"Well, our talents are a bit different. Yours came and went

erratically. I couldn't get away from mine. Every day I had to face it. Before I developed control there was no telling whose mind I was going to be sucked into."

She tried to imagine what that would be like and shuddered at the thought. My God, she'd had only a small taste of what he must have gone through with Trask, and it was the seed of which nightmares were born. "Yes, it would be different." Christ, she was actually feeling sorry for him, and that was a megamistake. No one was less deserving of sympathy than Brad Silver. He had faced his problems and found a way to solve them, but that didn't excuse him for invading her privacy. "But I didn't suck you into anything."

"True." He parked the car and opened the door. "You're the victim and I'm the bad guy. I don't expect you to forgive me."

"That's good." She jumped out of the car and let Sam out of the backseat. "Because I've no intention of letting you off the hook." She started for the terminal. "Come on, Sam."

"I just had a thought. How good a flier is Sam?"

"I've no idea. He's never been on an airplane." She gave him a malicious glance. "But he does occasionally get carsick."

This is your house?" Kerry gazed at the white-columned mansion with the same amazement she'd experienced moments ago when they drove through the iron gates that enclosed the Oakbrook estate. "I'm surprised. It doesn't look like you."

"How can you say that?" He opened the door and helped her out of the car. "Don't I impress you as the Rhett Butler type?"

"No."

"You're right. I inherited Oakbrook from Cam. He fit like a glove into the Old South scenario. But then, there weren't many places he didn't fit. He was one of those men who—" He stopped and cleared his throat. "He was a great guy."

And Silver had obviously loved him very much. "I'm sorry."

"Yeah, me too." He climbed the steps. "He always tried to mold me into his image. He thought it was safer for me." He smiled bitterly. "But it wasn't safer, was it?"

"No, I guess it wasn't."

"He was going to ask me to help in finding Trask. He tried several times to get me to see him, but I kept putting him off. I was too busy. When I finally did come, it was the night Trask decided to burn Cam into a cinder."

"But you didn't know he was in danger. It wasn't your fault."

"I'm not playing the martyr. I just wish— Hello, George," he said to the tall, dapper man who opened the front door. "How have you been?"

"Bored, sir." The butler gave Silver a resigned look. "Do you have luggage?"

"Yep." Silver handed him the car keys. "This is George Tarwick, Kerry. Ms. Murphy, George. George worked for Cam, and I'm a great disappointment to him."

"Not a disappointment." George gave him a faint smile. "More of a challenge. When you give me the opportunity. How do you do, Ms. Murphy? I'm delighted you've come to stay with us." He moved past them down the steps toward the car. "If you'll take Ms. Murphy into the library, I'll be right in to serve refreshments."

"Right." Silver took Kerry's arm. "Come on, Kerry. We've been given our orders. Mustn't upset George. He has his way of getting his own back."

"Absolutely," George murmured.

Kerry glanced back at the butler as she reached the door. George Tarwick was moving down the steps with an athletic grace and vitality that was at odds with his august manner. At first glance

Kerry had thought he was perhaps in his forties, but that stride and suppressed energy was that of a younger man. Thirties? His temples had just the hint of gray and his brown eyes were sparkling with intelligence and humor. "He's not exactly Mr. Jeeves, is he?"

"No way. Before he decided on his present career, he worked for two years with the Secret Service. He's a black belt, was once a commando, and is an expert marksman."

"What?"

"There are all kinds of discreet organizations that furnish butlers who serve as bodyguards. Four years ago I persuaded Cam to hire one. I thought it wouldn't hurt him to have a little protection. He was in the public eye and there are all kinds of nuts around." He smiled crookedly. "But George couldn't stop Trask. Neither of us could. We stood there and let Cam burn to death before our eyes."

"How did it happen?"

"Trask rigged the limo. It automatically locked so Cam and his wife couldn't get out, and then he turned loose a little Firestorm on them. So damn hot . . . They burned to death before we could get the car door open."

"Christ."

"So George and I have grown very close in the past months. We share a bond. Failure. And it bugs the hell out of us."

"Did you find any evidence that Trask was here when it happened?"

He shook his head. "The grounds were being watched by the Secret Service at the time. Cam wasn't the first victim, and the President didn't want any more 'incidents.' But there was no sign of him."

"I'd bet he was there. Maybe not close, but he likes what he does too much to set a trap and then walk away." She absently stroked Sam's head as she thought about it. "And your brother was a difficult target. Trask would have wanted to see his child take him out."

"His child." Silver grimaced in distaste. "Every time you say that it makes me want to throw up. It's ... obscene."

"Yes, but then, you must be familiar with a lot of concepts that are obscene."

"But they didn't touch someone I cared about." He opened the door of the library. "It gets beyond all the barriers I've learned to put up. I guess maybe I'm not as tough as I thought I was."

He was tough enough, she thought. And she didn't want to think about this streak of vulnerability. "No trace of Trask at the other crime sites?"

He shook his head. "You say he was a block away from your brother's house?"

"Yes, but he was having trouble controlling the fire. Do you know the range of Firestorm?"

"Theoretically, with a small transmitter it can be controlled from a distance of a thousand yards. A larger transmitter permits access of a mile or two. Unless he's modified it."

"Which is possible." She shrugged. "But I still think that he's going to want to watch. It's the one thing I believe he has in common with other pyromaniacs I've dealt with. There's nothing like watching, smelling." She moistened her lips. "And if he's there, I think I'll be able to know it."

"I'm banking on it."

"That's right. You've spent so many months monitoring me. It would be a great disappointment to you if I let you down."

"You're damn tooting." He paused. "But I don't think you will. You've come through with flying colors so far. I wasn't sure you'd even make contact for the first few encounters."

"This concerned people I care about. It could be an isolated incident."

"But you don't think so." His eyes narrowed on her face. "You think that you reached him—and that you can do it again. Exactly how does your talent work? Do you ever have contact before the act?"

She shook her head. "Once or twice I've seen it when it was going on. Other times I get a flash when I'm examining the crime scene." She paused. "But this was the first time I felt . . . inside. It was as if I *was* Trask."

"Welcome to the club."

She shivered. "I hope I never feel like that again."

"So do I. I wouldn't wish that feeling on my worst enemy." He grimaced. "Yes, I would. I'd wish it on Trask."

"Tea," George said from the doorway as he brought in the silver tray. "And sandwiches. Ladies like tea."

"Do they?" Silver turned to Kerry. "Do you like tea?"

"Yes."

"I didn't see any tea bags in your kitchen."

"And I didn't see your crystal ball." She smiled at George. "I like the ceremony more than the beverage itself."

"I told you so," George said to Silver. "Ladies have an innate appreciation for the delicacy and orderliness of tea. I've put your bags in the guest room at the top of the stairs, Ms. Murphy."

"Kerry."

He flinched. "I don't wish to be impolite, but it would violate my sense of what is proper. Suppose we accept your democratic good feelings and let it go at that." He glanced at Sam. "May I take that animal out and give it some water?"

"His name is Sam," Kerry said as she handed him the leash. "And I think he needs something to eat."

"Probably," Silver said sourly. "He threw up on the plane."

"I'll keep that in mind," George said as he led Sam from the room. "Definitely a light repast."

Kerry stared after him in bemusement. "You're sure he was a commando?"

"Oh, yes. But he was also raised in domestic service in England. He has firm convictions about the way things should be done, whether it's firing a Sam7 or serving a state dinner."

"Interesting." She lifted the cup to her lips. "I'm surprised he's still with you. I wouldn't think he'd believe you worthy of his efforts."

"Because I'm a slob? He's hoping to reform me."

"But that isn't all?"

"No. He wants to be around when we corner Trask. As I said, he doesn't like failure."

"What does he know about you?"

"Only that my brother thought I was a bit of a screwball who studied hydrostatics at the university." He took a swallow of tea and immediately made a face. "He did this to me on purpose. He knows I hate tea."

She smiled. "You know, I'm beginning to like George."

———

The bedroom she'd been given was as huge as the entire sleeping quarters at the fire station. It was decorated in blue and peach with restrained elegance, and again it jarred against her impression of Silver.

"You're right," Silver said. "I like warm colors and casual furniture."

"And Gwyneth Paltrow," she murmured. Then she stiffened and said, "Were you spying?"

"Nope. I told you that you were safe from me. But, considering how well I know you, it's not hard to read you." He nodded at the buzzer on the table. "Ring if you need anything. I'll ask George to bring you some supper in an hour or so. Until then why don't you make a call to your brother and then relax. Take a long shower and let it iron out some of those kinks in your neck. You probably need time to adjust. Things have been moving pretty fast."

She did need downtime, but she resented him realizing it. It was almost as bad having him so familiar with her mental processes and responses as it was to have him inside her head. "And what are you going to do?"

"I have a few calls to make."

"To Travis?"

"And other associates." He smiled. "My entire life doesn't revolve around Trask. It only seems that way."

She thought back to their first meeting. "Gillen? That's who you were on the phone with when I came into my kitchen that night."

He looked surprised. "You have a good memory. I didn't think you were paying any attention to anything but your friend Charlie's death that night."

"Oh, everything connected with you stands out crystal clear. Who is Gillen?"

"The present bane of my existence. But no one you should be concerned about."

He wasn't going to tell her. "And when are we going to talk about Trask's prospective targets?"

"Soon." He turned away. "You only brought one bag. If you need any other clothes, just tell George and he'll have anything you need sent here from the local shops."

"I have enough to get by. I don't intend to dress for dinner." She headed for the bathroom. "In spite of what George might think proper."

Two minutes later she was under the warm shower and muttering a curse beneath her breath. He was right. She did have kinks in her neck, and the shower was relaxing her. It was very annoying that he was so perceptive.

Yet why was she so sure that he hadn't lied to her about not going inside her mind? She should probably be uneasy. But somehow she wasn't uneasy and she did believe him. Instinct? Whatever it was, she had to accept it. She couldn't keep doubting her feelings. She had to be confident that she was strong enough to know when he was trespassing. Otherwise their partnership would be a nightmare.

Nightmare.

She drew a deep breath as the thought hit her. This was the first time she would sleep since last night, the night of the fire. The night when Silver had assured her that she wouldn't dream of her mother's death. She hadn't believed him then, but there had been no real test. Trask had seen to it that her dream of fire had become reality.

She closed her eyes. God, she hoped she had no dreams tonight. Her nerves were so taut that she was near to breaking. But she wouldn't break. She'd gone through these nightmare cycles many times through the years. She could do it again. So stop being a wimp. Get out of this shower and get something to eat and call Jason.

She'd worry about the nightmares later.

I brought you a steak, salad, and a lemon pudding," George said when she opened the door to his knock. "Substantial but not overpowering." He entered the room and set the tray down on the desk against the wall. "But I suggest you eat it, since you didn't touch a bite of the sandwiches I brought with the tea."

"I wasn't hungry." Good Lord, she was actually feeling guilty. This was ridiculous. "Where's Sam?"

"I left him in the kitchen playing with the cook's son. He seemed to be enjoying himself." He poured coffee into a cup. "He's very good with children."

"Yes, he visits the pediatrics ward at the hospital every week. The kids love him."

"Well, he certainly isn't going to intimidate them with his power and coordination. He almost knocked me down when I was filling his water bowl."

"He's a little clumsy."

"And he dripped water all over the kitchen."

"And a little messy." She stuck out her chin. "If you don't like it, bring him up to me."

"I don't mind him. And the cook is already enamored with the beast." He smiled. "He's just a surprise. Brad told me that he's an arson dog."

"You don't call Silver by his surname. Doesn't that strike you as improper too?"

"Certainly. But he won the match, so I gave in gracefully."

"Match?"

"Karate. He became annoyed with my politeness and told me to stop. When I expressed my displeasure, he told me that if I could put him down two out of three times, he'd drop the matter." He shook his head. "I only managed to put him down once. But I'm already preparing for the next encounter."

"He said you were a black belt."

He flinched. "Must you remind me of my humiliation? Yes, I should have been able to put him down. He took me by surprise. Mr. Cam told me Brad worked at a university think tank. Something to do with hydrostatics. Whatever that is." He grimaced. "He didn't learn those moves in college. He's a street fighter and a good one, and he's not above fighting dirty if it means that he'll come out on top."

"He told me he'd batted around the world and was something of a black sheep."

"He's certainly not like Mr. Cam." He held out the chair for her. "Mr. Cam would never have objected to me doing the right thing. He always allowed people to set their own code and live by it."

"Even his brother?"

He shook his head. "There was too much love there. It's hard to see someone wandering down a path that you think may lead to disaster."

"A think tank is disaster?"

"I don't know. All I can say is that Mr. Cam was always worried about Brad."

She smiled. "You say that name as if it's bitter on your tongue."

"Oh, it is." He moved toward the door. "But soon I'll be ready to make sure I no longer have to say it. Until then, there's always 'sir.' I never agreed to stop substituting 'sir.'" He opened the door. "I'll be back in forty-five minutes for the tray. I do hope you'll eat. It must take a lot of energy to handle that Lab."

"He keeps me on my toes. You can bring him with you when you come."

"I was planning on it. The cook may be fond of your Sam, but I'll bet she's not going to appreciate what he's going to do to her kitchen."

Kerry found herself smiling as the door closed behind him. George was a very strange individual, but she liked him. There were enough conventional people in the world, dammit. It was refreshing to run into someone who walked his own path and set his own rules.

Like Brad Silver.

The thought jumped into her mind but she immediately rejected it. Silver might walk his own path and certainly set his own rules, but there was nothing refreshing or likable about the path he'd chosen.

Or that had chosen him. He'd really had no more choice than Kerry, and his experience had been even more traumatic. He'd had to live with episodes every day, not just spasmodically. Could she really blame him for trying to find a way to survive?

Jesus, she was softening toward him.

The realization sent a ripple of shock through her. That mustn't happen. She could find a way to coexist, but she mustn't let herself feel sympathy. He was too powerful, and it wasn't a power she could trust.

But George was no threat. His strangeness was odd and amusing, not dangerous. She sat down at the desk and lifted the silver-domed lid. The steak did look good. And she was sure she'd hear from George if she didn't eat some of it.

Besides, maybe the food would make her lethargic. She wanted to give herself every chance to sleep deeply tonight.

Deeply and, pray God, with no dreams.

6

urning flesh. Burning flesh.

Pull away. Pull away.

She couldn't do it. He was dragging her into the fire.

She screamed!

"Wake up." She was being shaken. "For God's sake, wake up."

Silver.

Burning . . . smell of . . . burning flesh . . .

"No! You're not going back. Open your eyes. Now!"

Her lids flipped open to see Silver's face, tense, demanding, only a foot from her own.

He let his breath out in a relieved sigh. "That's better. Now, keep them open. No more burning." He pulled her out of bed. "We're going to go downstairs and have a cup of coffee. Where's your robe?" He spotted it on the bed and draped it around her. "Come on. Walk slowly and talk to me. What did George bring you for dinner?"

She tried to think through the heavy rolls of smoke surrounding her. "Salad."

"What else?"

"Meat."

He was leading her down the stairs. "What kind of meat?"

What difference did it make? *Smoke. Burning.*

"It matters. Think."

His voice cracked like a whip, cutting through the smoke like a sword. "Steak."

"Good. Now, where are you?"

Easier now. The smoke was clearing. "Stairs. Your brother's house. No, it's your house now, isn't it?"

"That's right."

"So sad. Your brother . . . the fire." She bent double as a sudden pain wrenched through her. "Can't smell. Hate it that I can't smell. Too far."

"Christ." He picked her up and carried her the rest of the way down the stairs. "I can't stand this. I'm coming in. Just for a minute. In and out, I promise."

Pain fading. Smoke fading.

They were in the library and he was dropping into a big leather easy chair in front of the fireplace, cradling her on his lap as if she were a small child. "You're awake. Nothing can hurt you. Pretty soon you're going to realize that. I'm going to sit here, and when you feel like getting up and going to the kitchen for that coffee, you tell me."

No smoke. No pain.

Warmth. Strength. The smell of a spice. Aftershave lotion.

"It's okay." He was stroking her hair. "Just relax. Nothing's going to happen. Come back to me. You want to do that, don't you?"

She nodded drowsily. She could hear the beating of his heart beneath her ear.

"Now release everything else. No smoke. No pain. It's gone. I'm coming out."

Strange. Empty. Peaceful.

Awake.

Good God!

She sat upright on his lap. "Shit!" She jumped to her feet.

"Not the warmest response I've ever had to a helping hand." He steadied her. "Are you okay?"

"No, you did it again, dammit."

He frowned. "Guilty. But I couldn't— You were hurting. What the hell else could I do?"

"What any normal man would do."

"It didn't work. I couldn't take— It wasn't that bad. Hell, I told you I was going to do it. And you were damn glad that I was there inside. So don't give me any bullshit."

"But I didn't want you to—" She broke off and drew a deep breath. Stop lying to him and herself. He was right. She would have been grateful for any way to stop that hideous pain. She had welcomed him. "Okay. It wasn't entirely your fault."

"That's a grudging admission if I've ever heard one." He stood up. "But I'll take it. Beggars can't be choosers. Let's go get that coffee."

"I don't need coffee."

"Well, I do. You've put me through hell tonight. I need either a drink or caffeine, and I think I'd better have a clear head."

She trailed after him out of the library and down the hall. Her bare feet were cold on the marble floor and she realized for the first time that he was also barefoot and dressed in a brown velvet robe. "I woke you up again?"

"Oh, yes. You could say that. All of a sudden I found myself being pulled down to hell and thrown in the fire and brimstone. Then I couldn't wake you up so that we'd both be able to break free." He opened the door of the kitchen at the end of the hall. "So, since I never want to go through that again, we're going to drink coffee and you're going to tell me what was going on in your head. Okay?"

"Do you think I want to go through—" She met his gaze and nodded. "Okay."

"Good." He went to the cabinet and took down a canister of coffee. "So sit down at the table and catch your breath while I put the coffee on." He glanced at her over his shoulder. "You're not shaking anymore."

She was still shaking inside. "I'm not usually a coward. It wasn't the—"

"For God's sake, I know what you were going through. I was *there*. Or at least on the fringe. I thought I'd put up a block so you wouldn't have that nightmare. I guess I'm not as good as I thought I was."

"Block? Sort of a posthypnotic suggestion? Is that how you do it?"

"Close." He turned the coffee on before coming and dropping onto the chair opposite her. "But hypnosis subjects have to be willing, and some of mine are fighting tooth and nail. I often have to execute a covert operation to avoid the battle."

"But you didn't have to do that with me tonight." It wasn't a question. She shuddered. "Christ, I wanted out of it."

"Pretty evident. You grabbed and held on." He studied her expression. "Your nightmares aren't usually that violent. I remember when I first started monitoring you, there was fear and horror, but it wasn't—"

"Because it wasn't the same nightmare."

He went still. "What?"

"It was Trask."

"I see." He got up and went to pour coffee from the steaming carafe. "The fire at your brother's place?"

"No. I think you know what it was about."

"You mentioned Cam." He brought the cups back and sat down again. "You said...so sad...and then something about not being able to smell."

She closed her eyes as the memory washed over her. "Not me. It was him. Trask couldn't smell your brother's burning flesh. He was too far away. He could see the burning limousine, but he couldn't smell it. He was in a rage as he thought about it, remembered it." She opened her eyes. "He's still in a rage."

"Still?"

"He was staring at this house and wondering how he could let the child loose on it. But he knew your brother had put in protective jamming devices to stall out Firestorm. It was the frustration that triggered his anger."

He was silent a moment. "You're not talking about a nightmare."

"It was enough of a nightmare for me. One minute I was sleeping and the next I was there with him, feeling what he was feeling." Her hand was shaking as she lifted the cup to her mouth. "No, it wasn't a nightmare. He was here tonight. He was standing in the trees beside the front gate."

"Shit!"

She shook her head as he half rose from his chair. "He's gone now."

"Why the hell didn't you tell me?"

She glared at him. "I wasn't in any shape to send out an alarm. If you'll remember, I could barely function. And I knew he wasn't there anymore after I did wake up."

He smothered a curse and then said with an effort, "Sorry. I just hate the idea he was that close and slipped away."

"Didn't you think he'd follow us?"

"Hell, yes, and George arranged to have security patrolling the grounds. How the devil did he get anywhere near the gate? The son of a bitch is like a ghost."

"He's no ghost, he's a monster. You were right about that." She wrapped her cold hands around her cup. "And I think we'd better go over the names of potential victims on his hit list."

"Now?"

She nodded. "He's angry after remembering his lack of satisfaction with your brother's death. He's hungry to experience the full range of the senses." She moistened her lips. "His child needs a good kill."

"How soon?"

"I don't know. I think . . . sometime tonight. He was thinking . . . before the night is over." She glanced at the clock. "But we may have a little time. He'd like it to be right away, but he has to wait for the setup."

"What setup?"

She shook her head helplessly.

"And you don't know who it will be?"

She shook her head. "He just thinks of him as the target. Everyone's a target. He doesn't think of them as people. Just fuel for Firestorm."

"You didn't catch anything else?"

She thought about it. "Water. There was an impression of water. Very vague."

"Lake? Ocean? Creek?"

She shrugged helplessly. "Dammit, I don't know. It's like being a sponge. I'm not like you. I haven't got any control. I can't make him think in specifics."

"I know. I know." He set his cup down on the table and rose to his feet. "So let's go to the library and we'll go over pictures and dossiers and see what we come up with. Maybe you absorbed more than you think you did."

"I hope so." She got to her feet. She could feel the tension and restless energy he was emitting, and she didn't want to deal with it yet. She needed a little time alone to pull herself together. "I'm going upstairs to get dressed. I'll meet you in the library in fifteen minutes."

He frowned. "Do you have to— Good idea." He glanced down at his robe. "I'll do the same. Come on." He was ushering her out into the hall toward the steps. "Thirty minutes. Take a quick shower. It may be a long night."

"To look through the dossiers?"

"And maybe to go to sites that look promising."

She should have known he'd want to go after Trask full steam ahead. Well, so did she. The thought of the urgency of Trask's threat was scaring the hell out of her. She just needed a little time to recover before she came in contact with him again.

"Okay?" He was studying her expression.

"Of course." She started up the stairs. "I'm fine now."

"No, you're not. You're scared." His eyes were narrowed on her face. "And I just remembered a little bit of that nightmare. You were being dragged into the fire. Not Cam. It was your flesh that was burning."

She nodded.

"Dammit, talk to me."

"What is there to say? What did you expect?" She didn't look at him. "I was an automatic target when he thought I was going to help you. But it got personal when his precious 'child' failed to kill me. He wants me very badly." Her lips twisted as she glanced at him. "Maybe more than he wants you, Silver. He's having fantasies about how I'll look, how I'll smell as he burns me to ashes."

"Jesus."

"But it's not going to happen."

"You're damn right it's not. I won't let it."

"Yeah, sure." She smiled mirthlessly. "I'd rather rely on myself, thank you. We've already established where your priorities lie." She opened the door of her room. "Thirty minutes, Silver."

———

Silver muttered a curse as he watched the door shut behind her. Why did he feel this sense of outrage and frustration? She was right. He had his priorities and he'd already decided that he had to use her. She was the key to Trask. Tonight had proved that beyond the shadow of a doubt. She had made contact with Trask during a period when there was no immediate danger of fire. According to her, it was the first time that had happened for her with any subject. She was getting closer and more knowledgeable about him with every encounter.

And every encounter was more painful and fraught with horror.

He could protect her. He'd managed to jerk her out of that mental quicksand tonight.

Barely.

No doubts. He could control it. If he moved fast, there would be minimal danger.

He hoped.

The phone was ringing as he opened his bedroom door.

"I beg pardon," George said when Silver picked up. "Though I don't see why I should apologize when you were the one disturbing me. As you know, my quarters are right below the kitchen, and it sounded like two horses galloping over my head. Now, I don't mean to interrupt a midnight tryst, but I thought I'd check to see if there is anything wrong or if I could be of assistance."

"You can fire your security team that's patrolling the grounds. Trask was out there tonight."

Silence. "You're sure? O'Neill didn't report any disturbance to me."

"I'm sure."

"How?"

"Dammit, I said I was sure. Now, why don't you stop questioning me and go see why O'Neill didn't do his job."

"Excellent idea. I do hope I find that you have a copious amount of egg on your face." George hung up.

———

Silver was spreading dossiers on the desk when Kerry came into the library. "Hello. You look more wide awake. Ready?"

She nodded. "Would it matter if I wasn't?"

He met her gaze. "Yes, it would. I hate like hell prodding you. And it surprises me as much as it does you."

She looked quickly down at the dossiers on the desk. "Well, I'm ready."

Silver came around the desk to stand beside her. "This is all that's left of Trask's hit list. One senator. Three scientists from the Firestorm project who Trask would consider a threat. Where do you want to start?"

"Who was his last target?"

"Senator Pappas. He burned to death in an automobile accident a few days ago."

"And before that?"

"Bill Doddard. Professor of molecular chemistry at Princeton."

"Then he's hitting randomly?"

"So it would seem."

"Then let's look at the scientists first." She opened one of the dossiers and studied the photo of a fortyish woman with short wavy hair and an engaging smile. "You've examined these?"

"Many times. The one you're looking at is Dr. Joyce Fairchild. She has a PhD in three fields and was instrumental in the completion of the larger dish. She wasn't at all pleased when the project went down the tube."

"Angry enough to try to take it out on her own?"

"Trask might think she was." He flipped open another dossier to reveal a photo of a plump, bushy-haired man in his sixties. "Dr. Ivan Raztov. He was in a think tank in Russia before the Cold War ended and he joined Firestorm. He was head of testing as well as making contributions to the development of the larger dish. According to his notes, Trask never trusted him. Of course, Trask didn't really trust anyone. He was too possessive." He handed her the last dossier. "Gary Handel. He's in his late twenties, a young wunderkind who is reputedly a wizard of a molecular engineer. He came in near the end of the project, but he's brilliant, ambitious, and definitely after the gold ring."

Handel was thin, sandy-haired, and looked as eager as Silver had described him, Kerry thought. "And the senator?"

"Senator Jesse Kimble. He's been in the Senate for over twenty years. He's a good old boy from Louisiana." He paused. "Cam liked him. They didn't agree on most things, but he said he had integrity."

"Evidently they agreed on Firestorm."

He nodded. "It seems they did."

"How well protected are these people?"

"Damn well. After the first murders they didn't take any chances. They were being shadowed anyway. The President decided that it wasn't safe to trust anyone connected to the project and set Homeland Security to intimidate them from talking or trying to continue the project. But since the first deaths, their residences have been protected by a jamming barrier and they've all been assigned a battery of Secret Service agents to guard them and their families."

"Which doesn't appear to have helped."

"It made it more difficult." He made a face. "But these are smart, savvy professionals who have their own share of ego. They think they can take care of themselves. They're not willing to be stuffed into safe houses until Trask is caught."

"I can understand how they feel."

He smiled. "Because you're probably more independent and stubborn than they are."

"I don't like trusting someone else with my well-being."

"Yet you trusted your fellow firefighters."

"That was different. Do you have a dossier on Trask?"

He nodded and handed her a folder. "There's not much here that I haven't told you. He was born and raised in Marionville, West Virginia. Brilliant child, brilliant adolescent. Kind to pets and sucked up to adults. Passed all the psychological tests they threw at him. Earned a Fulbright scholarship. Never made a false step until he took off with Firestorm."

"That's hard to believe. But maybe there's something here that will trigger a memory, something I didn't pay any attention to at the time. Besides, I want to see what he looks like." She flipped open the folder and glanced at the picture inside. A ripple of shock went through her. Trask was fortyish, with a receding hairline. Wide blue eyes stared out of a smooth, unlined face with childlike curiosity. He didn't look like a monster, and somehow that was even more terrible. She quickly closed the folder and put it back on the desk. She found she couldn't take more exposure to Trask at the moment. "Later. We're wasting time." She glanced at the clock. It wasn't one yet, but that didn't stop her sense of urgency. She handed Silver two of the dossiers, kept the other two for herself, and settled in the leather chair. "Water. We have to try to find some connection or location with water. . . ."

He sat down at the desk. "Then let's get to work."

———

No egg," George sighed as he entered the library. "To my intense humiliation and disappointment."

George was dressed in black jeans and sweater and looked very unbutlerlike, Kerry thought as she glanced up from the dossier she was reading. "Egg?"

"On my face," George said. "There were fresh footprints by the front gate. I took a cast and called in the gendarmes to check it against Trask's shoe size."

"It was Trask," Kerry said.

"You seem as certain as Brad." George gazed curiously at her. "How? Did you see him?"

"No." She glanced down at the dossier. "Ivan Raztov lives in an apartment in Baltimore. I checked the city map, Silver. Nowhere near any body of water. Joyce Fairchild has a house in the burbs of Fredericksburg. Ditto. No lakes or rivers nearby. But Gary Handel has an apartment overlooking the Potomac."

Silver nodded. "And Senator Kimble lives in a plush subdivision in Virginia called Twin Lakes. It's a possible."

"What's a possible?" George asked.

Silver was silent a moment before he said, "I have an informant who told me that the next Trask victim would be connected with water."

George's brows lifted. "Indeed? The same informant who told you Trask was here tonight?"

Silver nodded.

"Then don't you think it's time to share this informant with me and the authorities?"

"No," Kerry said.

"Oh, a 'deep-throat' type informant?" George nodded. "I understand perfectly. I'm hurt, but if that's the way—"

"Knock it off, George," Silver said. "If you're so hot to share information, why don't you call one of your Secret Service buddies and tell them to put their people on stakeout on the alert? They might want to do some checking to make sure everything's okay."

"They'll want to know who your informant is too."

"Too bad."

"They can get very nasty." He headed for the door. "But don't worry. I'll save you. I'll tell them I saw this vision in my crystal ball. . . ."

Kerry looked at Silver, startled, after George had left the room. "I thought you said he didn't know—"

"He doesn't." He frowned. "That remark might have been pure coincidence."

"Or that wonderful cover you told me about might have been blown and he knows your think tank has nothing to do with hydrostatics."

"Possibly." He smiled slightly. "It's never wise to underestimate George."

"I'm not underestimating him. You're the one who did that." She rubbed her eyes. Lord, she was tired. "So do we go check out the senator's place and Gary Handel's apartment and see if I pick up any trace of Trask?"

He nodded. "As soon as George checks and makes sure we don't already have a victim."

"I think we have time. It's too soon. He wanted it to come quickly, but he had to wait. . . ."

"But you think it's tonight."

She nodded. "I got the impression the setup would take hours. But we can't just sit and wait for a report." She got to her feet. "George can phone you while we're on our way to check out Handel and the senator."

He nodded and headed for the door. "I was just going to suggest that."

She smiled caustically as she followed him out of the house. "Maybe I read your mind."

"I hope not. Considering the slimeballs you seem to specialize in." He opened the car door for her. "Why don't you close your eyes and try to rest? You've already had a hell of a night."

Yes, she had. And to grab what rest she could would be a smart move. She needed to be fresh for whatever confronted them tonight. "I don't think I can relax. But if I fall asleep, you'll wake me as soon as George gets back to you?"

"Of course. You know I will. I need you."

That's right. How stupid of her. He needed her. . . .

The water was clear and tumbled over the smooth stones in a crystal flow.

A deadly flow, Trask thought. Deadly for Firestorm. It was frustrating that all the research he'd done had never brought a solution to this one element that could kill the fire. The only saving grace was that Firestorm burned so hot and so fast that most of the time it had done its work before water could be brought in to kill it. Oh, well, he still had time to work on Firestorm after he turned it over to the North Koreans. He would insist that his services be included in the deal in spite of their reluctance. Damn Asians thought their people were always superior. Yet they hadn't been able to develop anything nearly as sophisticated as Firestorm. They'd relied on nuclear when Firestorm was so much cleaner and just as deadly.

He climbed the oak tree and made adjustments to the small dish he'd set up a week ago on the third branch. He hadn't had a chance to make any changes in the dish since the failure at the house in Macon, but since it was going to be focused on one person there should be no problem. Then he settled down and made himself comfortable on the tarp he'd folded to cushion the hardness of the branch. Everything was prepared, and all he could do was wait. He could feel the adrenaline coursing through him as he thought about the kill to come. It had been agony to leave the house that now belonged to Silver without being able to touch Kerry Murphy. She was a symbol of failure for him and for the child.

No matter. The death of this target would ease him, and Kerry Murphy would be a joy all the more complete for the anticipation.

The moon was going down, but he could still see its bright reflection on the water.

Deadly, deadly water . . .

———

Wake up, Kerry."

"I think I've heard you say that before." She yawned as she opened her eyes. "I wasn't really sleeping. Where are we?"

"Twin Lakes." He got out of the car and came around to open her passenger door. "Senator Kimble's place is just around the corner. I thought you might want to take your time and approach the house gradually."

"Whatever works. I'm a complete amateur at this, and I've no idea what will and what won't." She glanced around her. If this was a subdivision, it was a subdivision of antebellum mansions. "Beautiful. Each of those houses must have at least ten acres surrounding it. I'm not sure that I'd vote for anyone who had this kind of money. I'd wonder where he got it."

"Private means. Inherited wealth," Silver said. "Cam said he was a pretty straight shooter." He pointed to the west. "See that glint through the trees? That's one of the two lakes. It's right in back of Kimble's property."

"And where are the Secret Service men who are supposed to be protecting Kimble?"

"I'm sure they can see us. I doubt if they'll show themselves unless they think it necessary. We have to hope that George was able to persuade them we're harmless."

"Then it would be a lie. You're not harmless." She stiffened as she saw two men detach themselves from the shadows of the trees. "And evidently they did find it necessary to decide for themselves."

"Stay here." Silver went to meet the two agents. "I'll talk to them."

She nodded. She certainly had no desire to deal with the authorities. She didn't even know what she could say to them. I'm here to see if I can pick up bad vibes? Christ, she had been trying to avoid appearing to be a nutcase her entire adult life, and now she'd been hurled in the middle of a situation where she had to be on the alert every minute.

Silver was smiling at the agents and then turning and coming back to her. "We're okay. They're just not taking any chances. I told them you're an arson expert and checking the grounds for suspicious objects. They'll be keeping an eye on us while they verify your credentials, but they won't interfere."

"Interfere with what?" She moved toward the house. "I don't have a clue what I'm doing, blast it."

"The first thing to do is not to get stressed out," Silver said quietly. "We both know this may work and it may not. All you have to do is give it your best shot."

She drew a deep breath. "You've dealt with this kind of thing before. What do real psychics do?"

Silver's lips twitched. "Kerry, you *are* a real psychic." He held up his hand. "I know. You don't think of yourself in that way." He shrugged. "Different strokes for different folks. Some concentrate. Others relax and try to let the impressions flow."

"You're a great help."

"It's up to you. I never claimed anything else. But, while you're trying to decide, why don't you kneel down and pretend you're looking for wires or something?"

She fell to her knees, her gaze searching the ground. "I thought you said the houses of all the potential victims were protected by that jamming barrier. Don't these Secret Service men know that?"

"No. Everything connected to Firestorm is on a need-to-know basis."

She looked up at him. "I feel like I'm praying. Hell, maybe that's not a bad idea." She closed her eyes. "I need all the help I can get."

He didn't answer. He probably didn't want to disturb her concentration. Okay, so try to concentrate.

Where are you, Trask, you son of a bitch?

Nothing.

Okay, then open your mind and let him come in. Breathe deep and steady. Relax.

Five minutes later she opened her eyes.

"Blank," she said. "Absolutely blank."

"Then maybe he's not here," Silver said. "Maybe Kimble's not the target."

"And maybe he is and I can't sense Trask." She got jerkily to her feet. "I told you I was no good at this."

"Easy." He took her elbow and nudged her back toward the car. "Are you willing to go and see our wunderkind who lives on the Potomac?"

"Why not? I can't do any worse. I have to try." She felt a ripple

of panic as her gaze went to the east where the sky was just beginning to lighten. It would be dawn soon, and Trask had meant to
make his kill before the night was over. Her pace quickened. "How
long is it going to take to get to wunderkind's place?"

"Thirty minutes maybe."

"Let's hurry."

"Don't worry." Silver opened the car door. "I'm not going to
waste any time, Kerry."

7

It was almost five-thirty. The target should be on the move by now.

Trask's gaze narrowed on the highway some distance away. The target's Volkswagen had come to a stop and he could see the Secret Service car pull up a short distance away.

He smiled in amusement as he saw the agents get out of the car. So serious. So official. So completely inept outside their limited experience. It only made the challenge more exciting to know that they were there.

The tension was building inside him as he made a final adjustment to the dish.

Come on. Let's get to it. I'm ready. . . .

Relax." Silver glanced sideways at her. "You're tense as a strung wire. Another fifteen minutes."

She glanced at the eastern sky. It was brighter, more gray than black now. "You're sure George let everyone know to be on the alert?"

"What do you think? George isn't someone who makes mistakes. Kimble's bodyguards knew we were coming."

He was right. She didn't believe George would be careless or take anything for granted, but it didn't keep her nerves from screaming. Panic had been growing since she had left Kimble's house. Dammit, she felt so helpless. "Maybe I was wrong. Maybe it was the Kimble place."

"Do you want to go back?"

"Yes. No. I don't know. But this doesn't feel . . . right."

"What doesn't feel right?"

"I don't know." She moistened her lips. "Perhaps I'm just tired."

"Are you sensing anything?"

"No. I'm blank. Maybe that contact with Trask was a fluke. Maybe I interpreted it wrong. Maybe I'll always be blank to him from now on." She shook her head. "Just hurry up and get there. Okay?"

"Okay." He was silent a moment. "But I don't think you should doubt yourself. First impressions are usually the true ones, in my experience."

"Well, I don't have any experience to go by," she said fiercely. "I could only tell you what I felt. He wanted a kill and he was going to get it. He was hurting and furious with me and he was glad he was— Oh, my God." She sat bolt upright in the seat. "Christ in heaven."

"What?"

"It's a woman. The target is a woman." Her lips were trembling. "It has to be Joyce Fairchild."

"Why?"

"He wanted me, but it was going to be okay. Substitution. Another woman instead of me. Don't you see? That would please the child."

"You're beginning to sound like him. You never mentioned a woman target."

"Don't you think I know that? He never consciously thought of her as a woman. She was a target. I only got impressions of water and that it was going to be all right that he couldn't give me to the child to burn. The target wasn't going to be perfect, but it might be close."

"Water. Her place isn't on the water."

"Dammit. I don't care. Turn around and go to..." She tried to remember. "...Fredericksburg. Isn't that where she lives?"

He nodded as he looked for a turnoff. "Get on my cell phone and call George. He's in my directory. Tell him to check with her guards to make sure she's still okay."

The target was running down the path toward him.

She was running fast, smoothly, seemingly covering the ground with no effort. But then, Joyce had always been a runner. He could remember when the rest of them had pulled all-nighters at the lab, she'd insist on breaking for her morning run. She said it cleared her head and increased her creativity.

Stupid bitch. She didn't know the meaning of creativity. She'd ridden on his coattails for the entire project. But that wouldn't prevent her from taking credit and whatever else she could steal.

But he could prevent her from doing it.

Joyce Fairchild goes for a run in Tyler Park every morning," George said curtly when he called Kerry back. "She's there now. Agent Ledbruk is in charge of the security arrangements and he's on his way. I've told them you're coming and to tell his men to go after her and bring her back."

"Call us when they have her safe," Kerry said, and hung up. She turned to Silver. "She's in Tyler Park. She's a runner. They're trying to bring her back. How long until we can get there?"

"Ten minutes."

She was beginning to feel the burn, Joyce thought as she increased her pace. In a moment she'd be in that place where running was pure euphoria.

The burn. Her lips curved in amusement. So many everyday phrases had to do with fire, and this was one she loved. Every muscle of her body felt stretched and alive, and the wind on her cheeks was like a brisk caress. Like a mother's gentle chastisement of a beloved child.

Child. That was what that nut Trask had always called Firestorm. His child. His creation. No credit to anyone else. Bastard.

Was someone calling her name?

It was those Secret Service agents who trailed her. They were probably upset because she was leaving them in the dust. She'd slow and let them catch up soon. But not now. Not yet.

Her lungs had stopped hurting. Her head was crystal clear.

Just a few more steps and she'd reach the burn.

She was there!

She could feel it explode inside her.

No. *Pain.*

Something was wrong. . . .

Oh, God," Kerry whispered.

The road bordering Tyler Park was jammed with vehicles. Silver pulled in behind an EMT truck and jumped out of the car. Kerry was already out the passenger door and running toward the path, where she could see a cluster of men and women gathered.

"Wait." Silver caught up with her.

"Wait for what?" she said fiercely. "It's probably already too late. Do you want me to—"

"Stop right there." A tall young man in a navy jogging suit stepped before them. "This is as far as you go. Get back to the road."

"Brad Silver. And this is Kerry Murphy." He glanced at the ID tag on the man's jacket. "Agent Ledbruk. We had George Tarwick contact you."

"Identification."

Silver handed him his wallet.

Ledbruk scrutinized the ID carefully before handing it back.

"For Christ's sake, what happened?" Kerry asked.

Ledbruk looked beyond her. "Son of a bitch, the media are arriving already. How the hell did they find out so soon?" He called to another agent a few yards away. "Keep them out of the area until we can get that body out of here. I was hoping to have this under wraps before—"

"What happened?" Kerry said through her teeth. "What body?"

"You're with the fire department? Come on. Maybe you can tell me." He turned and started down the path. "Damnedest thing I ever saw. And I never want to see anything like it again. We were running after Fairchild trying to stop her. Stubborn woman. We told her that it would be hard to protect her on these morning runs, but she was arrogant as hell. She said if we did our job she'd be safe. We tried, dammit. We sent agents over her route every day to make sure there were no snipers. But it's seven miles of wooded terrain. Too easy to miss someone. But she wouldn't listen. The park was her favorite run and she was—"

"Water," Kerry said numbly.

"What?"

Kerry's gaze was on the narrow trickling brook that had suddenly appeared as they turned a bend. "The path runs beside a stream. Water."

"So?"

Brad's hand was beneath her arm. "Just a comment, Agent Ledbruk. She's an arson investigator, and naturally she—"

"Jesus, that smell." Kerry's eyes closed as waves of sickness washed over her. "I can't—"

"You don't have to go any farther," Silver said. "Stay here and I'll—"

"No." Her eyes opened and she drew a deep breath. She started up the path again. "What happened to Joyce Fairchild, Agent Ledbruk?"

"She . . . ignited. One minute she was running ahead of us, and the next she was . . . blazing." His lips tightened. "Spontaneous combustion? It's crazy. I don't know what—"

"Did you try to put the fire out?" Silver asked.

"Do you think we're stupid? Of course, we—" He swallowed. "See for yourself. She's right ahead."

At first, Kerry didn't see her. A policeman was already stringing the familiar yellow tape, and several forensics experts were carefully going over the scene. One white-coated man was bending over a heap of—

Bones. Blackened bones.

"Dear God," Kerry whispered. She moved closer until she was standing over the woman. Or what had once been a woman. No trace of flesh or organs remained. There was only skull and skeleton. "She looks like she's been burning for over twenty-four hours."

"Five minutes," Ledbruk said. "It couldn't have taken us more than a couple minutes to reach her. It was as if she was exploding from the inside, melting, dissolving, and the flame was so hot that we couldn't get near her. One of my men tried to wrap her in his jacket, but it ignited before it touched her. A few minutes more and she was like this." He looked at Kerry. "So you're the expert. You tell me how this happened. Because my ass is on the line."

"Did you search the area for Trask?" Silver asked.

"No sign of anyone. Footprints near a drainpipe that led out of the park about a mile away."

"Kerry?" Silver asked.

"He's not here anymore," she said dully. "Why should he be? He got what he wanted. The entire sensory experience. He saw her die and he was probably close enough to smell her burning flesh. He'd like that."

"But how did it happen that fast?" Ledbruk asked. "We couldn't do anything."

"Maybe your lab will be able to tell you." She had to get out of here. "I can't." She turned and started back toward the road.

Silver caught up with her. "Are you okay?"

"Of course I'm not okay." She jammed her hands in her jacket pockets. "Do you mean am I going to keel over or anything? No. I've seen more gory cadavers than that over the years."

"This is different."

"You bet it is," she said jerkily. "She's dead because I let him kill her."

"Bullshit."

"I should have thought it through. I must have shied away from thinking about the threat to me or I would have realized she was his target before it was too late."

"You can analyze. You can agonize. You can tear yourself apart. But the fact still remains that Trask is to blame, not you." He opened the car door for her. "You did your best. We tried to stop him and we didn't succeed."

"Tell that to Joyce Fairchild." She got into the car and looked straight ahead. She had to keep her muscles locked. She had to keep him from seeing that she was starting to shake. She had told the truth. She had seen more-horrible sights, but this one had struck her to the core. "Could we go home, please? I'm very tired."

He studied her for a moment and then muttered a curse beneath his breath. "For someone who's not about to keel over, you look like you're pretty close." He pulled away from the curb. "We'll be home in thirty minutes."

———

You look like you could use a nice cup of tea, Ms. Murphy," George said as he met them on the steps. "Or maybe a good stiff bourbon."

"No, thank you."

George glanced at Silver. "I haven't been able to contact anyone at Tyler Park since I warned them. That isn't a good sign."

"A lousy sign," Kerry said as she climbed the steps. "Yellow tapes, agents all over the place, and EMT trucks, and no one who could help."

"She's dead?"

"Burned to a crisp. Now, if you'll excuse me, I think I'll go to my room." She passed George and went inside the house. The staircase seemed to stretch on forever. Just get up the stairs and into her room. She'd curl up under that lush comforter and the shaking would stop. Then, after a little while, she'd be able to face what had happened to Joyce Fairchild.

———

She's not good," George murmured as he watched Kerry slowly climb the steps. "And I'd judge her to be a tough cookie. It must have been one hell of a night."

"Yes, and she's had an emotional overload for the past week," Silver said. "Today was the icing on the cake."

"No trace of Trask at the scene?"

"Footprints near a drainage pipe." He hesitated and then made a decision. "I'm going to see how she's doing."

"Don't you think you'd better let her have a little time to herself?"

"No." George might be right, but Silver didn't want to wait. That silent drive home had bugged the hell out of him. He hated feeling this helpless. "Where's her dog?"

"In the kitchen. Where else? You think you need protection? You chose the wrong animal."

"I need a buffer." He headed for the kitchen. "And Sam has got to fill the bill."

———

It's Silver. May I come in?"

She huddled deeper under the comforter. "Why?"

"I brought Sam." He opened the door. "I thought you could use a little canine therapy."

"It's not the—" She broke off as Sam hurled himself across the room, landed in the middle of the bed, and began licking her face. "Stop it, Sam. I'm not in the mood." But she automatically started stroking his head. She glanced warily at Silver over the dog's head. "I don't need therapy, Silver."

"You need comfort, and it comes close to the same thing." He sat down in the chair beside the bed. "I figured it couldn't hurt. I knew you wouldn't accept it from me."

"You want to comfort me?" She smiled without mirth. "Will wonders never cease."

"This kind of situation frustrates me. I'd rather go in and fix what's wrong. It's what I *do,* dammit. It's what I'm good at. But I made you a promise." He made a face. "So I brought you Sam."

"Sam would rather be in the kitchen and follow the food chain."

"Too bad. He has a duty to you." He reached over and tucked the comforter tighter around her. "Everyone has to do their job. Are you cold? You look like an Eskimo."

"I'm a little chilly."

"Shock." He got up and headed for the bathroom. "I'll get you some instant coffee. There's a hot-water dispenser in the bathroom."

"I don't need—" She was talking to the air. She could hear the water running and a moment later he returned with a steaming cup. "Why are you doing this?"

"I told you." He handed her the cup. "My prime job is to fix what's broken, and this is the only way you'll let me do it."

She took the cup and cradled it in her hands. The heat felt good on her cold palms. "Fix what's broken . . . Is that really what you try to do?"

"It's what I prefer to do." He sat down in the chair again. "I can't deny I've done my share of spoiling. I'm not perfect and sometimes I get off on other tracks, but putting things back together gives me the most satisfaction."

"By interfering."

He shrugged. "I can't deny it. But when I decided to take charge of my talent, I had a choice to make. I could either use it destructively or constructively, and either way I couldn't pussyfoot around. It's not my way. So what you see is what you get." He leaned back and gazed at her. "Right now you're pretty messed up, but I think you can work it out for yourself. I just wanted to tell you that I'm here if you need me."

She nodded slowly. "Thank you. That's very kind of you."

He grinned as he rose to his feet. "And you're shocked as hell. You've been thinking of me as the bogeyman. Well, I'm a selfish son of a bitch and I'm not always pure as the driven snow." He headed for the door. "But I have my moments."

Evidently he did. These last few moments had completely surprised her. "And you came up here to try to make me feel better?"

"Yes." He opened the door. "But I also have a hunch you're at a crossroad. I wanted to give you all the information you need to decide which path to take."

The door closed after him before she could reply.

He was wrong. She was upset and shocked, but she wasn't torn by indecision. She just needed a little time to recover her balance after the death of that poor woman. Why had he thought she was? She rejected immediately the answer that occurred to her. He hadn't broken his promise.

How could she be sure? Of course, she couldn't be sure, but she was beginning to know Silver.

Putting things back together gives me the most satisfaction.

Those words had rung true. An important missing piece of the puzzle that was Brad Silver.

And she believed he was trying to keep his promise.

So if he seemed to have insight into her thought processes, it was because he probably knew her better than anyone on earth.

And he thought she was at a crossroad.

Sam whined and rolled over on his back for a belly rub.

She absently stroked him as she lay back down on the pillows. Having Sam here was a comfort. Another thing that Silver had guessed. That didn't mean he was right about her inner turmoil. Perhaps he was nudging her toward this mythical crossroad.

But she was beginning to think he was right about that too, dammit.

─────────

You look more rested," Silver said as he watched her coming down the staircase with Sam at her heels. "I peeked in your room a couple hours ago and you were sound asleep."

"I went to sleep almost immediately after you left." She grimaced. "So if you expected me to lie there and soul-search, you batted out."

He shook his head. "I'm glad you slept." He took her arm. "Come on. I'll ask George to have the cook make you something to eat."

"A sandwich will do. And I don't need a cook." She glanced at him. "Did you sleep at all?"

"A little. I don't need much."

"Is there anything on the news about Joyce Fairchild?"

He shook his head. "Ledbruk must have managed to cover it. God only knows how." He gestured to the kitchen chair. "Sit down. I'll make you something. Ham and cheese okay?"

She nodded. "I can make it."

"I know where everything is." He went to the refrigerator. "It's more efficient if I do it."

"Then by all means."

He glanced at her over his shoulder. "You're being very agreeable."

"You're offering me a service." She smiled faintly. "And you're making sense. As you said, it's more efficient."

He stopped, then turned and leaned back on the refrigerator. "Are we still talking about the sandwich?"

"Among other things." Her smile faded. "Damn you."

"And that means?"

"It means that Michael Travis was right. That you were right."

She moistened her lips. "And that if I'd had more control instead of just being a damn sponge, I might have been able to save Joyce Fairchild."

He didn't answer.

"You're not going to argue with me?"

"Do you want someone to soothe you and tell you lies? It won't be me, Kerry. There's a strong possibility that you're right. On the other hand, it might still have gone down the same way. Who the hell knows?"

"I know. I have a gut feeling."

"Then it's probably true. I believe in gut feelings. So where is this taking us?"

"I think you know. You said you fix things. Can you also build things?"

"Maybe. What do you want me to build?"

"A wall to keep out all the flak and poison Trask throws at me. It's like being in the middle of a tornado. I can't sort out what's important and what's not. All I can do is try to keep from drowning in the slime."

"That's not too difficult to do. It's what Travis wanted to teach you to protect yourself years ago."

"And while you're at it"—she met his gaze—"do you think you can show me how to influence Trask, push him to do what I want him to do?"

He shook his head. "I've never run across anyone who had the same talent I have."

"I know I can't change his reality. All I want to do is push him a little, maybe find a way to slow him down or divert him so that we can catch the bastard. Is that possible?"

He thought about it. "I don't know. It's possible, I suppose. It depends how well you can defend yourself."

"Defend?"

"Even if he's unaware of what you're doing, the psyche's defenses are automatic. You'd be safer not trying anything fancy."

"Will you try to teach me how to do it?"

"If that's what you want."

"That's what I want."

"Are you sure you know what you're getting into?"

"Hell, no, I don't have any idea. Tell me."

"You want me to teach you. I can't be subtle. I can't sneak in and just change everything. You're going to know I'm inside your mind and you're not going to like it. I'm going to have to show you. There's nothing more intimate or intrusive. Do you understand?"

"Do you think I didn't consider every disadvantage you could dream up? You're damn right I'm not going to like it. I'm going to feel like kicking and screaming. I'm going to *hate* it." She paused a moment to gain control. "But I don't see any other way I can handle this. I won't let anyone else die if I can find any way to prevent it. There are three more people at risk out there."

"Five. You forgot about you and me. Not to mention the thousands who might be victimized if Trask sells Firestorm to an unfriendly nation."

"So stop warning me and worry about how you're going to teach me to push."

He shook his head. "Defense first." He paused. "And you're going to have to learn to trust me."

"I'll try. You can't expect me to—"

"I expect everything from you. Just as you'll have to expect everything from me. Total interdependence."

"Is that supposed to intimidate me? I can handle it."

He smiled. "But you're scared shitless."

"That doesn't change anything. Let's go for it."

"Right now?"

"Now. This minute. I don't want to put it off."

"Like a dose of castor oil. It doesn't work that way. I set the pace, Kerry."

"I don't see why I can't—" She shrugged. "So how do we begin?"

He opened the refrigerator door. "We begin with a ham-and-cheese sandwich. Do you like mayonnaise?"

What the hell happened in Tyler Park?" Dickens asked when Trask called him. "The feds were all over the place."

"How do you know?"

"Did you think I wasn't going to keep an eye on what was going on? I'm the one who did the legwork scoping the park out for you. I'm the one who might be remembered and recognized." He paused. "What did you do?"

"You don't want to know."

Dickens swore softly. "I didn't buy into anything that might get me hung out to dry. I'm not getting paid to take those kinds of risks. Ki Yong said that all I had to do was some basic tailing and bugging."

"But I'm sure Ki Yong said you were to obey my orders. I don't think you'd like me to tell him I'm not happy with you. He might decide to finesse you into Guantánamo with those other terrorist suspects."

"Jesus, I'm no terrorist."

"It's a fine line. I don't consider myself a terrorist either, but Homeland Security might have a different view. And you're my accomplice, aren't you?"

"Accomplice to what?" He paused. "Did you kill her?"

"Of course. You knew it was going to happen. That's what makes you an accomplice." His tone hardened. "Enough, Dickens.

It's over. I didn't call you to discuss what happened in Tyler Park. I need to know about Kerry Murphy. What have you found out?"

Dickens was silent a moment. "You know about her brother and his wife. Her father, Ron Murphy, is still alive, but she doesn't see much of him. He's a journalist and seems to be closer to his son. She has friends, but no one very close. You're looking for a hook?"

"No, I'm looking for bait. Someone to draw her out and away from Silver."

"I thought Silver was your next—" He stopped. "You had me find out everything I could about him."

Trask chuckled. "You see, you are an accomplice. So stop wobbling, Dickens. Silver is a target, but Kerry Murphy has a special appeal for me." And excitement. He'd thought that the Fairchild killing would cause that excitement to abate, but it hadn't happened. What was it about Kerry Murphy that made him feel this sense of closeness to her? The fact that Silver had brought her here to track him down? The fact that he had failed in killing her and her family that night?

No, it was something else, something he couldn't put his finger on. Oh, well, it would come to him. "I'll stay in touch, Dickens. Keep on the woman. Don't just tail her. I want to know everything about her. Watch her, get a tech van, and monitor her phone calls. Let me know when you find a hole in her armor."

"If I find a hole."

"No, Dickens, when. Everyone is vulnerable—even you." He hung up before Dickens could reply. He didn't want Dickens to have a chance to stammer or ask questions. It was important to strike just the right note with people of his caliber. You had to instill fear and never let them get the upper hand. Ki Yong had furnished him with a tool that was only adequate and had to be constantly sharpened.

Until it was worn out and had to be destroyed and tossed away.

can't see you right now, Gillen. Perhaps in a day or two. Just be patient and—" Silver looked up as Kerry marched into the library and plopped down in the visitor's chair in front of the desk. "I'll call you back." He hung up and stared warily at her. "May I help you?"

"You're damn right. It's been two days," Kerry said. "And I'm tired of waiting for you to start teaching me something useful. I thought we'd agreed on what needed doing."

"And I told you that I was running the show. Just be patient."

"That's what you just told that Gillen person on the phone. I'm not buying it. While I'm being patient, Trask is probably setting up his next kill."

"No doubt. But Fairchild's death had a sobering effect on the other people on Trask's hit list, and they're being much more careful. We have a little time."

"But it doesn't make sense that we don't move ahead and—"

She broke off as she saw he was staring at her with a complete lack of expression. It was like talking to a wall. "Damn you." She stood up and started for the door. "I'm not going to wait forever. I want your help, but if you stall me much longer, I'll go after Trask on my own. I can't *take* this."

Silver flinched as the door slammed behind her.

He had been expecting a blowup from her, but he'd hoped he could put it off for another day or so. Well, he hadn't gotten lucky. It had happened and now he had to deal with it.

A discreet knock and then George opened the door. "I beg your pardon, sir, but I ran into Ms. Murphy on the stairs. I'm forced to advise you that you're handling her with incredible stupidity."

"Oh, am I? And would you like to tell me how I should handle her?"

"I wouldn't presume." George shrugged. "Well, actually, I would. She's a woman who's used to action, and this inactivity is driving her crazy. I can fully sympathize." He met Silver's gaze. "Because I feel the same way. So when are you going to get off your duff and do something?"

"I am doing something."

"You'll forgive me, but I see no sign of it." He added thoughtfully, "Yet I judge you to be a man who hates to spin his wheels. You could be telling me the truth."

"Thank you."

"Sarcasm isn't necessary. People who try to make a mystery of their lives should expect both skepticism and questions."

"Mystery?"

George smiled. "I'm not really complaining. I enjoy a good whodunit. It stimulates my mind and imagination." He turned to leave. "And I've been stimulated with some rather bizarre ideas since I met you."

"Would you care to discuss them?"

"Presently." He opened the door. "But I'm not your primary worry right now. I assume Ms. Murphy is important to you, and you may be losing her."

"I won't lose her."

"Such confidence. It makes one wonder on what it's based. . . ."

The door shut behind him.

Damn it all. Silver grimaced as he rose to his feet. George was too perceptive and his instincts were sharp. He was coming very close to the truth about Silver, and Silver didn't know whether that would be good or bad. Privacy had been a way of life to him for too long.

But George had been right about Kerry. He couldn't afford to lose her even though she might not be ready.

And it was too dangerous letting her simmer while he waited for the ideal time and situation to come together.

He might have to go for it.

Damn him.

She strode over to the window and stared blindly out at the driveway below. She should have known better than to try to budge Silver when she knew what an arrogant bastard he could be.

No, she'd been right to confront him. She hated this lack of control in their relationship, and she didn't like the idea of this delay. Trask might be moving closer to his next victim. How could Silver be so sure that they had time?

She was getting upset again. She should probably go for a walk or something and stop letting this impasse eat at her.

The hell she would. She wasn't going to trot meekly off and try to forget that she was right and Silver was wrong. She was feeling angry and hurt and helpless and there was no way she was going to stay that way.

She went to the closet, pulled out her suitcase, and tossed it on the bed.

There was a knock on the door. "Kerry."

Silver.

She didn't answer it.

"Kerry?" He opened the door and stood watching her throw two T-shirts and underwear into the suitcase.

"May I ask where you're going?" He answered his own question. "For God's sake, be patient. You can't go after Trask by yourself."

"I'm not going to be patient." She threw a pair of jeans into the suitcase. "I'm going to do something."

"What?"

"Oh, don't worry. I was angry with you downstairs. I'm not going to go after Trask and risk losing him." She closed the suitcase and snapped the lock. "But I can't sit around and wait for you to teach me how to get to him. You just take your time. When you're ready, you come after me."

"Where are you going?"

"Marionville."

"The place where Trask grew up? Why? Surely you don't think he's gone to ground there?"

"No, but his roots are in that town, and I may learn something about him that wasn't in that dossier. Knowledge is power, and I need all the power I can get. I don't like feeling this ineffectual." She gave him a fierce glance. "And don't tell me to be patient again. I'm sick of it."

"I gathered that you were. What do you think you're going to learn?"

"How the hell do I know? Maybe the way he thinks. Maybe a clue to what makes him tick so that I can push the right buttons."

"You do know there's a possibility you may be followed?"

"And that might not be bad either. At least it would mean something was happening." She dragged the suitcase from the bed and started toward the door. "I'll see you when you get around to doing what you promised."

"You'll see me before that." He took the suitcase from her. "I'm going with you."

"You're not invited."

"I'm used to barging in where I'm not wanted. It's a way of life to me." He opened the door for her. "So stop spitting at me and let's get going."

"I don't need you. Ledbruk's agents aren't going to let me go anywhere without surveillance. If you think you're going to protect me, I can—"

"Oh, I know, you think you can protect yourself. Well, maybe you can. But that's probably what all of Trask's deceased targets thought," he said. "Anyway, it wouldn't stop me from worrying, and I'm not going to go nuts wondering what's happening to you. I'd rather be on the spot and know." He started down the stairs. "So are we going to take Sam?"

She stared at him for a moment before she slowly followed him down the stairs. "No, he'd be in the way. We'll leave him with George." It was clear he was absolutely determined, and it didn't really matter whether he came with her or not. Maybe it would give him a nudge to start working with her. "I don't intend to be gone more than a day or two."

"I noticed you didn't take much more than the bare necessities." He put down her suitcase by the front door. "Now, can I trust you not to jump in the SUV and take off while I run upstairs and pack an overnight case?"

"What would you do if I did?"

"Go after you."

She shrugged. "Then it would be a waste of time and effort."
She leaned against the door. "I'll wait for you."

She's left the estate," Dickens said when Trask answered the
phone. "She and Silver took off about three hours ago in the SUV
and took Highway 66 and then 81. They just crossed the West Virginia border. I followed them, but I had to be damn careful. The
Secret Service was right on their tail."

"Highway 81," Trask said thoughtfully. "Now, why would they
be going..." He started to chuckle. "Of course."

"You know where she's going?"

"Yes, I know. It's always smart to know your enemy."

"You want me to stay with her?"

"For the time being." My God, Marionville. He hadn't been
back to that one-horse town since he'd left it to go to Europe on his
Fulbright scholarship. He'd thought he'd put those memories far
behind him, but they were suddenly bombarding him. All the bitter humiliations and the delicious triumphs... "Yes, I want to
know where she is every minute."

"You can't touch her. I told you, she's being followed by—"

"I heard you. I'll get back to you." He hung up.

Marionville.

He could visualize Kerry Murphy digging, searching, stirring
the embers of long ago. The image was curiously alluring. Maybe
that was her intention, to draw him into following her.

Marionville...

Drop me off at the local library," Kerry said. If this tiny town *had*
a library, she thought in discouragement. It was hardly a bustling

metropolis. The sign they'd passed when they entered Marionville had laid claim to eleven thousand people, but that could have been an old sign. It appeared that half the stores were closed on the main street winding through the center of the town. "I want to go through back newspapers and see if I can find any reference to Trask."

"How far back are you going?"

"All the way. I'll start the year he was born."

"I doubt if he was into any shenanigans in the cradle."

"I don't care. I want to know everything about him."

Silver nodded. "Well, I noticed an elementary school when we first hit town. Schools and libraries usually go together." He turned the corner and doubled back. "If we don't see the library, we'll ask at the school."

"Okay." She gazed out the window as they passed several small shotgun houses with peeling paint and rickety front porches. "This is depressing. It looks like the town's dying."

"It probably is. Evidently when the mines closed down so did the town." He pulled into the school parking lot and got out of the SUV. "I'll be right back." He glanced over his shoulder to make sure Ledbruk's surveillance car was within view. "This shouldn't take long."

She watched him go up the steps toward the front entrance. The elementary school was red brick but still managed to look as old and shoddy as the houses they'd passed. Had the town been this decrepit when Trask was growing up?

Silver came out of the school ten minutes later and walked up to her side of the SUV. "I found out the only local newspaper is the Marionville *Gazette*. It's been in business for the last seventy years. The library is two blocks from here. You turn left at the corner and it's on your right."

"You're not coming?"

"I decided to check back records while I was in the office, and Trask went to grade school here. The chances were good since this is such a small burg. I thought I'd get copies of his records and then check out his high school. It's in Cartersville, about five miles from here."

"They'll give you access to his records?"

"I'll persuade them. I'm a very persuasive guy." He stepped back. "I'll call you when I'm done and you can pick me up." He turned and went back into the school.

She scooted over into the driver's seat. That had been a stupid question. Of course Silver would be able to get the information. *Persuasive* was definitely an understatement.

The computer at the Marionville library was a dinosaur. She did a search on Trask. After the first hour the work went smoother. It was still slow but not excruciating. It took Kerry nearly thirty minutes just to stumble through the first year of Trask's life in the newspaper she'd chosen to access. Not that there was anything there but a birth announcement that Charles and Elizabeth Trask were now the proud parents of a healthy baby boy.

The next mention of Trask was when he won a local spelling bee at age seven. Two years later he came in first at a statewide science fair. There was even a picture of him holding the blue ribbon, with his parents beaming with pride. After that there were numerous mentions, as he took prize after prize that the academic community offered. Until the final awarding of the Fulbright.

She leaned back and rubbed her eyes. A brilliant student, a son to be proud of. No indications of any false steps. But this couldn't be the true picture. Trask couldn't have gone through his entire maturing years as a role model and then turned around and become a monster. The seed had to be there.

The seed.

She sat up straight in her chair.

And in this case the seed was the obsession that dominated Trask's life. Silver had said that it went back only fifteen years, but she had told him that she knew it went back much, much further.

She leaned forward and typed in one word.

Fire.

She didn't pick Silver up when he called her from Cartersville High School. "I've found something—I think. Call Ledbruk to come and get you. Check into a motel and call me and let me know where you are. I'll meet you there as soon as I'm done."

"I'll get to a motel on my own. I don't want you left alone." He paused. "I'm glad one of us has gotten lucky. With a few exceptions, all I've learned is that Trask was a golden boy."

"I want to hear about those exceptions." She glanced back at the computer screen. "I've got to go. I have two more years to cover and the library closes in an hour." She hung up and leaned forward, her finger clicking on the mouse as she went through the newspaper page by page. She stiffened as her gaze fell on an article on the back pages of June 3.

There was another one. . . .

She pressed the print button.

So what did you find?" Silver asked when he answered her knock at his motel room. "It took you long enough."

"I persuaded the librarian to keep the library open an extra hour." She dropped down on the couch and handed him the papers in her hand. "And I didn't have to use any of your 'persuasiveness.' All I said was please."

"Sometimes that works too." He looked down at the papers she'd handed him. "What's this supposed to be?"

"Articles about fires that occurred in Marionville and surrounding towns during the twenty years Trask lived here. I've marked the ones that interested me." She rubbed her temple. "No, interested isn't the right word. Horrified is closer."

"You think that Trask started these fires?"

"I told you that I sensed he'd started to be obsessed a long time before he made Firestorm his career. But I couldn't find anything in his background that indicated he was anything but Mr. Clean."

Silver nodded. "The golden boy."

"I still can't find any proof. And I don't even have the info to make a connection." She grimaced. "So tell me about these exceptions you ran across in his school records."

"There wasn't much." He sat down across from her. "You look beat. Want to go out and get something to eat?"

"No, I want to make a connection, dammit. I want to know the bastard."

He nodded. "You know he was brilliant. He was a fantastic student and made the effort to make himself likable to his teachers. But he wasn't the most popular kid with the other students. This was a tough, gritty mining town, and he was generally thought of as a king-size dork. There were a couple incidents when he went to the principal because kids were bullying him."

She sat up straight. "Who?"

"Wait a minute." He went to the bed and opened a folder he'd tossed there. "Tim Krazky. Fourth grade. The principal had a talk with the kid and that was the end of it."

"Maybe. Any other problems?"

He flipped a couple pages. "He was beat up by one of the football players in high school. Dwayne Melton. The school was going to suspend Melton, but Trask stepped up and defended him. Which made Trask even more popular with the academia."

"Dwayne Melton—" She jumped to her feet and took back the papers she'd handed him. "When did that happen?"

He glanced down at the record. "June fourth, 1979."

She put the pages down on the table and frantically riffled through them until she found the one she was looking for. "October third, 1981." She handed him the article. "Dwayne Melton died in a fire when the oil drum at the gas station where he was working blew up."

"Two years later," Silver said. "Trask would have had to be a damn patient kid."

"Like a spider spinning his web. He had no intention of being caught. I doubt if Trask was even in town when it happened." She went back through the other papers. "What was that other kid's name?"

"Tim Krazky."

She found it. "Oh, shit."

"Fire?"

"His house burned down and he and his entire family were killed." She read the last paragraph. *"No suspected arson. A kerosene space heater ignited the curtains in the living room."* She shook her head. "His entire family, Silver."

"Less suspicious."

She shivered. "Horrible." She sat back down. "Give me those school records. I want to see who else offended that son of a bitch."

He sat down beside her. "I'll read off the records. You go through the newspaper articles."

———

They found only two more cases that were blatantly suspicious. A gym teacher who'd embarrassed Trask was killed in a private plane crash the year Trask left on his Fulbright scholarship. The principal who had not punished Tim Krazky for bullying Trask was burned to death when his car ran off the road and crashed into a tree.

"Patience again," Silver murmured. "No wonder he wasn't suspected. He sat back, planned, and waited until his motives would have been forgotten before he went after them."

"And there's no telling how many more people he killed over the years." She gazed blindly down at the articles. "He was a perfectionist. He probably did some practicing before he went after his targets. Talk about bad seeds."

"Isn't this enough for you?" He took the papers from her. "You're not going to know the bastard any better by unearthing his entire list of victims."

"Yes, it's enough," she said dully. "No conscience. Not even when he was a child. But clever. My God, how clever to avoid any hint of suspicion."

"Then, if you're satisfied, why don't we go home tonight? This motel isn't the Ritz."

She thought about it, gazing down at the articles. "No, I'm not satisfied. This is all too remote. I need to touch him. Feel what he was feeling."

"And how are you going to do that?"

She shrugged helplessly. "I don't know. I just can't leave without—" She picked up the article about the death of Tim Krazky and his family. "Will you find out where this boy's house was located? I want to visit there tomorrow morning."

"It was a long time ago. They've probably built something over the ashes."

"Try." She rose to her feet. "He must have hated that little boy to have destroyed his entire family to get to him. I want to see it, feel it."

"No, you don't," he said roughly. "It's going to tear you up. You can't even think about that fire without getting sick."

"Then I'd better learn. I'd better learn everything about him and the way he thinks so that I don't flinch away every time he gets too close." She moved toward the door. "And I can't do it by keeping my distance. What's the number of the motel room you booked for me?"

"Nineteen. It's next door." He reached in his pocket and brought out a key. "Adjoining. You get spooked, you come running."

"I won't get spooked. I'm too tired."

"And you don't think Trask is near."

"No, but what do I know? I can't even be sure I'd sense him." She smiled mirthlessly. "That's what this exercise is all about. Getting inside his skin. Will you help me?"

"You know damn well I will." He turned and picked up the phone. "Though it's going to be difficult to find out anything at this time of night. Towns this small roll up the streets by eight o'clock."

"Call George. He'll consider it a challenge."

"That's who I'm calling." He smiled. "You must have read my mind."

"God, I hope not. The only mind reading I want to do is Trask's." She paused before admitting, "Actually, you've already helped a good deal."

"Of course I have. We're in this together."

"That's true." She gave him a cool glance. "And I probably never would have decided to do this if you'd helped me in the beginning."

"Maybe. But Trask is becoming an obsession with you. Somewhere along the road you'd have wanted to visit here."

"He's not an obsession. I just want to be prepared for—"

He held up his hand. "I've no objection to you being obsessed. It can only help me. It was just a comment."

"Trask is the one who's obsessed. I'm just trying to—" She drew a deep breath. "It could be you're right. At any rate, I'm feeling too blasted helpless." She opened the door. "The situation has to change. Good night, Silver."

Obsession.

She didn't permit herself to think about Silver's words until she'd let herself into her room and closed the door. She'd said Trask was the one who was obsessed, but ever since that first contact with him she'd been driven. Was it possible that when she'd been drawn into Trask's sick mind, she'd not really been able to free herself? Perhaps some of his poison still lingered.

She shuddered at the thought. The idea of being a part of Trask in any way was a horror.

But the idea of being unable to stand against him in another encounter was worse. Screw worrying about Trask's influence on her. Just take one day at a time, one step at a time, and tomorrow she'd sink deep into his past and the filth she'd uncovered.

Fire.

Screams.

Tim Krazky and his family trapped in that burning house.

Jesus, she hoped she could take it.

———

The Krazky family had not lived in town. Their farmhouse had been located on the Oscano River five miles from Marionville. It was a pretty site, surrounded by Bartlett pear trees.

But the ruins of the Krazky house were not pretty. Even decades later the foundations were still crumbling, blackened, and scorched. A brick chimney was the only part of the house that still stood.

"I was surprised that the ruins were still here," Silver said as he parked the car. "I guess the heirs couldn't get a buyer in such a poverty-stricken area. Or maybe they didn't have the heart to disturb the site of a family tragedy. Do you want to get out and walk around?"

"Yes." She already had her door open. "But you don't have to come with me."

"I'll come. Why shouldn't I—" He stopped. "You don't want me to come. Any reason?"

"I don't think..." She shook her head. "I don't know. I just want to be alone to..." She got out of the car. "I won't be long."

"Wait a minute." He glanced around the area. "It's pretty open. No place for anyone to hide." He nodded. "Okay, don't go out of sight."

"Why would I do that? Everything I want to see is here." She walked toward the ruins. It was even more desolate at closer view. Patches of grass were struggling for life among the rotting timbers. That pitiful effort to overcome the destruction only underscored the brutality of the fire that had ravaged the house.

Five people had died on this spot. A family had lived and clung to one another the way families did all over the world. Had they clung together that night when they were trapped in Trask's inferno? Or had they died separately in their beds, suffocated by the deadly smoke? She felt suffocated herself at the thought, suffocated by horror and sadness and anger.

"Okay?" Silver called from the car.

She straightened her shoulders. "I'm fine." She stepped over a timber and made her way toward the chimney. She wasn't fine. She wanted to get away from here and the memory of Tim Krazky and the hell he'd brought down on his family by offending Trask.

Stop whimpering. Do what you came to do. Think about Trask. Think about what he did. Imagine what he'd feel. Remember that night she'd touched him, and bring it all together. Learn him.

She reached out and tentatively touched the brick of the chimney. It was warm from the sun. It wouldn't have been warm that night. It would have been hot. Hot from the flames.

Hot. Hot. Hot.

Screams.

Lousy son of a bitch. Burn in hell.

No, burn here tonight.

They were trying to get out the front door, but he'd thought of that and tied a hemp rope to the doorknob and fastened it to the porch post. He'd anticipated everything, he thought proudly. Yesterday when they were at church he'd gone to every window and painted them shut, and tonight he'd crept into the house and started the fire first in Krazky's parents' room so that they'd be overcome with smoke first. Then all he'd had to do was wait here and make sure that that asshole, Tim, didn't manage to break a window and get out. But he'd seen no sign of Tim, and now the house was full of smoke. It wouldn't take long before they were too weak to—

He could see a face at the window. Tim's sister, Marcy. Crying. Beating her fists on the glass. She'd always had more guts than Tim. Where was Tim? Probably hiding under a bed.

Marcy was sliding to the floor, her hands clutching at the windowsill.

No more pounding on the glass.

He hurried across the porch and loosened the rope he'd tied around the doorknob. Then he ran around the back and untied the kitchen door.

The house was blazing. He could feel the heat on his face as he stared at the conflagration.

Die, you bastard.

He wished he could smell the oily prick's flesh as it burned. He'd only smelled burning flesh once before. Those two hoboes sleeping in the woods he'd set on fire last year when he'd been experimenting with ways to get at Tim. The scent had been like roast pig, only curiously different, more pleasing. Maybe if he broke a window, he could—

No, he had to get across the river to the woods and then home. Someone might have seen the blaze by now. Though he'd made sure there would be no way to rescue them in time. He'd burned the telephone wire leading into the house earlier in the evening. Tim's father had almost caught him when he went outside with the garbage.

Garbage. They were all garbage now. Less than garbage.

The water was cold as he left the bank and started across the river. But he didn't feel cold. He felt flushed and full of strength and exhilaration.

He'd done it.

So easy. The fire had taken care of everything. Killing. Destroying. Like a wonderful genie who had popped out of the bottle to do his bidding.

He looked over his shoulder, and his heart started pounding with excitement again.

Flames. Beautiful, beautiful, flames—

"Kerry." Silver was shaking her. "Kerry, what the hell?"

Fire. Let the prick burn in—

"Kerry?"

Fight it.

"I'm . . . okay." She jerked away from Silver. But then she had to lean against the chimney as her knees gave way. The brick was warm again, not hot like that night when—

Fight it.

"Tell . . . Ledbruk. Trask." She had to stop to steady her voice. "The woods across the river. He's there now."

"What?"

"Don't . . . ask me . . . questions. Just get someone across the river."

He glanced across the river. "And get you back to the car." His hand was beneath her elbow, pushing her across the ruins. "You're sure that—"

Hot. Hot. Hot.

"Do you think that I was communing with some kind of childhood spirit?" she asked fiercely. "There's no reason I'd suddenly be able to pull that off when I've never been able to do it before. I tell you, it was *him*. He has to be there. He felt safe in those woods that night. He'd feel safe hiding there watching us. He must have followed us from the motel. Call Ledbruk."

"I'm calling him."

She hadn't noticed he had his phone out and was dialing.

"Hurry. He's there. I know he's there."

"Easy." He opened the passenger door. "Get in and out of sight."

She collapsed into the passenger seat and listened dazedly as he talked to Ledbruk.

"They're on their way," he said as he hung up. "But the bridge over the river is five miles away."

"He didn't take the bridge that night. He swam across." She took a deep breath. "I don't feel him any longer."

"Try."

"Dammit, I am trying. I tell you, I don't feel him any longer. He's not there."

"It's a long way." He gazed at the woods across the river. "You lost him fairly quickly when he started moving away in the other two encounters. I'm surprised you could sense him at all at that distance."

"So am I. It must be because this memory was so important to him." She added bitterly, "It was his first kill and he was half out of his mind with joy. He didn't count the two hoboes. They were just a learning experience." She straightened in the seat. "Let's go after Ledbruk. Maybe I can help."

"I don't like the idea of you getting any closer to that bastard."

"I'm not afraid. He doesn't like to make any moves without preparation and he doesn't take chances. He had this fire planned down to burning the telephone wires so that no one would suspect he'd cut them."

"That doesn't mean he might not change. He followed you here. That was a big chance. Why would he do that?"

"I don't know." Her hands clenched. "I don't know everything. Maybe he was looking for a chance to take his shot at me. Perhaps he thought it was worth running the risk. Let's go ask him. That's what you want to do, isn't it? Forget about me. You know Trask is the only thing important to you right now."

He didn't speak for a moment, and she could see a myriad of expressions crossing his face. "Hell, yes." He shrugged and started the car. "I'm glad you reminded me. What was I thinking? Let's go get him."

Trask was no longer in the woods by the time they got across the bridge. Ledbruk's agents were scouring the area when Silver drew up behind their car.

"You're sure you saw him?" Ledbruk was frowning as he walked toward them. "How the hell could you tell it was him from that distance?"

"I could tell." Kerry got out of the car. "He was here."

"Past tense," Ledbruk said sourly. "I've got a bad feeling that we've missed him again. God, I'm tired of it."

Kerry had the same feeling. "You're probably right. He knows this countryside. He grew up here." She gazed at the heavy thatch of trees. "But you've got to try."

"Do you think I don't know that?" Ledbruk said. "I do my job. No stone unturned to find that snake." He turned and walked away.

"He's not in the best humor," Silver said. "Not that I blame him. He's done as well as he could, and it must be frustrating as hell to be let in on only part of the picture." He glanced at her. "Any vibes?"

She shook her head. "I don't think he's here." She leaned back in the seat. "But we're not leaving until Ledbruk confirms it."

"Suits me." He gazed after Ledbruk. "We'll wait until he gives up on the bastard."

Ledbruk didn't give up for another four hours. "No sign of him. I'll leave two men here to keep searching, but I don't believe they're going to find him. You might as well go home."

Silver looked at her inquiringly. "Kerry?"

She nodded wearily. "Let's go home."

9

Y ou look exhausted," Silver's glance was on Kerry's face as he drove through the gates of the estate four hours later. "And you haven't said a word since we left Marionville."

"What is there to say? We lost him."

"But you didn't expect to even have a chance at him. Think positive: You did what you set out to do. You became more familiar with the son of a bitch's psyche. That kind of concentration might even have helped you to increase your distance capability of contact. Those woods were pretty far away."

"Distance capability. Lord, you sound scientific." She shook her head. "I know you're trying to encourage me, but I can't think bright and happy thoughts right now. I'm too close to that poison that Trask was slinging at me." She opened the door as he stopped before the front entrance. "Maybe tomorrow. Right now I'm not seeing how much progress I might have made. All I can remember is how it felt to stand there and have Trask ripping me with his venom and to know I didn't have any control. I couldn't fight back. I was just a damn vessel." She started up the front steps. "And I'm remembering that you could have helped me and you didn't. If you'd done what you promised, I might have had a chance to be something besides a whipping boy for him." She opened the door. "So, if you don't mind, leave me the hell alone for a while."

"For a while," he said quietly. "Not for long, Kerry."

She slammed the door behind her and headed for the staircase. No, he wouldn't leave her alone. She was too valuable. He needed her. But that need had to be satisfied his way. He had to be the one in control. Well, she'd had enough of being—

The house was curiously silent, she realized suddenly. Where was George? She'd become accustomed to having him pop out of the library with one of his dry comments. He'd become a welcome buffer between her and Silver.

Maybe it was just as well he'd absented himself. She wasn't in the mood for humor, dry or otherwise. She just wanted to go to bed and not think of Trask or that poor Krazky family or her own sense of helplessness.

She had kicked off her shoes and was unbuttoning her blouse when her cell phone rang.

Probably Jason. He'd called two nights ago to tell her that Laura would be leaving the hospital soon, and she'd asked him to phone when they were settled at the hotel.

"Kerry?"

Her hand tightened on the phone. Her father was the last person she wanted to deal with right now. "Hello. What a surprise."

"It shouldn't be a surprise." Ron Murphy's tone was faintly sardonic. "I asked Jason to tell you I wanted to see you. He told me you were going through a bad patch."

"It's Jason who's been having a bad time. I'm fine."

"That's what you always said. Every time I tried to help, you closed up on me."

"As I recall, the last time you tried to help, I ended up in Milledgeville."

"For God's sake, you were—I thought it for the best." He drew a deep breath. "Let it go, Kerry. Life's too short to hold grudges. I've found that out lately."

"I'm not holding a grudge. I'm just wary." This conversation was becoming unbearably painful. It had to end. "Why did you call?"

"You're my daughter. Isn't it reasonable I'd want to make sure you're safe and well?" When she didn't answer, he paused. "And that fire at Jason's house was . . . unusual."

She stiffened. "Do you think I set it? My God, I *love* Jason."

"Don't be ridiculous. You're jumping to conclusions. I never said anything about—"

"But isn't it what you'd expect from a nutcase? Isn't that why you put me away?"

"I put you away because I wanted to get you well. And I know you'd never intentionally hurt Jason or Laura."

"Intentionally?"

"I've been nosing around, and there's no doubt the fire was arson. But other than that fact, I haven't been able to discover anything else. The lid's been closed down tight and no one's talking. Then I hear that you're taking an extended leave from your job and are out of town. Now, I know damn well you'd rather be close to Jason and Laura at this time. So what's happening, Kerry?"

"What do you think is happening?"

"I think you might be getting into something that might prove dangerous. I ask myself why an arsonist would wait to burn down Jason's house until the night you came."

"And what did you answer?"

"You deal with crazies all the time. Maybe one came out of the woodwork and decided to get even. But that doesn't tell me why the arson investigation has been put under wraps. Or who did it."

"And all your journalistic contacts are coming up with no info? How frustrating for you."

"It's more than frustrating. For God's sake, I won't be shut out of this, Kerry." A hint of anger layered his voice. "Jason is my son and I was looking forward to being a grandfather. I'm mad as hell and I want to find out who did this. I think you may know who it is. Tell me, dammit."

"So much for calling to make sure I'm safe." She interrupted wearily when he started to speak. "I don't blame you. Why should you be worried about me? We're not even on the same wavelength. Never have been. And I think you're probably telling the truth about your concern for Jason."

"Thank you," he said sarcastically. "I'm glad you believe I have some human feelings."

She had never doubted he could feel affection. She had just never been able to reach out and touch him. And after Milledgeville it was the last thing she wanted to do. "Jason and Laura are safe. I made sure of that. I'm safe too. Stay out of it."

"The hell I will. Where are you?"

"Stay out of it," she repeated, and hung up.

Christ, that had been difficult. She felt raw and hurt and angry, as she always did after she talked to her father, and tonight she hadn't needed that additional aggravation. Close it away. Don't think about him.

She half expected to hear the phone ring again. As a father, Ron Murphy might be hesitant. As an investigative reporter, he had no such compunction. And he wanted to protect his son and get to the bottom of the fire that had hurt him.

The phone didn't ring.

Good. Now go to bed and forget about him and all the

memories he had resurrected. He was no longer important in her life. The only problem he might pose was getting in the way of her finding Trask.

Go to bed and forget him....

———

Y*ou never forget him. He's always there."* Silver was leaning against the weeping willow tree beside the lake. *"Because you refuse to deal with him."*

"The hell I do. What do you know about—" She stiffened in shock, her gaze circling the all-too-familiar scene. *"What the devil are you doing to me?"*

"You know what I'm doing. What you asked me to do." He looked out over the lake. *"I didn't really want to use this scenario, because I was afraid it would bring unpleasant memories, but you gave me no choice. It was either this or barge in and risk doing damage."*

"Damage?"

"You weren't ready. Two days' infiltration wasn't enough. I needed much more. But you're so resentful now that I can't wait any longer."

"Infiltration." She repeated the word as if it had a bitter taste. *"What's that supposed to mean?"*

"Your mind has too much resistance. I had to slide in on the sly and undermine the barriers." He smiled. *"Even now it's going to be an uphill battle."*

"On the sly." Her lips tightened as she worked it out. *"You broke your promise."*

"I didn't break it. I was invited, remember?"

"I didn't expect—For the past four days you've been—You didn't give me warning, dammit. I was willing to let you help me, but it's not fair of you to—" She drew a deep breath. *"What have you been doing to me?"*

"Just what I told you. You thought you were ready, but you were

wrong. It would have taken me weeks to get anywhere. We don't have weeks." He picked up a stone and threw it skipping across the lake. "This last encounter with Trask bruised you. You need healing. You were comfortable here with me before, so this is where we stay."

"It's not real."

"But it's comforting. You like the sun on your face and the flowers and the lake. It's all very soothing, and you're going to need comfort."

She couldn't deny that. She felt . . . exposed, naked.

"I told you that you wouldn't like it." He turned to look at her. "There's nothing more intimate than what we're sharing. You're afraid of intimacy."

"We're not sharing. You're invading. I don't see you letting me go prancing through your mind."

"Good point. I'll make a bargain with you. When you're ready, I'll let you have a peek." He chuckled. "If you can take it. My mind isn't nearly as clean as yours."

"I can take it. Am I asleep now?"

"Yes, it's easier getting through to you. It may take a while to reach you in a waking state."

"I hope to God you're never able to do that." She braced herself. "Okay, we're here. Start teaching me."

He shook his head. "Easy and slow. Relax."

"How the hell am I supposed to do that?"

"I could help."

"No, you can't." She tried to ease the stiffness of her muscles. "There's only one kind of help I want from you."

"Then do it yourself." He yawned and leaned his head against the trunk of the willow tree. "And while you're at it, start thinking about your father."

"What?"

"He's one of the barriers we have to get rid of."

"He has no place in what we're doing."

"Yes, he does. I have to clear the path." He closed his eyes. "Or you have to clear it yourself."

She stared at him in disbelief. "Are you going to sleep?"

"Probably. I'm tired. I haven't had any sleep in the last two nights, and we can't go any further until you get used to the idea that we're together."

"And you're just going to leave me here?"

"I'll be with you. I can maintain the scenario." He smiled faintly. "I know you so well I can do it in my sleep."

"I don't know if I want you to maintain—"

"Too tired." He yawned again. "Wake me if you have any questions...."

He was asleep, she realized with indignation.

Of course he was asleep. She was asleep too. This was only another one of Silver's manipulations.

And the concept was too confusing to cope with right now.

She gazed out at the lake. It looked blue and deep and clean. She wondered if she'd be able to feel the water on her hand if she touched it. Probably. Silver was nothing if not thorough.

But she didn't want to test him. She was tired and on edge and wanted nothing more than for Silver to stay asleep so that she didn't have to deal with him as well as his damn scenario.

And, okay, at least it was a pleasant escape from reality. She could feel a soft breeze blowing her hair gently away from her temples and bringing with it the scent of spring violets. He had this dream world down to the last detail. How did he do it?

Stop worrying about Silver's talent. It existed, and she must use it as he intended to use her.

Are you listening, Silver?

No response. Maybe he really was asleep.

A little of her tension eased as she stared at him. His lips were soft and slightly parted, and his body reminded her of the boneless relaxation of a cat at rest. He didn't look nearly as intimidating as he did when he was awake.

Had he left some posthypnotic command to make her think that? she wondered suddenly.

"No." He opened his eyes. "Just got rid of the barriers. You wouldn't trust me if I messed around with anything else." He closed his eyes again. "Now will you let me sleep?"

"How did I wake you up?"

"Sharp . . . We're linked now and I can feel the sharpness. . . ."

Linked.

She felt an instinctive rejection. She didn't want to be linked to him in any way. "I didn't think it would be—I don't like it."

"Too late . . . We'll talk about it later."

Too late.

Because she could feel it too. Just a ghost of a tether, but it was there.

All right, she had asked for it. Accept it.

She forced herself to look away from him and out at the lake. Relax. Get used to it. The sooner she learned what she needed, the sooner the bond could be broken.

Open your mind. Close your eyes. Relax. Ignore that strange feeling of being joined to Silver. . . .

———

I'm leaving you now," Silver said.

She opened her eyes to see the sun going down over the lake and the light mellowing to soft twilight. How long had she been here? she wondered. She had drowsed and woken and drowsed again.

"Long enough." Silver smiled at her. "And now you're going to sleep deeply and wake calm and rested."

"That sounds suspiciously like a posthypnotic suggestion."

"Just a suggestion. Take it any way you want."

"You don't ever use hypnosis?" she asked skeptically.

"I told you, not with you. I promise. Sometimes I'm forced to use a form of it with a disturbed mind."

"For instance?"

"Gillen."

"The man you talk to on the phone. Who is he?"

"One of Travis's walking wounded. He's in an asylum in upstate New York. I've been working with him. He's a tough case. He was already unstable before he was injured and went into a coma. I use everything I can with Gillen."

"To put him back together."

"If I can. Sometimes it doesn't work. Good night, Kerry. . . ."

He was gone.

No!

Good God, she felt lonely. She wanted him back, she realized with shock. It was as if a part of her had been torn away.

Linked.

She was frightened at the thought, but that wasn't all she was experiencing. She hadn't expected to feel this sense of loss.

Empty. So empty.

The lake was darkening and so was the sky. Everything was becoming hazy. . . .

Her father called her tonight," Dickens told Trask when he picked up. "I don't think there's anything you can use there. She wasn't exactly friendly with him. They have issues. He evidently had her committed to a booby hatch several years ago."

"She's unstable?"

"She was at one time. No indication of it in her present life.

Unless you'd call her obsession with catching pyromaniacs a sign."

"Obsession isn't always a weakness," Trask said. "I've been called obsessed myself."

"Did you get my dossier on her?"

"Yes, very interesting." He looked down at the photo of Kerry Murphy on the desk in front of him. She was looking straight ahead, and there was a touch of bold defiance in her expression. "I need to know more. Keep on her."

"What about the surveillance of Raztov?"

He thought about it. He needed to move forward with tying up those loose ends, but Murphy was too alluring. "Put him on hold for now. Find me a way to get to Kerry Murphy." He hung up, his gaze still on the photo.

Kerry Murphy was probably an indulgence he couldn't afford, but the more he learned about her, the more he was enticed. As he'd stood watching her at the Krazky ruins, he'd felt an odd sense of empathy and familiarity. It had been very strong and caught him completely off guard. It was probably that, in her way, she was as enthralled with fire as he was. It had dominated her life as it had his. It made him feel very close to her. Almost as close as he'd been to Helen. . . .

His finger traced the curve of Kerry Murphy's cheek in the photo. It was strange to feel this mixture of emotions where she was concerned. His rage and desire to destroy in the most painful of ways were becoming tainted with an almost sexual attachment.

Because, even though she didn't realize it, he knew she didn't hate the fires she fought. She was fascinated by them; they possessed her.

And that possession formed a strong bond between them.
Linked.

———

Pardon me, Ms. Murphy. But it's after noon and Brad said that you needed to eat."

Kerry opened her eyes to see George standing by her bed with a breakfast tray. "Oh, he did." She yawned and sat up in bed. "I'm surprised you went along with him."

"Oh, I agree with him on occasion." He put the tray on her lap. "You haven't been eating decently since you came here. And he seemed convinced he was right. I thought it was worthwhile going along with him." He tilted his head. "You look very rested. Sleeping late did you good."

She felt rested. And calm. Damn Silver. She still wasn't entirely sure he hadn't left some sort of suggestion when he'd—

"You're frowning. Don't you like pancakes?"

She smiled. "I love pancakes." She picked up her fork. "Thank you, George."

"Thank Brad." He turned to the door. "It was his suggestion."

"I'm a little wary of his suggestions at the moment."

"Indeed?" He glanced over his shoulder. "Would you care to elaborate?"

"No."

"Too bad. I'm sure there were all kinds of layers to that remark."

She suddenly remembered something. "You weren't here last night when we arrived. Or maybe you were. Did you go to bed early?"

"No, I took a little trip of my own."

"Where?"

He smiled. "You might call it an exploratory journey. Brad wanted me to ask you if you'd see him after you got dressed."

He wasn't going to tell her where he'd gone. Perhaps she shouldn't have asked. Everyone had a right to their privacy. "How very polite of him." She took a bite of pancake. "You can tell him to come up now. I want to see him."

"He's on the phone. From what I overheard he evidently got a call from someone who needed soothing." He made a face. "It's weird to see Brad in that kind of nurturing mode. Like watching a tiger protecting a goat. I find myself waiting for him to pounce."

"Was it Gillen?"

He shrugged. "I've no idea. You know this particular goat?"

"I just know about him." She sipped her coffee. "And I don't think you need to worry about Silver devouring him. Maybe he's not as ruthless as we thought."

"Don't count on it." He studied her. "Do I detect signs of softening?"

"No, but he's like everybody else. I'm sure he has a good side and a bad side."

"Yesterday you would have argued with me if I'd tried to tell you that. What changed you?"

"I was angry yesterday. I've had a good night's sleep and now I'm more reasonable."

"And Silver is looking more like a pussycat than a tiger to you?"

She chuckled. "No way."

He breathed a sign of relief. "You were beginning to worry me. I was afraid you were having a serious lapse of judgment."

"Are you trying to warn me about Silver? It's not necessary, George." She leaned back against the pillow. "And I'm surprised you'd try. I think you like him."

"Oh, I do. I've always liked him. I admired his brother, but I've always felt a sense of empathy with Brad."

"Because you're a tiger too?"

He shook his head. "We have similar savage instincts, but I'd consider myself more of a leopard. Less straightforward and very changeable."

"Changeable..." Yes, she could sense the volatility beneath George's calm surface. "Yet you've chosen a profession that requires the utmost in trust and reliability."

"That's my Dr. Jekyll persona." He smiled. "And, as you've said, no one is one-dimensional."

"But you're not Mr. Hyde either."

"Are you sure?"

"Yes."

"Then that's more than I am."

"Believe it. Lately I've come too close to a monster not to know one when I see it."

"Trask."

She nodded. "And your choices seem to have always been on the side of the good guys. Silver told me you were a commando and then worked for the Secret Service. Why did you decide to go to work as a butler?"

"Why not? I'm very good at it and the pay is extraordinary."

"Because..." She frowned, trying to put her thought into words. "I can't see you...It's too...confining."

"Exactly." He laughed as he saw her troubled expression. "Stop trying to put me in my own niche. I'm the one who likes everything done properly." As her expression failed to lighten, his own smile faded. "Some people should be confined, Kerry. When I was a boy growing up in a family of servants, I hated the idea of being like them. I couldn't stand the concept that everyone has a place in society. I ran away and sowed my wild oats, and in the process I learned a good deal about myself."

"Such as?"

"I'm not at all civilized. I *like* violence. Yes, I chose the good guys, but given time I would have slipped. Violence is permitted, even applauded, in some professions. I had to find a cage where it was hard to break free."

"A cage . . ."

"A cage isn't that bad as long as it's self-chosen." He turned to go. "And I permit myself a few perks to liven it up."

"What kind of perks?"

His eyes glinted as he glanced over his shoulder. "Like curiosity. I have an insatiable curiosity and it has to be satisfied. Do remember that, Kerry." He opened the door. "I'll tell Brad to come and see you if he's off the phone."

"Okay." She stared thoughtfully at the door as it closed behind him. George's demeanor toward her had definitely changed as evidenced by the familiarity of calling her by her first name, and that last remark had definitely been a warning. George didn't like to be closed out, and he was evidently more formidable than she'd thought. Not that she actually considered him threatening, but his dry wit and bland manner had thrown her off guard even after Silver had told her his background. From now on she wouldn't make that mistake. In his way he might be even more dangerous than Silver.

No, just the thought that she was discounting Silver's power was disconcerting. She was becoming too confident of him.

The hell she was. How many doubts about him had attacked her since she'd woken today? But she'd dismissed them almost immediately.

Because she wanted him to be one of the good guys. She wanted to trust him. Oh, shit.

She pushed aside the tray and jumped out of bed. Stop fretting. Last night had been bizarre and unsettling and she was craving both explanations and reassurance. She probably had time to wash her face and brush her teeth before he showed up. She needed to feel alert and pulled together before she faced him.

Fat chance. She hadn't felt confident and pulled together since the moment she had met Silver.

———————

Silver was staring down at her breakfast tray when she came out of the bathroom ten minutes later. "You ate almost your entire breakfast. Good."

"I'm glad you approve." She dropped down on the bed and shoved her feet into her slippers. "How is Gillen?"

"Not good. I may have to go see him. I can't put him off much longer." He sat down in the easy chair. "How are you today?"

"You sound like a shrink. I'm fine. Just fine."

"Stop bristling. It was just a question."

"I'm not Gillen. I don't need your 'services' to put me back together. There's only one thing I need from you and you didn't give it to me last night."

"I told you it wouldn't happen overnight. Next time we may make more progress."

"And we may not. If you're going to have to wait until I go to sleep, it may take weeks before—"

"I won't have to wait for REM cycle after we're together the next couple times. It was just easier for the first time. All it takes is for you to relax and I'll be there."

After we're together. I'll be there....

The words struck her as almost unbelievably intimate. Or maybe it wasn't the words; maybe it was the memory of how she'd felt watching him sleep, his head resting against the trunk of the willow tree. She moistened her lips. "It will be that easy for you?"

"If you help me."

"You didn't need help last night. You were totally in control."

"And you resent it." He sighed. "You can't have it both ways, Kerry."

She looked away from him. "It scared me. I didn't know I was going to feel like that."

"Go on."

"I don't have to go on. You probably know how I—" Her glance shifted back to him. "I felt...connected. I felt part of you. You didn't tell me I'd feel like that."

"It's different every time. I knew there would be intimacy. I warned you about it. I wasn't sure you'd feel the bond. I didn't know I'd feel it."

"Well, I did feel it, dammit," she said fiercely. "Will it go away?"

"Probably."

"When?"

He shrugged. "I'm not sure."

"Don't tell me that. Has this happened before for you?"

"Twice. When I first started experimenting. Not this strong. Weak. Very weak."

"Who were they?"

"A ten-year-old boy and an old Italian lady."

"And what happened then?"

"The old lady died a couple years later. Neither of them even realized the connection was there."

"And the little boy?"

"It faded."

"But didn't disappear entirely?"

"No, but it didn't interfere." He scowled. "You're not the only one involved here. What do you want me to say? I'm not Superman. I don't know everything. Hell, I don't know a tenth of what's going on in your mind. As I said, everyone is different."

"I don't want it to get any stronger," she said through her teeth. "Make it *stop*."

"I'll try." He stared directly into her eyes. "But I can't promise. If that doesn't satisfy you, then you'd better opt out right now."

It didn't satisfy her. But she wasn't about to opt out. She'd gone too far to back away now. "No." She pulled her gaze away with an effort. "Just try to make it stop. It scares me."

"You said that before." He leaned forward and covered her hand with his. "It will be okay, Kerry. We'll find a way to make this work for you."

His hand was hard and warm against her skin, and she suddenly felt secure and yet . . . not safe.

Disturbed.

Heat.

Oh, Jesus.

She moved her hand and got jerkily to her feet. "I've got to get dressed and go find Sam. He needs to go for a walk."

"He's in the kitchen."

"All the more reason to take him for a walk." She headed for the bathroom. "He's probably been fed nonstop. I'll see you later."

"Yes." His tone was abstracted and so was his expression as he slowly rose to his feet. "Later."

He knew what she was feeling. How the hell could he not know? Close. They were so blasted close that she couldn't take a breath without him knowing. She stopped at the door. "It doesn't mean anything. It's just this . . . togetherness—it doesn't mean anything."

"I know that," he said quietly. "You don't have to explain anything to me."

No, she didn't, she thought in frustration. Because he knew her too damn well. "It *will* go away. I'll make sure of it." She slammed the door behind her.

10

I've been having complaints about you, Dickens." Ki Yong's voice was silky soft. "Trask isn't pleased with you."

Dickens's hand tightened on his phone. "Then get someone else to do his dirty work. I don't like the idea of risking my neck to please that crazy son of a bitch."

"You think he's crazy?"

"What do you think?"

There was a silence at the other end of the line. "You may be right. I've noticed signs of instability. But it's of no importance as long as he's kept under control. That's why I have loyal men like you to keep an eye on him."

"They'll catch him. He takes too many chances. He doesn't give a damn about the risk as long as he makes his kill."

"He's very clever. He has a chance of doing what he wants and surviving."

"How many kills? He's lost focus. He took me off Raztov and put me on Kerry Murphy. And then last night he told me to scout around the wharf district for a deserted warehouse."

"Indeed? How curious. I wonder what he could be planning."

"Whatever it is, he doesn't give a damn whether I get stung."

"I'm sure you're wrong. You know too much. He wouldn't want you caught." He paused. "How much do you know, Dickens? Have you found out where we can find Trask?"

"How could I do that?" Dickens didn't try to hide the frustration in his voice. "When he wants to see me, he doesn't let me know until thirty or forty minutes before the meeting, and it's always a different place. Most of the time he communicates by phone. He's damn careful."

"There must be some way to do it. If you could arrange a meeting with him on some pretext, I would be very grateful. And you would become very rich."

"You've told me that before. He won't go for it."

"Continue to try. The ideal situation would be to have him willing and cooperative, but I don't want him caught by the authorities. The simplest way to prevent that from happening is to take him off the scene."

"Before he makes his kills?"

"I don't care about his revenge. I care about plucking the prize he's holding under my nose. I can do that if I can catch him."

Dickens was sure Ki Yong could. In his dealings with the North Korean, he had always found him to be a cold-blooded son of a bitch. He could almost pity Trask if Ki Yong ever got the upper hand.

Almost.

"I'll do the best I can." He was silent a moment. "He's got a bug in his ass about Kerry Murphy. I might be able to use her to get to him."

"Kerry Murphy..." Dickens could almost hear the wheels turning in Ki Yong's mind as he went over everything Dickens had reported to him on the woman. "It's possible, I suppose. But there's really no revenge factor involved. Would there be enough emotion involved to spur him to an indiscretion?"

"How the hell do I know? But he took me off Raztov."

"And that alone is enough to explore the situation," Ki Yong said. "You may have hit on a way to benefit both of us, Dickens. Do keep me informed." He hung up.

Dickens pressed disconnect and thrust the phone in his pocket. Arrogant son of a bitch. He disliked Ki Yong as much as he did Trask, but the Korean paid well and he'd rather deal with his icy ruthlessness than Trask's volatility. He could judge which way Ki Yong would jump, because he was always motivated by cool logic. Trask was brilliant, but vengeful men were often erratic, and Dickens distrusted unpredictability. Dickens couldn't see where Trask was leading him, and if he wasn't careful, the bastard could get him killed.

Like tonight.

He parked the car and sat there looking at the row of deserted warehouses that lined the street. Two were condemned, and he'd be lucky not to have the floor give way and send him crashing into the basement.

What the hell was he doing here, anyway?

Doing what that crazy bastard told him to do. He got out of the car and headed for the first warehouse. Get it over with and get out.

This couldn't go on. He needed to put an end to being at Trask's beck and call. He had to find a way to serve Trask up to Ki Yong on a silver platter, line his own pockets, and get out.

But to do that he might have to find a way to stake out Kerry Murphy for Trask....

———

Why do you hate your father?" Silver picked a blade of grass and chewed thoughtfully on it.

"I don't hate him. I just don't like him." Kerry looked out at the lake. "And you should know why I'm not fond of him. He stuck me in that asylum."

"You didn't like him before that. Your relationship with him has always been troubled."

"Not all children get along with their parents."

"But you're very affectionate. You believe in maintaining family ties. You forgave your brother. Why not your father?"

"I'd rather not talk about it."

"Okay, then just think about it."

She looked at him in exasperation. "That's the same thing as—" His expression was alight with mischief, and she found herself smiling grudgingly. "Stay out of my business, Silver. I don't want my relationship with him glued back together."

"Why not? Don't you think you should ask yourself that question?"

"No." She rolled over and sat up. "I think I should ask you why you seem happy to lie around and ask me stupid questions instead of teaching me. When are we going to make some progress?"

"This is only the third time we've been here. And I am happy." He stretched and reached for another blade of grass. "And so are you. You like it here."

What was not to like? Delphiniums and green grass, a glittering lake and this man who had become a part of her. "You probably brainwashed me."

He shook his head. "You've just gotten used to me. Having me here isn't so bad, is it?"

She had gotten used to him. It was strange how comfortable she was with him now. She actually was beginning to look forward to opening her eyes and seeing him sitting by the lake and smiling at her. "Yes."

"Liar." *He chuckled.* "You like me."

Jesus, she loved his laugh. His voice was deep, but there was a note of boyish enjoyment. "Sometimes."

"Most of the time."

"When you don't interfere in my business." *She frowned sternly.* "Stop it and get to work."

"I'm already working."

She stared at him warily. "Have you been messing with me?"

"Just building a few barriers. I wanted to protect you."

Don't soften. "Then why didn't you tell me what you were doing?"

"I didn't have to have your help. The defenses will be automatic. When you need them, they'll be there."

"Just like that?"

He nodded. "Just like that."

"Show me."

"Trust me."

"Show me. I want to see what—"

She screamed as pain tore through her.

---

*D*addy!

Fire. Smoke.

Mama. Help Mama.

Couldn't help her. Couldn't help her. Couldn't help her.

The man was looking down at her and there was something in his hand.

No! Go away! Go away!

———

Gone.

"Sorry." She opened her eyes to see Silver's face above her. "Are you okay?"

"No." She couldn't stop the tears from running down her cheeks. "What the hell did you do to me?"

"I showed you," he said simply. "I attacked and you fought back."

"Shit."

"You wouldn't have thanked me for being gentle. I had to hit you where it hurt."

"You did that." Her lips were trembling and she tried to keep her voice even. "It hurt like hell."

"I know." He reached out and gently touched her cheek. "But you can stop it sooner next time, now that you know you're capable of doing it."

She drew a deep breath. "All right. You found a way to protect me, now find a way to show me how to push."

His hand fell away from her. "You're pretty pushy as you are. You just learned something pretty darn big. Absorb it before you leap forward."

"I don't want to absorb it. I want to build on what I've learned. Teach me."

"I told you I wasn't certain I could help you out there."

"Screw being certain. I've got to try to learn. Tell me how it works with you. How do you make people do what you want?"

"First, you have to make sure the subject isn't closed to you."

"Trask isn't closed to me. He erupts like a volcano every time I'm near him."

"Then you have to go in and block out all the distractions and try to find the path."

"What path?"

"You'll see. When you go into the psyche, it's like a twisting tunnel with offshoots everywhere. Most of them are short and some are blocked. But there are some that go all the way to the center of influence. When you find one, settle in and start pushing. Don't try commands. Suggest."

"Suggest what?"

"If you want him to go jump in the lake, suggest he's hot and wants to go for a swim."

"And he'll do it?"

"It works for me." He held up his hand as she opened her lips. "Yeah, I know. It has to work for you."

"And I can't practice on anyone, dammit. I can't go into anyone but Trask."

"You can go into me."

"And there's no way you'd let anyone control you."

"It's all I can offer. It's a pretty big concession for me."

She sighed. "Okay, I'll try."

"At least you'll get the basics. But don't get impatient if you don't have a breakthrough right away. Concentrate and pretend there's a wall before you and you have to chip away at it to get to the other side. . . ."

I told you that it wasn't going to be easy," Silver said. "We might as well stop for now."

The lake and field disappeared in darkness.

She opened her eyes to see Silver sitting beside her bed. "Why didn't it work?" Her hands clenched into fists. "I tried so hard."

"Maybe too hard." He stood up. "We'll try again tomorrow."

"You want me to keep chipping away at that imaginary wall?"

She grimaced. "I feel like blowing it up. Was there any progress at all?"

"A little." He smiled. "I could feel you plugging away at it." He headed for the door. "As I said, we'll try again after you get some sleep. You need the rest."

"What time is it?"

"Three forty-five in the morning." He glanced back over his shoulder. "You'll find you're pretty exhausted. Sleep late."

She shook her head. "I'm wide awake."

"You'll wind down soon. It will be like pulling a plug out of a dam."

She made a face. "You're just full of similes tonight. Walls and now dams."

"I'll try to be more original in the future. Good night."

"No, I want to try again. I can do it. I know I can do it." She added hurriedly as she saw he was going to refuse, "Just one more time. Please."

"You're relentless." His lips lifted in a half smile. "Okay, once more."

———

She was in!

"Congratulations. Now find the path."

"Don't nag me. I'm still getting used to—"

What?

Shadows.

"You're not like Trask. I can't feel what you're feeling. You're . . . hidden."

"I know. That's exactly the way I like it. Do what you can, learn what you can. Now, find the path."

"I can't see anything."

"Feel it. Concentrate. You wanted this. Now, see it through."

"Stop barking at me. I can't help it if I'm intruding where I'm not wanted. Well, maybe I can, but you deserve it. Now you see how it feels."

He was silent. "You're right. I deserve it. But that won't keep me from bitching."

"Obviously."

"So get your ass in gear and find that path."

I didn't do it, did I?" She got out of bed and walked over to the window. "I found your damn path and I settled into your damn influence center and zilch."

"I warned you it might not work with me."

"It might if you'd lowered your blasted protective barriers just a little. Would that have been too much to ask?"

"Yes. I gave you all I could." He was silent a moment, his gaze on her tense back. "You've learned a lot, and you'll learn more with practice."

"But I don't know if it will work with Trask. Maybe he'll know I'm there. Maybe I won't be able to find my way through that cesspool of a mind. Maybe when I thought I was pushing with you, it wasn't happening."

"You were pushing."

"How much? Enough?"

"I don't know."

"Neither do I. It's like stumbling in the dark, and I won't be sure until I run into Trask."

"That's what I've been trying to tell you." He headed for the door. "And now I'm going to bed. You may not realize it, but you wore me out."

"Yeah, keeping me from seeing anything, keeping me from making a dent, you secretive bastard."

"I'm glad you're beginning to understand me so well. See you after you've had some sleep."

She watched the door close behind him.

Loneliness.

Jesus, it wasn't bad enough that she felt a sense of desolation when they separated mentally. Now she was feeling physically lost when he wasn't in the same room.

Get over it. It was all a part of this damn togetherness. Or if she couldn't get over it, just ride with it until she could bow out of his life.

Loneliness.

Pretend it was another wall to overcome. Chip away, and maybe she'd be better at pushing the loneliness away than she was at being on the attack.

But there was no way she was going to be able to sleep right now. She'd done too much, and too little. So much for winding down. She felt as tense and strung out as a dope addict trying to go cold turkey. Hell, perhaps that merging between them was addictive. She'd become aware that the time she spent with Silver by the lake was lazily seductive, almost sensual in its beauty.

Because he wanted it that way for her.

Stop thinking about him. He was already dominating too much of her life. Take a shower and relax.

She turned and headed for the bathroom. That was the right idea. A hot shower and she'd be fine. She'd be able to go to sleep and practice the control Silver had given her to push away all thought of him.

She was out of the shower and drying off when her phone rang. She froze. It was after four in the morning. Jason?

She hurriedly wrapped her towel around herself and ran out of the bathroom to pick up her cell phone on the night table.

"You sound very alert for this hour of the morning. Am I keeping you awake, Kerry?"

Not Jason. The man's voice wasn't familiar. It was deep, smooth, every syllable precisely enunciated. "Who is this?"

"I believe you can guess. No, that's a childish game, and we're not children. This is James Trask."

Shock ripped through her.

"You're not speaking," Trask said. "Don't you believe it's me?"

"Yes." She had to steady her voice. "What do you want, Trask?"

"I thought it was time we talked. I've been thinking about you a good deal lately."

"I can imagine. You're probably salivating over the idea of incinerating me like you did Joyce Fairchild."

"Oh, I'm way past that stage. I admit that was my first impulse. I was very annoyed that you managed to escape when I set Firestorm loose on you in Macon."

"My sister-in-law didn't escape. Her baby died."

"Do you expect me to regret that? They were in the way." He paused. "It's really your fault the baby died. You shouldn't have teamed up with Silver."

"And that's your excuse?"

"I don't make excuses. I'm just commenting."

His voice was casual, without expression, and she had to take a moment to smother the flare of anger. "Why did you call?"

"I wanted to hear your voice. I've been sitting here looking at your photograph and thinking how alike we are."

"Bullshit."

He chuckled. "You sound so indignant. But it's true, Kerry. Think about it."

"You're a murderer. I don't have to think about it."

"Is that supposed to make me angry? Murder is only a word. You could probably kill given the right circumstances. Can't you think of one?"

"No."

"What if you were able to kill me?"

She drew a deep breath. "I'm going to hang up."

"I don't think you will. You're too curious about me. Just as I'm curious about you."

"I'm only curious about how a bastard like you justifies murder."

"The trick is not to try to justify, just accept. And your curiosity extends beyond that question. Why else did you go to Marionville?"

She didn't answer. "Why did you follow me?"

"For the same reason that drove you. I'm beginning to believe we're kindred spirits."

"No way."

"Did you enjoy the Krazky house? I was particularly proud of my work there."

"Three children died in that fire."

"Tim Krazky was a bully. I don't like bullies."

"So you killed him and his family."

"Fire cleans and destroys all the ugliness. Tim Krazky was very ugly." He chuckled. "Though you'd think he was even uglier after the fire got through with him."

"My God, you're sick."

"I'd be insulted if I thought you really meant that. But I know it's just part of the battle you've been fighting all your life. You got off on the wrong path and you're blind to the truth, but that's okay. I'll teach it to you. Unless Firestorm has to kill you. I find I'm regretting that possibility. Isn't that strange?"

"The battle I've been fighting is against people like you."

"There is no one like me. Except perhaps you." He paused. "But you didn't answer me. If you had the opportunity to kill me, would you take it?"

"Yes."

"That was difficult, wasn't it? Most people find it hard to admit the capacity to kill. It's so much easier once you face your true self."

"Is this conversation going somewhere?"

"You're cutting to the chase." He chuckled. "I'd do the same. I knew we were alike the moment I watched you standing in those ruins at Marionville. I felt a closeness to you that I've never felt with anyone else before. We're two sides of the same coin."

"You don't know what you're talking about."

"I know exactly what I'm talking about. We both love the child."

"Child? Fire. You're talking about fire?"

"Of course. You probably think you hate fire, but it's not true. It's dominated your life, and you can't help but be fascinated by it."

"You're crazy."

"No, you're just not seeing clearly. I believe it's my duty to open your eyes before the child takes you. My duty and my pleasure."

Smother the anger. "Then meet with me."

"You're not ready yet. You need to be seasoned. You need to feel the power of life and death and know that you're in control. There's nothing like that emotion on the face of the earth."

"I don't know what you're talking about."

"You will. How is your dog?"

The change of subject threw her off guard. "What?"

"I've decided to let your wonder dog get in a little practice. I'm having to run a few tests to correct some problems in one of my pieces of equipment. It didn't work properly on your brother's house in Macon. I think I've made the right adjustment, but I need a trial run."

She felt as if she'd been kicked in the stomach. "Trial run? One of the people on your hit list?"

"Oh, no. I have something else in mind. Something that will

bring us together. I have a challenge for you. Do you know how many warehouses there are in the Washington area?"

"I've no idea."

"Then you'd better find out. Or let your dog sniff it out. Now, what's his name? Oh, yes—Sam."

"You're saying you're going to destroy a warehouse."

"Yes. But it wouldn't be a true test unless there was something besides real estate to burn." He paused. "I'm choosing very carefully. I want someone young, with her whole life before her. Maybe a teenage girl . . ."

"You bastard."

"Yes, I can almost visualize her. A little plump, with long dark hair. Lovely, silky olive skin. If she wasn't wearing those hideous torn jeans, she'd look like a young Mona Lisa. So much potential and so little judgment."

"Who is she?"

"Find the warehouse and maybe you'll find her."

"And expose myself so that you can kill me."

"There's always that possibility." He sounded amused. "But how exciting it will be for you to find out if you value your own skin more than that poor innocent teenager. It will be a journey of self-discovery."

"Why are you doing this?"

"It could be I'm bored and want to challenge myself and you. It could be that I want to draw you close to Firestorm and burn away all the lies you've been telling yourself." He was silent a moment. "Or it could be because I'm lonely. You're the first woman I've felt this close to since Helen. It doesn't really matter which is true."

"Helen?"

He ignored the question. "I'm hanging up now. I've enjoyed talking to—"

"Wait. When are you—how much time do I have?"

"Two days. Midnight. The infamous ticking clock. Isn't that exciting?" He hung up.

Christ.

She threw the phone down and ran toward the door. She had to get to Silver.

Two days . . .

———————

For God's sake, stop shaking." Silver grabbed a blanket from his bed and wrapped it around her. "It's going to be okay."

"You didn't hear him." She clutched the blanket closer. Lord, she was cold. "He'll kill her."

"He may not even have a target in mind."

"He knows who she is. He's already decided who he's going to kill. I could *feel* it."

"A teenager. A warehouse." Silver's forehead creased. "A runaway using a warehouse as base?"

"It makes sense. Unless that's what he wants me to think." She lifted a shaking hand to her temple. "But I don't think he was lying. He was enjoying it too much. He wanted me to know how bold and clever he is. He practically drew me a picture of her."

"Then maybe we can find her," Silver said. "Or the warehouse."

"He asked me if I knew how many warehouses there were in this area. There could be hundreds, thousands."

Silver nodded. "But if this teenager is using the warehouse to live in, then she'd have to feel secure in the knowledge that she wouldn't be discovered. That means no security guards or people working in the place."

"Which doesn't narrow it down very much."

"We'll take what we can get." He reached for the telephone. "And we need some help with those statistics."

"Who are you calling?"

He was dialing quickly. "George."

————

He didn't give you any other hint, Kerry?" George asked. "It's not much info to go on."

"We've already established that fact," Kerry said. "And I've told you everything Trask said. Judge for yourself."

"We are a bit testy, aren't we?"

"There's a teenage kid who may die in order to draw me to that warehouse. You're damn right I'm testy."

"Easy," Silver said.

She whirled on him. "Stop that soothing bullshit. Nothing is easy about this. It stinks." She turned back to George. "We're going to find that warehouse. Hell, he wants me to find it."

"Then he should have given you more information."

"But then it wouldn't be a challenge for me. Can't you see?"

"He may call again."

She shook her head. "Only after he burns her to death."

"You seem certain."

"I'm beginning to know him. He'd call me and crow if I didn't find her. He might give me a second chance to stop another fire, but it would be too late for her." She drew a shaky breath. "So narrow down those warehouses for us. Get on the phone and call all those computer gurus in the Secret Service and get me a list we can work with."

"The Washington area could include Baltimore and several towns in Virginia and—"

"Then you'd better get on the ball, hadn't you?" Silver asked.

George smiled. "I just wanted to point out what a difficult task you've set me. I wouldn't get any pleasure out of success if you didn't appreciate that failure is such a strong possibility. But don't worry, I'll persevere." He turned to the door. "You'd better get her a cup of tea, Brad. She looks like she can use it."

"I don't want tea. I don't want any of your little civilized niceties. I'm feeling as barbaric as Attila the Hun at the moment."

"Ah, that's when you need those niceties the most," he said as he shut the door behind him.

"He didn't tell us how long it would take." Kerry shook her head. "What am I thinking? How could he even know?"

"I'll check with him after he talks to Secret Service headquarters. He'll have an idea then. It shouldn't take that long."

"It's just that there's no time. Trask's damn ticking clock." She closed her eyes. "I can hear it. It's like a heartbeat. Her heartbeat."

"No matter what happens, it's not your fault, Kerry."

"That's not going to help if I have to watch her burn to death." Her lids lifted. "Who is Helen?"

"The woman he said he'd been close to?" He shrugged. "I don't know. There's nothing about her in the dossier I received on Trask."

"I know." After Joyce Fairchild's death Kerry had forced herself to go over every detail of Trask's dossier. "But she meant something to him. Maybe she still does. I need to know about her."

"I'll call Travis and see if he can tap some of his sources and dig deeper."

"I'd think they would have already done that."

"Me too."

"It doesn't make sense." She thought about it. "Unless they don't want anyone to know who she is. Maybe she's under the witness-protection program or something."

"There's no use guessing. We'll find out. No last name?"

She shook her head. "I've told you everything." She grimaced. "Not that you probably wouldn't have known anyway. But this is one time I don't want to keep anything to myself. I'm scared to death."

"You have a right to be."

"Oh, not because this is probably an elaborate trap. It's because he said we were alike." She stopped. "It was a lie. I'm not like him."

"Of course you're not."

"When I dream of fire, it's a nightmare. Just because I keep having those dreams doesn't mean I have some sort of sick fascination."

"You're preaching to the converted." His gaze searched her face. "Why are you even dwelling on that bastard's fantasies?"

"I don't know. He was so . . . sure." She tried to smile. "And he hit on the one insecurity that dominates my life."

"If he's sure, it's because he's talked himself into it." He grasped her shoulders. "Take it from someone who knows. You have all sorts of guilt feelings, but your horror of fire is real. It's not some kind of charade you're hiding behind."

She drew a deep breath as relief rippled through her. Yes, Silver would know. Not that she'd really had any doubts. It had just been a thought triggered in that hideous conversation. "Thank you." Another thought occurred to her. "He says he's never felt closer to anyone than he does to me. Do you suppose on some level he's aware that I'm reading what he thinks?"

"It's possible. It would be one explanation for his fascination with you. But you can be sure that it's not because you're soul mates."

"That's good to know." She was suddenly aware of the warmth of his hands on her shoulders. Acutely aware. And even more aware of the response of her body to that touch. Dear God, not now. "Evidently you're not the only one who was able to tamper with my mind." She stepped back, and his hands slowly fell away from her. "I have to go get dressed. I'll see you in the library after you've talked to Travis?"

He nodded. "You're sure you don't want to try George's favorite antidote to the trials of life?"

"I don't want tea."

"Then I could think of another antidote."

"No." She grasped the blanket around her as she headed for the door. "I don't want you monkeying around in my head and try-ing to make everything all right."

"I had no intention of monkeying around in your . . . head."

She faltered in midstride. Don't look back at him. She didn't want to see what she knew she'd see.

Hell, she didn't need to see his expression to know what he meant.

She opened the door. "I'll find my own antidotes."

11

*J*esus, she was hungry.

It would go away, Carmela thought as she made her way carefully up the rickety staircase to the third floor of the warehouse. Just think of something else right now. Tomorrow she'd go down to the Salvation Army on Third Street and let them feed her.

God, she hated the idea of being a charity case. She'd had such big hopes when she left her mom's place in Louisville. It wasn't supposed to be like this. She was going to be on her own and not have to take all the lies her mom and her new boyfriend had thrown at her. She'd had enough money to last a couple weeks, and getting a job would be a cinch.

But the money hadn't lasted more than a few days, and no one wanted to hire a fifteen-year-old for anything but sex. Yeah, she'd run across plenty of pimps who were willing to help her sell her body.

Screw them. She wasn't stupid. She knew that whoring was a

one-way street, and she wasn't going down it. She'd take the charity and then she'd keep on looking for work. She wasn't beaten yet.

Not beaten, but chilled and lonely and scared. This dark, drafty warehouse smelled of tobacco that had been stored here years ago and the sour stench of rot. Every step she took caused the wood floor to creak, and there were other sounds, she thought with a shiver. Rats scurrying in the walls, and last night she'd thought she heard footsteps when she was roused from sleep.

Imagination. No one but her would be desperate enough to stay in this condemned building. But it had made her frightened enough to go out to the park this morning to find a branch to use as a club. Her hand tightened around it now as she pushed open the door to the tiny accounting office where she'd set up her quarters.

She lifted the flashlight, and the beam danced around the room.

Nothing was there but a desk, chair, and the pallet she'd made of the clothes she'd pulled from her suitcase. No reason for her to be scared. She grabbed the chair and pushed it under the handle of the door before she moved across the room and huddled down on the pallet. She forced herself to turn off her flashlight to save the batteries, and darkness overwhelmed her. Don't panic. She was safe. There was nothing here that could hurt her, except maybe those rats she could hear scampering in the walls.

If she could sleep tonight, she'd get stronger, and tomorrow she'd have a meal and she'd be stronger still. She'd find a job and everything would start going her way. Life didn't always suck. It was just pretty lousy right now.

But, Jesus, she was hungry.

———

Fourteen hundred commercial warehouses in the D.C. area," George said as he came into the library. "At least two hundred thirty-four are unoccupied at present. There may be more. Some owners don't like to report a lack of occupants to the insurance company."

"Shit." Silver grimaced. "No wonder he felt safe telling Kerry a warehouse was the target."

"He's not safe," Kerry said. "You told the Secret Service they had to search those warehouses right away, George?"

"I didn't have to tell them. They want Trask as much as we do. But that's a lot of territory to cover." He looked at the pile of telephone books on the desk in front of Kerry. "And you're not going to find him in the yellow pages."

"I don't know that. I think he wants me to find that warehouse. But he won't make it easy. I thought maybe I might see something that would strike a chord." She rubbed her eyes. "But no luck so far."

"Then what's next?" Silver asked.

"We go driving around and see if I can sense the son of a bitch."

"Sense?" George asked.

She ignored the question. She had made a slip, but she was too tired to follow it with a lie. "Will you get us the list of unoccupied warehouses, George?"

"I have it printing from the list Ledbruk gave me right now." He turned and left the room.

She turned to Silver. "Will I be able to sense Trask?"

"Possibly. If he's around. He may be waiting until the last moment to put in an appearance."

"We've got to try. I can't wait until he—" She broke off as her cell phone rang.

"Her name is Carmela," Trask said when she picked up the phone. "She's not of Italian descent after all. She's Hispanic."

She went rigid. "I thought you weren't going to call me back, Trask."

Silver straightened in his chair.

"I couldn't resist when Dick—when my employee called to tell me that he'd found out some information about our sweet little girl."

"And how did he do that?"

"He followed her around town today. She's trying to get a job, but she's only fifteen and she evidently doesn't have the money to buy phony papers. Poor child. She's having a hard time."

"Then why don't you give her a break?"

"Because she's perfect. She's turning out to be everything that I could want for Firestorm."

"You're sick."

"And knowing Carmela is trying so hard to make her way in the world is making you admire her and want to keep her alive. It's giving you additional incentive, isn't it?"

"I didn't need incentive." She paused. "At least tell me a general location."

"Are you getting discouraged? I told you that it wasn't going to be easy. So many warehouses . . ."

"You *want* me to know, dammit. You want me there."

"Maybe I'd get just as much satisfaction out of having you find Carmela after the fact. No, you have to work for it, Kerry. Now, don't sulk. After all, you can always have the wonder dog try to sniff her out."

She tried another tack. "Who is Helen?"

"Helen—" He was silent a moment. "That's right, I did mention her, didn't I? It shouldn't surprise me. I've been thinking of her a good deal since you came on the scene."

"Why? Do I look like her?"

"Not at all. She was brunette and quite beautiful. Don't be offended, but you're merely interesting-looking."

"Who is she?"

"An exceptional woman. She loved Firestorm almost more than she did me."

"Past tense? Did she leave you?"

"Don't be inquisitive."

"You're the one who barged into my life and turned it into hell. Don't I have the right to know about you?"

"Only what I wish you to know. But it encourages me to realize that I'm dominating your thoughts. We're growing closer, aren't we?" He hung up.

She turned to Silver. "Her name is Carmela. She's fifteen, Hispanic, and looking for a job." She swallowed hard. "And he can't wait to feed her to Firestorm."

"He didn't tell you a general location?"

She shook her head. "The bastard told me to tell Sam to sniff it out. Dammit, there's not much time. One more day if he told me the truth. It could be sooner." She had to drown the panic fostered by that thought. What else had he said that might help? "One of his employees was following Carmela. He broke off right away but I think he said . . . Dick."

"A first name?"

"I don't think so. It sounded like he cut it off. Maybe a last name with that as first syllable?" She shook her head in frustration. "I don't know. It could be a first name. Even if it's not, it may not be a help."

"And then again it may. Anything else?"

"He spoke of this Helen in the past tense. She was brunette and beautiful and had some involvement with Firestorm. Trask said she loved it almost more than she did him. If they were that close, why isn't there a mention in the dossier?"

"Travis is trying to find out," Silver said. "He'll get back to us as quick as he can. Carmela. No last name?"

"No, but if she's fifteen and a runaway, somebody must have

reported her missing. There are all kinds of databases these days for missing children. We *have* to find her. Maybe she called somebody and told them where she was and what she was doing. Probably not her parents, but maybe a friend?"

"It's a long shot." Silver got to his feet. "But I'll get George working right away. In the meantime, we'll get busy on those warehouses. I'll meet you at the car in ten minutes."

It's time to go home, Kerry," Silver said quietly. "It's almost three A.M. and we both need some sleep. We'll start out again in a few hours."

Kerry shook her head. "We should keep on going. We've only covered seventeen warehouses in all these hours. There are so many to—" She broke off and gazed at him in despair. "Too many. We're not going to be able to find her, are we?"

"We may have to get lucky," Silver said gently. "Maybe Ledbruk's team will locate her."

"And maybe they won't." She stared blindly out the window of the car. "I thought we might have a chance. But even if he'd been at any of those warehouses we went through, I might not have been able to sense him."

"No guarantees."

"Then what good is this damn talent?" she asked fiercely. "You'd think that there would be some benefit, something worthwhile connected with it."

"For God's sake, stop feeling sorry for yourself," Silver said. "Don't you think your years of zeroing in on arsonists were worthwhile? You wouldn't have been nearly as successful if you hadn't used your talent. You have to take the bad with the good."

The bluntness of his words jarred her, and for an instant anger flared. "I'm not feeling sorry for myself. I just don't—" She stopped and ruefully shook her head. "Maybe I was feeling a little sorry for myself. That's not allowed?"

He shook his head. "It's self-destructive. You know that. That's why you fight so hard. That's why you've made yourself into one tough lady." He started the car. "Now do we go back to the house and get some rest? We may need it later."

He thought she was tough, but she didn't feel tough right now. She was scared and discouraged, and he wasn't helping.

Or maybe he was. Maybe he knew that his harshness would be a prod that would spur her onward. He knew her well enough to know that she wouldn't respond nearly as well to pity.

Pity? The mere thought caused her hackles to rise. She drew a deep breath and straightened in the seat. "Not yet. Two more warehouses. Then we go back to the house and hope that George has been able to find out something to narrow down the search."

"Okay. That sounds like a plan." He smiled faintly as he backed out of the parking space. "Check the list and tell me where we go next."

Any luck?" George asked as he met them at the front door.

"That's what we were going to ask you," Silver said. "We came up with nada."

"Too bad." His glance shifted to Kerry. "You didn't 'sense' the bastard?"

She had almost forgotten the slip she had made last evening. "I'm not in a mood to have you make fun of me, George."

"Perish the thought. I wouldn't think of mocking you. I'm merely intrigued." He smiled. "And I can see you're a tad despondent. Maybe I can raise your spirits."

"Progress?" Silver asked.

"Not a breakthrough or I would have called you. But definitely progress."

Hope flared. "They've found the warehouse?" Kerry asked.

He shook his head. "No, but the results have come in on the missing-child database. Only three Carmelas are on the missing-person list. One was reported in 1997 and would be twenty now. The other one is seventeen and was reported missing in Dallas. The last was Carmela Ruiz from Louisville, Kentucky. That's not all that far from here."

"How old?"

"Fifteen. Her mother reported her missing over a month ago." He held up his hand as Kerry opened her mouth to speak. "Ledbruk's already sent someone to interview her mother and try to find out if she's been contacted and get the names of Carmela's friends. We should be getting a report back anytime."

"Thank God."

He nodded. "I'll second that." He turned back and moved toward the library. "Now if you'll excuse me, I'll go back to my command post and see if I can find out anything more from the agents in the field. I hope you realize it's not easy to balance running a perfect household and acting as a listening post as an extracurricular duty."

"We're duly impressed," Silver said. "Anything from Ledbruk's men?"

"No. Except a good deal of frustration and obscenities. The larger warehouses are like rabbit warrens." His voice trailed off as he went into the library. "Not at all easy to search . . ."

"But we have progress." Silver turned to Kerry. "Carmela has a last name and a mother. We just have to hope her mother knew her friends and that Carmela wasn't a loner."

And her mother might not be aware of who her daughter's

friends were, Kerry thought. If they'd been close, then Carmela would probably never have run away.

She wouldn't be pessimistic. They'd found out a treasure trove of information about Carmela, and there was still time to find out more.

She hoped.

"Take a nap," Silver said. "I'll stay here and call you if we hear anything."

She wasn't going to be able to sleep, but she'd try to rest. She started up the stairs. "And I'll call you if I hear anything from Trask." But she didn't think he'd call again. Trask had given her all the help he was going to give her. It was up to them to sort through the bits and pieces and come up with answers.

And cross her fingers and hope that everything would go right for Carmela.

———————

He was following her.

Carmela's heart jumped as she saw the tall man in the suede jacket standing by the Starbucks shop across the street.

It was the third time she'd seen him today. It was now late afternoon and she'd first noticed him this morning at a bus stop and again at the hot dog stand in the park.

A thief? Some sexual weirdo who preyed on girls like her?

It didn't matter. Just walk fast and try to lose him.

She turned down the next street and broke into a run. Two blocks later she turned left and then right again.

She waited.

No sign of him. She must have lost him, she thought with relief. Just to be sure, she'd go another three blocks down this street before she turned back and started for the warehouse. It was only six blocks away.

Funny how things changed. Last night she'd been scared to death of the darkness and creaking of the warehouse. She'd been thinking of trying to find someplace else to stay. But now she couldn't wait to get inside her little room on the third floor, where she'd be safe.

Baltimore," Silver said when he threw open Kerry's door. "Carmela Ruiz was in Baltimore two weeks ago."

Kerry jumped to her feet. "How do you know? Her mother?"

He shook his head. "Carmela has a sister, Rosa, and she was there when Ledbruk's man, Bushly, was questioning her mother. Evidently he was pretty convincing about the seriousness of Carmela's situation. He said Rosa didn't say anything while he was talking to her mother, but she ran after him and caught him at his car. She was pretty scared. She told him Carmela had called her twice and told her she was in Baltimore and having trouble getting work."

"Did she tell her where she was staying?"

He shook his head. "Just that it was Baltimore."

"How many of those warehouses on our list were in Baltimore?"

"Forty-seven. Come on. Let's go. Ledbruk's men are already on their way to start a search, and he's called in some of the local police to help, but time's running out. We have four hours if Trask wasn't lying to you."

She was already on her way to the door with Sam at her heels. "Where's Ledbruk starting?"

"South. We'll begin in the north side of town." He was running down the stairs. "Unless you have a better idea."

She shook her head. "I don't have a clue." She made a face as she glanced at Sam, who was skidding down the staircase at top speed. "Hell, maybe we should follow Trask's advice and take Sam to sniff out the son of a bitch."

"Not a good idea." Silver smiled as he opened the front door. "I'd rather rely on you."

"So would I." She turned to George, who had just come out of the library. "Will you have someone take care of—" She stopped. "Never mind. We're taking Sam with us."

"Why?" George asked.

"I'm not sure." A hunch? She signaled to Sam. "But it just occurred to me that Trask mentioned Sam in both conversations with me. It probably didn't mean anything, but I don't want to take a chance that he might have been trying to—" She headed for the door. "We're taking him."

———

Sam was barking in ecstatic greeting as Kerry and Silver climbed back into the SUV.

"Oh, for Pete's sake, shut up, Sam," Kerry said in exasperation. "You just saw us fifteen minutes ago." And it was fifteen minutes too long. This was the fourth warehouse they'd searched, and they weren't moving fast enough. She grabbed the list and checked off the two warehouses they'd searched on this block. "There's another warehouse ten minutes from here. Giliad Storage on Baker Street."

Silver nodded as he started the SUV. "Call George and check and see if Ledbruk has found anything."

"He said he'd let us know." She dialed the phone anyway. Maybe they'd gone through a dead-zone area for her cell. At this point she'd reach for any straw.

"No break," George said when she reached him. "I contacted Ledbruk ten minutes ago. They hadn't found anything, and he was pretty uptight." He was silent. "It's getting close to the wire."

"We know that," she said jerkily. "Let us know if you hear any-thing." She hung up. "Ledbruk hasn't found anything. Hurry."

"I'm hurrying." He glanced at her. "We still have an hour. A lot can happen in an hour."

"Yeah, Carmela Ruiz could burn up in that warehouse." She aimed her flashlight on the list. "There's another warehouse about ten minutes from Giliad. We should try— Stop that, Sam." The dog had jumped up on the back of the seat and was nuzzling her ear. "I don't want to play. No games."

"We should have left him at home," Silver said. "We don't need—"

"Game." Kerry sat upright in the seat. "This is a game Trask is playing with me, and he had to give me a clue if he wanted me to find that warehouse. He wouldn't want me to bring Sam to muddy up the situation, but he suggested I do it twice. Why?"

Silver's eyes narrowed on her face. "You tell me."

Her gaze was flying down the list. "I don't know. But maybe he— Samson Tobacco Storage." Her eyes widened with excite-ment. "Sam. Samson."

"It's a stretch."

"Do you have a better idea?"

He shook his head. "Where is this warehouse?"

She checked the address against the map. "On the waterfront. Thirty minutes."

"Get on the phone and have Ledbruk send some agents there." His foot pressed the accelerator, and the SUV jumped forward. "They might be able to reach it before we do."

———

Trask checked his watch.

Ten more minutes.

She should be here by now, he thought in disappointment.

Perhaps she wasn't as clever as he'd thought. He'd been sure that she would make the connection. *He* would have put two and two together, and they were so much alike.

Come on, Kerry. Let me show you my power.

Five more minutes passed.

He made a final adjustment of the dish that he'd aimed at the window of the third floor of the warehouse across the street. Carmela was in a little cubbyhole down the hall, but if the dish was working properly, the fire would block her exit route.

Where are you, Kerry?

Ten more minutes." Silver's foot pressed on the accelerator. "And Ledbruk may already be there, Kerry."

"And he may not." Kerry's teeth bit down on her lower lip. "All I could tell him was that I had a hunch. He may not consider a hunch valid enough to rush over there."

"He's not an ass. Trust him."

She shook her head, reached for her telephone, and started to dial.

"Who are you calling?" Silver asked.

"Someone I do trust."

Sirens.

Trask went still, his gaze on the flashing red lights of the three fire trucks at least seven blocks away. There was no question they were coming in this direction.

"Good girl," he murmured. She hadn't failed the test—yet. Kerry had figured out where the warehouse was located, but she wasn't going to get here in time to save the target. All he had to do was press the switch in his hand and get out of here. Too bad he couldn't stay and enjoy the fruits of his planning, but there would be firemen and police all over the place in minutes.

Kerry had cheated him out of that pleasure. It was strange that he felt no anger toward her. In fact, there was pride mixed with his disappointment. A pride resembling the way he felt when he saw Firestorm at work.

But he had to inflict the same disappointment, to make her realize that she hadn't really succeeded. It was only fair.

He pressed the red switch.

Smoke!

Carmela woke with a start, struggling for breath.

The office was filled with smoke so thick she could barely see. But what she did see terrified her. A red glare outlined the door across the room.

Fire.

Holy Mother of God, she was going to die.

No. She wouldn't die. Find a way out.

She was on her feet, running toward the door.

She threw it open.

The hall was a blazing inferno. The flames were eating the stairs going down to the first floor like a hungry beast. The fire was traveling at an incredible speed, already igniting the second floor.

But the stairs going up to the roof were untouched—so far.

She started toward the staircase.

Heat.

Searing heat.

She reached the stairs and started up them. She could see a door at the top of the winding staircase.

What if that door was locked?

No choice.

Sweet Jesus, the steps behind her were blazing.

Oh, God, let the door be unlocked.

Kerry and Silver were still five minutes away when Kerry heard the distant wail of sirens.

Relief soared through her. "They're on their way. They must be almost—"

Pain.

Tearing through her temples.

Swirling down into darkness.

Ugliness.

Filth.

Fire. Fire. Fire.

"Kerry?"

She couldn't answer. Fire was licking, swirling around her and . . . him. Trask. They were together, and Firestorm was—

"Kerry." This time it was a demand from Silver. "Fight it. Fight him."

Fight him. Yes, she couldn't be pulled into that darkness. She struggled. Hard. So hard.

Free.

Yet not free.

"What's happening?" Silver asked.

"He's done it," Kerry whispered. "He wanted to wait until I got there, but he was worried about being discovered."

"He ignited the warehouse?"

"Yes. He was in the building across from the warehouse, but he's out in the street now."

"Where?"

"Back door. Not the street where the warehouse—" She closed

her eyes. "Jesus, he's thinking about Carmela. He's wishing— No way out for her. But he wanted to see it."

"Why isn't there a way out for her?"

"He started the fire on the floor where she was sleeping. Firestorm travels too fast . . ." She was shaking. "She's going to die. He knows she's going to die."

"I'm going to call Ledbruk and see if he can intercept Trask. Tell me where he is."

"She's going to die," she whispered.

"Kerry."

"He's two blocks away and getting into a dark-gray van. He's driving away. He's looking back over his shoulder and he can see the warehouse. It looks like one big pillar of fire. No one could get out of that building. He's very satisfied. He's imagining Carmela in the fire. Her flesh is burning, blackening—"

"Okay, get away from him."

"She's going to die."

"Kerry, can you see the license number of his van?"

"No, I can only see what he sees."

She was vaguely aware of Silver dialing, talking on the phone. Then she couldn't hear anything but Trask.

Firestorm. Biting, tearing, devouring. The child was doing well. He hoped Kerry had reached the fire and could feel the power. Someday they would have to stand together and watch—

He was gone.

And the darkness and pain vanished with him.

"Out of range?"

She realized Silver's gaze was fastened on her face. "I guess. He's not there anymore."

"You stayed with him a long time."

"Did I?" She hadn't been aware of the passage of time. "Did you reach Ledbruk?"

"Yes. They've put an all-points bulletin out on a gray van. Can you remember any of the streets he passed?"

She shook her head. "Not when he was thinking about Carmela. It was too— Oh, my God." They had turned the corner and she saw the warehouse. "He's right," she whispered. "A pillar of flame." She could feel her stomach knot. How could anyone survive in that fire?

Stop being a defeatist. She'd fought enough fires to know that many times people miraculously survived in conditions that seemed impossible.

Carmela needed a miracle.

"She's not dead yet," Silver said as he parked a short distance behind the fire truck. "Scared shitless, but not dead."

Her gaze flew to his face. "You're sure?"

"I couldn't help but be sure. Her mind's screaming bloody murder. I couldn't close her out if I wanted to."

In Kerry's desperation she'd forgotten for the moment that Trask's ability to block Silver's intrusion was the rare exception. Of course he'd be able to reach Carmela. "She's all right?"

"Her back is burned. She couldn't get the door to the roof open. She thought it was locked, but it was only stuck. But it took her long enough that the fire reached her. She had to roll on the cement once she broke out onto the roof."

Her gaze searched the top of the building. The entire warehouse was engulfed, and she could barely see the low brick parapet surrounding the roof for the billowing clouds of smoke. "She's up there? Why doesn't she come to the edge and try to call out?"

"She's scared and almost in shock. She's curled up in the corner behind an air-conditioning unit." He paused. "But she doesn't have much time. She's thinking the roof is hot beneath her legs. She doesn't realize it's going to cave."

"Then tell her."

"It's not that easy. I'm dealing with hysteria, and I'm not familiar with her mind."

"You said you liked to fix things. Well, fix her, dammit. Save her. Make her do what you want her to do."

"Then tell me how those firemen can get her down."

She tried to think. "No helicopter. Too dangerous with those flames practically engulfing the roof. No ladder. She'll have to jump."

"Where?"

"Not much choice. South side of the building would allow them more room to set up. If the wall keeps standing."

"And if I can talk her into jumping. The parapet has to be scorching hot, and there are flames licking at it. She'll know there's a good chance she'll be burned."

"Are you saying you won't try?"

"No." He got out of the car. "I'm saying that you'd better get your ass in gear and try to talk those firemen into setting up for a jump. If I do get her off that roof, I want someone ready to catch her." He leaned against the SUV, his gaze on the roof. "Move."

12

Hurt.

Carmela whimpered as she drew closer to the air conditioner. The metal was turning hot. The whole world was turning hot.

It's not hot down in the street.

Can't get there. Stairs are gone.

Jump. They're waiting for you.

No, someone will come. I heard the sirens.

Not in time. The roof is going to go any minute. You know it. You can feel the heat.

She looked at the flames licking over the parapet surrounding the roof.

They'll come.

A sudden pain shot through her scorched back.

Hurt!

It will get worse. Unless you get off the roof.

No.

She cried out as another ripple of pain jolted through her.

Yes. You need help. Move toward the south wall.

I can't do— She screamed. Hurts!

Then crawl toward that parapet. They'll take care of you when you reach the street.

Hurts too much.

The pain will stop when you jump.

It will kill me.

Staying here will kill you.

Afraid. Always been afraid of heights.

Not anymore. I promise when you jump you won't be afraid.

Can't do it . . .

Then you'll hurt.

Pain. Pain. Pain.

———

There's no one in that building," Commander Jureski said impatiently. "I checked with the owner. The warehouse is vacant."

"That doesn't mean there couldn't be trespassers," Kerry said. "You know that as well as I do. There *is* a trespasser. A young girl. She's on the roof."

"You saw her?"

She jerked her head toward Silver leaning against the SUV. "No, but my friend did."

The commander glanced at Silver. "He seems really concerned," he said sarcastically. "He looks like he's working out an algebra problem."

"He saw her," she repeated. "She was at the south wall, but she's afraid to jump. You make it safe for her."

"It won't be safe no matter what we do." He frowned, his gaze on the roof. "Christ, there's no way she can jump without going through those flames. I've never seen a fire like this."

"It's her only chance," Kerry said desperately. "Just get ready for her. Please, Commander."

He hesitated. "You're sure she's up there?"

"I'm sure."

"Shit." He turned and strode toward the truck as he reached for his phone. "We'll get ready and we'll focus the hoses on that area. I hope to hell you're right about her wanting to jump. That roof's going to go any minute."

"She'll jump." Kerry prayed she was telling the truth. She'd done all she could. She turned and went back to the SUV, but she wasn't about to talk to Silver. His expression was intent, abstracted, and there was no way she wanted to disturb him. She stood on the other side of the SUV, staring up at the roof.

Oh, God, get her down, Silver.

---

*G*et closer to the wall.

It's too hot. Carmela shuddered as she saw the flames leaping up to melt the tar on the parapet. *I'll catch fire. I should wait for them to come.*

You can't wait. You have to jump now.

A sudden spray of water leapt over the wall.

See, they know you're here. They're trying to help you to jump. Now, get under that spray and get wet. You'll be less likely to catch fire when you jump.

Carmela edged closer until she was under the spray. She cried out and recoiled as the water sprayed her burned back. *Hurts.*

It will hurt more if you don't jump. I promise you. Now, move.

Take a deep breath, run, and dive over the wall. Don't think. Just do it.

She didn't move.

Do it!

Kerry held her breath, her eyes on the roof.

Come on, Carmela.

Christ, how terrifying the idea of jumping must be to that scared girl on the roof. There was so much smoke, she doubted if Carmela could even see the ground. She'd have to dive through smoke and fire, not knowing what lay beneath her. Could Silver make her do it?

There was a rumble as the north side of the warehouse began to crumble.

Oh, God, jump, Carmela.

Jump! Now!

No.

No more time. You're going over.

The hell I am.

The hell you aren't.

And Carmela found herself running toward the south wall. God, what was she doing? This was crazy. She had to stop. But she couldn't stop.

Dive over the edge. Dive over the edge.

She dove over the edge and was enveloped in spray and flame as she hurtled toward the ground.

A scream tore from her throat as the fire reached out, enveloping her.

———————

She's down." Kerry grabbed Silver's arm. "I saw her hit the mat. Come on."

"Right." He shook his head to clear it. "Let's go." He strode toward the crowd of firemen and medics gathered around the mat.

"Is she alive?" Kerry asked as she caught up with him. "Do you know if—"

"She's alive," Silver interrupted. "I don't know how badly she's hurt. I broke with her after she jumped." He pushed through the crowd until he could see Carmela. She was lying still and pale, curled up on the plastic as the medic placed an oxygen mask over her mouth and nose. Her clothes were in tatters, and the hair around her face was charred.

"She looks terrible," Kerry whispered. "Poor kid."

"Stubborn kid," Silver said grimly. "I thought I'd never get her to dive off that roof. I finally had to go in and take over."

"Why didn't you do that to begin with?"

"I didn't want to damage her. It's always possible when force is an issue."

She looked at him. "And did you?"

"We'll see when she wakes up."

"If she wakes up." Kerry turned back to watch the medics working over the girl. *Don't give up, Carmela. Trask wants you to give up. Don't let him win.*

———————

She's going to make it," Silver said as he came back into the waiting room after talking to the emergency-room doctor. "Some second-degree burns on her back. Shock. Smoke inhalation." He paused. "Mental disorientation."

Kerry stiffened. "Damage?"

"I won't know until she rouses again. I don't think so."

"But you don't know?"

"What do you want me to say? I'd like to reassure you, but I can't." His lips tightened. "Hell, I'd like to reassure myself. Do you think I want that guilt hanging over me? She's only a kid."

She felt a rush of sympathy as she saw his face. "You had to do it. You had no choice. She would have burned to death."

"That's what I'm telling myself." He moved over to the window. "You don't have to stay here. It may be hours before she wakes. I'll call you."

He was hurting, and she suddenly knew she couldn't stand abandoning him. "I'll stay."

"To hold my hand? That maternal streak surfacing again? I don't need it, Kerry."

"Shut up." She sat down again. "I'm staying."

He looked back at her and then shrugged. "Suit yourself."

He was tough, gruff, and often surly, but now she knew what lay beneath that defense. She leaned back against the wall. "Don't worry, I will."

Carmela didn't rouse for another eight hours.

Kerry was half dozing when she saw Silver suddenly go rigid in his chair. "What?"

He didn't answer, his expression holding the same intensity he'd shown when Carmela was on the roof.

She waited, holding her breath.

It was ten minutes before Silver looked at her and smiled. "She's okay."

Kerry let her breath out in a little rush. "No side effects?"

"No damage. She was a little worried because she thought she was hearing voices on the roof. I was able to convince her that it was shock that made her imagination go haywire. When she wakes up again, she'll believe that jumping was entirely her idea."

"Good. I haven't seen her mother. Where is she?"

He shook his head. "She hasn't shown up."

"Then maybe Carmela had good reason to run away. What mother would leave her daughter sick and alone in a hospital?" She stood up. "Let's go and ask if we can see her."

"She won't know who we are."

"That doesn't matter. I'll tell her we're from social services or something. I've thought about her, worried about her, ever since Trask told me he'd chosen his victim. I can't walk away without seeing her up close and personal."

He rose to his feet. "Then by all means let's go visit the kid."

———————

I don't want to talk to you." Carmela was gazing warily at Kerry. "And I'm not answering any questions."

"No questions." Kerry smiled. "We just dropped in to see if there was anything we could do."

"You can get me out of this hospital. I can't afford it."

"You don't have to worry. Your bill is being paid by the owner of the warehouse. He's just hoping you won't sue him."

She frowned doubtfully. "Really?"

"I promise you won't get a bill," Silver said. "Just concentrate on getting well."

She was silent a moment. "Is he really worried I'll sue him? Do you suppose you could get a settlement from him?"

Kerry felt a twinge of disappointment. "Possibly. What did you have in mind?"

"Not much. Just enough to set me up in an apartment and keep us going until I get a job."

"Us?"

"I want my sister, Rosa, with me." Her hands clenched on the sheet. "I promised her."

"And how old is Rosa?"

"Twelve."

"Then she's a minor just as you are," Kerry said. "The courts aren't going to let her leave your mother. They'll probably insist on you returning."

"No!" She drew a deep breath. "I'm not going back."

"Why not?"

"I don't have to tell you anything. I just don't want to."

"That's not an acceptable reason."

"She won't want me back. I was in the way." She moistened her lips. "Rosa's in the way too. She's better off with me."

"Why is she in the way?"

"She just is." She gazed at Kerry defiantly. "Now, you find out if you can get that money out of that warehouse owner. But don't tell my mother."

"Because she'd take it?" Silver asked.

"I didn't say that," Carmela said. "Don't you try to get my mother in trouble. None of this is her fault."

"Then whose fault is it?" Kerry asked.

"The boyfriend," Silver said suddenly. "What's his name? Don . . . Harvey?"

Carmela eyes widened. "How the hell do you know about Don?"

Kerry glanced at Silver.

He shrugged. "The police had to go to the apartment to inform your mother about what happened to you. Harvey lives with your mother. Right?"

She hesitated. "Yes."

"And that's the reason you left home."

"It's not her fault. She needs someone and she can't help— She's lonely. We're not enough for her."

"You don't like him?"

She glared at him. "I don't want to answer any questions about Mom and Don."

"Your mother's not here. She's had plenty of time to make the trip after she was told you were injured."

"She's got a job. They probably wouldn't let her off work."

Kerry was beginning to actively dislike Carmela's mother. "I'm sure you're right."

"I don't want to talk anymore." Carmela closed her eyes. "If you want to help, you just see if you can get me that money."

"We do want to help," Kerry said gently. "You rest and do what the staff tells you and we'll see what we can do." She gestured to Silver as she started for the door. "Maybe there's a way out for Rosa."

"You don't have to find a way out. I found it. I'll take care of my sister. If you can't get her out, I will." Carmela's eyes opened as the door started to close behind them. "Now, you find me money to support her."

"What happened with her mother?" Kerry asked Silver as they walked down the hall. "I assume you didn't find out about her boyfriend from George or Ledbruk?"

He shook his head. "It's all she can think about right now. She's worried about her sister."

"Let me guess. Her mother's boyfriend raped Carmela?"

He nodded. "And her mother wouldn't believe her when she told her. She didn't want her relationship jeopardized by an uncomfortable truth. Carmela took off two days later, but she's afraid for her younger sister."

Kerry felt sick. "She's only twelve."

"And Carmela is fifteen. Not much difference."

Kerry shook her head. "But refusing to face facts and rejecting a daughter who's been hurt are two different things. I can't believe she didn't come when the authorities told her that Carmela was here."

"Believe it. She made her choice. In her eyes, Carmela was trying to destroy her relationship with Harvey. She's probably built up an entire scenario for herself why she was better off without Carmela. I'd bet in her mind Carmela is a liar and a threat and deserves to be cast out."

"Some mother."

He smiled. "Some women aren't as maternal as you are, Kerry."

"Then some women should be tarred and feathered. It's common decency to do the—" She stopped. There was no use giving in to anger. "You know, children are so vulnerable. And they hate believing their parents are scum. I'll bet Carmela will fight to protect her mother to the last breath."

"No bet. She's very loyal."

"We're getting Rosa out of that house."

"Yes."

"And we're finding a place for Carmela where she'll be safe."

"Yes."

She grimaced. "You were going to do it anyway, weren't you?"

"Was I?"

"Yes, you feel a certain...closeness with her. For all your claims of keeping detached, you weren't able to do it with her. I wonder how often you manage it."

"Ah, you've found me out. Busted."

"You're joking, but I'm not." She met his gaze directly. "I found out tonight that this thing between us isn't one-sided. It couldn't stay that way when you're so attuned to me that I can't take a breath without you knowing how deep. I doubt if you'll ever let me take that peek you promised, but it may not be necessary."

His smile faded. "No?"

"No. I'm beginning to read you." She pressed the elevator button. "But this isn't the time to explore the situation. We have Carmela and her sister to worry about, and I'm not even sure Trask won't try to kill her again when he finds out that she's still alive."

"I'm not either. I've called and asked Ledbruk to put a guard in front of her room. He said he was on his way." He stepped aside to let her go first as the elevator doors opened. "Is that good enough?"

"Do you mean is Trask anywhere around?" She shook her head. "Nowhere near. I don't know how far out this psychic radar goes, but he's not in the hospital."

"You're very sure." His brows lifted. "Do I detect confidence at last?"

"It's about time." She leaned wearily back against the wall of the elevator as it started down. "Trask practically drowned me in his filth tonight. I either had to survive and deal with it or go bananas. Hell, yes, I'm confident. I may not be able to jump into anyone else's mind like you do, but I'm getting to be an expert on Trask."

"That's good. That's all that's important." He pressed her shoulder. "Now forget about him for a while—if he'll let you."

"He'll let me. Until he finds out Carmela's alive. He won't like losing status in my eyes by not completing what he promised. Carmela was the challenge and he failed."

"Then on the whole, the night's not been a total wash."

She shook her head. "No, because I found out something else while I was wading in that muck he calls a mind."

"What?"

"The name of the legman he uses to set up his kills is Dickens."

Dickens," George repeated. "What a fine literary name for a piece of crap. It hardly seems fair, does it?"

"I'm not concerned about fairness," Kerry said as she took the leash off Sam. "Certainly not in the abstract. All I want you to do is find out what you can about him. You haven't done very well with this Helen."

"You're accusing me of inefficiency? You stab me to the heart. But I'll forgive you since you've obviously been under a great strain. By the way, how is our young Carmela?"

"She was sleeping when we left the hospital," Silver said. "I'm sure she'll be fine."

"I'll take your word for it." George turned and headed for the library. "And I'll give this bit of information on Dickens to Ledbruk right away. You wouldn't like to tell me where you got it, would you?"

"No."

"I didn't think so. I'll tell Ledbruk it was a trusted but anonymous informant. He won't like it, but he hasn't liked much about this assignment." He disappeared into the library.

Kerry made a face. "Well, this trusted and anonymous informant is going up to bed." She looked around the foyer. "Where did Sam go?"

"He was heading for the kitchen." Silver smiled. "I think you can assume he'll take care of himself."

"That's a given." She started slowly up the stairs. Lord, she was tired. "I just wanted to make sure he wouldn't be in anyone's way."

"He won't be. Sam knows he's got a home here."

"Does he?" She yawned. "Yeah, Sam thinks he's welcome anywhere. You'll let me know if George finds anything about Dickens?"

"Of course. Good night, Kerry."

She glanced back at him. He looked exhausted. He'd gone through just as much stress as she had. Perhaps more. She had no idea what kind of tension he'd undergone trying to get Carmela to jump off that roof. "Aren't you going to bed?"

"Soon. I have to call Gillen."

"Can't it wait until tomorrow?"

"Could Carmela have waited until tomorrow?"

"You can't heal the entire world, Silver."

"No, but I can put on a Band-Aid or two." He turned away. "I'll see you in the morning."

A Band-Aid.

Not likely. There was no question he'd saved Carmela's life. And maybe by calling Gillen, he might save the man's sanity. She'd never thought about the awesome responsibility Silver faced every time he stepped in to "fix" someone. It must be a little like playing God with no divine safety net to fall back on. He was just a man trying to come to terms with a talent he'd never asked for and didn't want.

She felt an overwhelming sadness as she started up the stairs again. Christ, stop thinking about him. Waking or sleeping, he was occupying too much of her thoughts. She didn't need the burden of feeling herself bleed for him at a time when she was so weary she could barely function.

Rest. Sleep. And, for God's sake, don't dream of Silver.

———

Jagged teeth tearing, mutilating.

Swirling blackness.

Agony.

Silver. She had to get to Silver.

Kerry threw the covers back and ran for the door.

In less than a minute she was down the hall and throwing open his bedroom door. He was still fully dressed, sitting on the side of the bed, staring down at the telephone. "Silver, what's the—"

And then she knew. "Gillen?" she whispered.

He didn't glance up. "I couldn't get in touch with him. I've been trying all night. I finally reached his father. Gillen hanged himself last night."

"Dear God." She walked slowly toward him. "I'm so sorry, Silver."

"Me too." He cleared his throat. "I thought I had a chance with him. But it's not as if it's the first time I've lost someone. It goes with the territory. You win some, you lose some. I got used to—"

"Shut up." She knelt down on the floor in front of him, her arms sliding around his waist. "Stop mouthing all that philosophic nonsense. Do you think I don't know what you're feeling?" She pressed her cheek to his chest. "And you've got to stop hurting. I don't think I can take much more. You're not to blame for Gillen's death. Why would you believe that?"

"I knew he was spiraling downward," he said dully. "I should have gone to see him. I should have kept in closer contact."

"Jesus, every time I turned around you were on the phone with Gillen. It's not as if you abandoned him."

"No." His hand was stroking the back of her head. "But I did make a choice. I thought Carmela's problem was more urgent. Or maybe I thought my revenge was more important. Who the hell knows?"

"I know." She sat back on her heels to look up at him. "Who should know better? It seems I know you better than I do myself." She tried to smile. "You saw to that."

"I did, didn't I?" His mouth tightened. "I didn't have too much control there either."

"Oh, for God's sake. I didn't mean—"

"I know." He was silent a moment and then shrugged. "Sorry. If I remember correctly, I told you that self-pity wasn't allowed, and I seem to be drowning in it. I guess it's a case of do what I say, not what I do. But it's over now, so you can go back to bed and try to—"

"Bullshit." She jumped to her feet. "It's not over." She went around the bed, pulled down the sheet, and lay down. "And I'm not leaving you. So turn out the light and lie down."

He went still. "I beg your pardon?"

"Lie down."

"Why? Is this some kind of bizarre sexual therapy?"

"Trust a man's mind to go straight to sex. At the moment I don't believe you're in any mood to screw anyone, even Gwyneth Paltrow. You're sad and tired and maybe want to hold on to someone." She met his gaze for a long moment before holding out her hand. "I could use someone to hold on to too."

He hesitated and then took her hand. "And your maternal protectiveness is flying banner high."

She smiled. "Or maybe I don't want to have to bother to come back here if you have another emotional jag. You woke me out of a sound sleep."

"Now you know how I feel." He turned off the lamp and lay down beside her. "And I refuse to feel sorry for you."

"Aren't you going to take off your clothes?"

"No." He pulled her close so that her head tucked into his shoulder. "This is fine. This is good."

Yes, it was. She felt warm and safe and sheltered against him. She'd wanted to give comfort but found herself taking it. Or sharing it? They were as close mentally as they were now physically, and it was difficult to define the emotion. "It's all right with me, you know. Living in a firehouse gets rid of any prudery."

"I'll keep my clothes on, thank you. Though it's more of a reminder than a barrier." His lips brushed her forehead. "Because you were right."

"About what?"

"That a man's mind goes straight to sex." His hand stroked her hair as he whispered, "And you can never tell when his mood might change."

Crystal blue lake.

Soft breeze blowing through the high grass.

"What the hell?" Silver stood up and moved away from her. "I don't know what happened. God, I swear I never meant to do this, Kerry."

"I know you didn't." She smiled. "But I did."

His gaze shifted back to her. "What?"

"Oh, I haven't discovered a new talent. There's no way I could build a scenario like this. But I'm close enough to you now to be able to tap into your memory bank. I wasn't sure I could, but a little exploration and there I was...." She looked out at the lake. "Here. Where I wanted to be. Where I wanted you to be."

"Good God, I've created a monster."

"No such thing. But you should have expected me to grab hold and run with it."

"I suppose I should have." He smiled. "But why? Why did you want to come here?"

"Because this is the place you brought me to to take away pain. I thought it might help. You wouldn't do it for yourself. It would have been too much like self-indulgence. Heaven forbid you give yourself a break."

"Oh? And where did you get the idea I was that self-sacrificing? I

assure you I can be as selfish as they come given the right circumstances."

"Then be selfish, dammit. Where can you find more ideal circumstances?"

"I can think of a few."

She inhaled sharply as a wave of heat shocked through her. He was looking at her as he had that other day, and she became acutely aware of the tension of his muscles, the movement of his chest as he breathed in and out, his eyes . . .

"You shouldn't have brought me here," he said thickly. "You didn't think far enough ahead. You blunt the pain and you remove the distraction. Believe me, I needed the distraction."

She wasn't about to pretend she didn't know what he meant. Sex. Raw, hot, urgent. All the more powerful for the bond they shared. She wanted to touch him. She wanted to move her hands on his back and feel him tense against her. How would it be to have him sink—

"Don't even think about it," Silver said harshly. "I'm trying to keep this thing between us on an even keel. Do you think this is easy for me?"

"I don't care about your even keel." She got to her feet and moved toward him. "You know what I want."

"Hell, yes. And I don't know whether I purposely caused it to happen." His hands reached out and grasped her shoulders. "I tried not to do it. But I wanted you and I might have made sure you wanted me."

"Don't be so conceited. I believe I'd be able to know whether or not you'd manipulated me when it came to sex."

"But you can't be sure."

"I learned when I was fighting fires that there comes a time when you just have to trust your instincts."

"Listen, you're feeling all warm and soft because you're sorry for me. But unless you back off now, I'm not going to give a damn about the whys or wherefores."

"Good. Because no matter how this started, it's pretty clear to me that I don't want to go to bed with you because I pity you." She grimaced. "Maybe I'm just using it as an excuse. Take a peek and you tell me."

He muttered a curse. "I'm not getting any closer to you than I have to, either mentally or physically. It's not fair to you. In spite of what you say about your wonderful firefighter instincts."

"Screw being fair to me." Her fingers touched his lips. They were warm and firm, and a tiny shock of sensation rippled through her. "My instinct tells me that I want this because I find you sexy as hell and that I'd want you if I was blind to that damn talent of yours."

"What if your instinct is—" A shudder ran through him as she stepped closer and pressed against him. "Shit." His arms closed around her. "You definitely know how to clinch an argument." His head bent until their lips were only a breath apart. "Okay, but I have only one qualification. No buffer. No dream-lake scenario."

Darkness.

Swirling heat.

Skin against skin.

She opened her eyes to see him above her on the bed. It took her a moment to come to full wakefulness. "You took your clothes off. . . ."

"You bet I did." He pulled her sleep shirt over her head and threw it aside. "I don't want anything between us. Not a piece of material, not a—" He broke off as his chest touched her breasts. "Jesus."

She knew how he felt. Her skin was flushed, burning, taut, and ready. "I can't— Come here." Her legs curled around his hips and drew him toward her. "I need you to—" She arched with a cry as she felt him move against her.

"I know. I will." He bent over her. "Anything you want."

Anything she wanted, she thought dazedly. He was already

giving her what she wanted. But there was something she had to know, something she had to ask. "The lake," she whispered. "Why did you take me away from the lake?"

"Because I couldn't stand for it to happen there." He moved between her legs. "Because it's got to be real. . . ."

13

Well, was it real enough for you?" Kerry rose on her elbow to look down at him, trying to catch her breath. "If it wasn't, then you're out of luck. I don't think it gets any earthier than this."

"We could try again and see." His hand covered her breast. "I believe in frequent reality checks."

She chuckled. "I can see why you'd need them." She flopped back down on the pillow and stretched lazily. "Give me a little time to get my breath. I didn't expect—I don't know what I expected, but it wasn't this. You're very . . . strong."

"I didn't hurt you?"

"Don't be ridiculous. You know how much I liked it." She reached out and rubbed his chest. She loved the prickly feel of hair against her palm. She loved the *feel* of him, the rough, smooth textures, the hardness. Jesus, how she loved that hardness. "It was just different."

"I love the way you feel too. Different?"

She laughed. "How can you ask? I've never made love to anyone who knew what I was thinking every minute. It was incredibly exciting."

"It could have gone either way." His hand covered her hand on his chest, stilling it. "And I tried to block you out. I thought it would be fairer to you. It didn't work. The bond was too strong."

"It didn't matter." It was difficult to be critical at the moment, since this sexual encounter was probably the most intense she'd ever had. He'd known every thought, every emotion, and had been able to meet and escalate them to the height of sensuality. She could still vaguely sense him, but it was the shadow presence to which she'd become accustomed. "I may feel differently tomorrow, but tonight it was definitely a plus."

"Too late. You can't back out now." He pulled her closer to lie against him. "You're the one who seduced me. You even turned my own scenario against me. Now you've got to live with it."

There was a note in his voice that made her stiffen. "What do you mean?"

"I told you I was a selfish bastard. I'm also chock full of the usual testosterone. I'm not giving this up."

"That has to be a mutual decision."

"You made your decision." He was silent a moment. "I . . . like what we are together. I'm usually pretty much of a loner. I have trouble getting close, even in sex. I guess it's because my work forces me into an intimacy that's sometimes suffocating. But it's not like that with you. I felt—Hell, you know how I felt. So I don't care if your decision was based on pity or curiosity. I'm going to do everything I can to keep this happening."

"And how do you intend to do that?"

"Don't sound so wary. I'm not going to try to force you." He took her hand and pressed the palm to his lips. "But I learned a lot about you tonight. You can't blame me for using it to make the pleasure so intense you won't want to give it up." His breath was warm on her palm, and every word was sending a ripple of heat down her arm. "You like this, don't you? Your palms are very sensitive."

"I like it." The heat was spreading throughout her body and her breath was quickening. "And I like having sex with you. That doesn't mean I'm going to let you dominate me. I can still take what I want and then walk away. So you just take your best shot, Silver."

"Oh, I will." He chuckled as he moved over her. "I can't thank you enough for the invitation...."

The girl was alive.

Trask gazed at the picture of Carmela Ruiz in the newspaper in angry disgust. How the hell had she escaped Firestorm? He'd been sure that the fire would travel too fast for her to get away before the flames devoured her. He'd been wrong. She'd managed to get to the roof and somehow whipped up her courage to jump.

And Kerry Murphy had made sure that those firemen were there to catch her.

That didn't mean he'd failed and Kerry had won. The warehouse had still burned to the ground and he'd walked away free and powerful as ever.

Screw the warehouse. He wouldn't lie to himself. It had been Carmela who was to be the pièce de résistance of that delicious event, and she'd escaped. And it had been Kerry who'd called the firemen who'd saved her so she could claim the victory.

His hand clenched on the newspaper as fury tore through him.

Calm down. It was only the opening gambit. No, it wasn't. He'd failed at that fire in Macon at her brother's house. Two failures chalked up to Kerry Murphy. It was an unbearable humiliation. No, he could bear it because it would only make him stronger and more determined.

But she had to be shown that he was the one with a power that could reach out and scar and twist her life. Carmela? Or go after Kerry herself? He'd have to think about it. He'd have to reconsider a good many things in light of this defeat. His priorities had been clear before Kerry came on the scene, and he'd allowed her to disrupt and disturb those plans. Should he ignore her and go on as if—

No! The rejection came with unexpected violence.

Very well, then certain adjustments might have to be made.

He reached out and punched in Dickens's number.

———

Dickens." George walked out of the library as Kerry and Silver were coming down the stairs the next morning. He waved a sheaf of fax papers in his hand. "Donald William Dickens. Age forty-two, and every year after the age of ten devoted to petty and not so petty crime. Theft, rape, suspicion in two murder cases. According to the dossier the FBI managed to pull up, he grew up in Detroit and was associated with the Mafia for a few years, but then broke away and started to freelance. He's not supposed to be the sharpest tool in the shed, but he has the reputation of being very thorough and reasonably loyal to his employers."

"The FBI had a record?" Kerry asked. "But how did Trask get hold of him?"

George shrugged. "Dickens spent twelve years in Asia involved in drug and artifact smuggling before he came back to the States. He had a lot of contacts in North Korea."

"You're thinking he was a gift to Trask from Ki Yong?" Silver nodded slowly. "It's possible. Trask could have made the providing of help a part of his price."

"Where is he?" Kerry said. "Now that we know who he is, can we find him?"

"We're trying," George said. "Remember, he's a professional, and it won't be easy."

"Nothing's easy," Kerry said. "Do we have a photo?"

"I wouldn't fail you." He handed her the sheaf of papers in his hand. "The second sheet down. The third is his rap sheet."

Dickens was a heavyset man with bulldog jowls and unruly red hair sprinkled with gray. She handed the sheet to Silver. "Since he doesn't know that we know who he is, it should help."

He nodded. "And Trask must have had him doing the legwork before he approached you. I don't think there's a question that he'll have him on your heels when he finds out that Carmela is still alive." He glanced at George. "Is her rescue in the papers yet?"

"You've got to be kidding," George said. "Pretty, homeless teenager rescued from a fiery death by our city's finest? It's a story made in media heaven."

"Then Trask knows about it already." Kerry had to make an effort to keep from shivering. It was stupid to feel this bolt of fear that had come out of nowhere. It wasn't as if she hadn't expected Trask to learn that he'd failed to kill Carmela. "You're sure Carmela is well guarded?"

"I'm sure." Silver handed the sheaf of papers back to George. "But Trask may not think it's worthwhile to target her again. She was only a random victim."

"Random." The word left an ugly taste in Kerry's mouth. It was a cold word for a cold act. The idea of anyone casually choosing a victim as Trask had chosen Carmela was terrible. She moistened her lips. "Maybe you're right. But I'm not a random victim, and there's not a chance in hell that Trask won't go after me. And he'll probably need Dickens's help."

"Probably."

"So maybe we should make sure I'm accessible."

"No way," Silver said flatly.

"Wait a minute." George's eyes narrowed on Kerry's face. "I don't believe she's talking about making herself a martyr. What do you have in mind?"

"Just moving around town a little. Dickens isn't going to show himself as long as I'm barricaded behind these walls. If I make a few trips, it will give him reason to follow me. And that will give Ledbruk's agents a chance to identify or apprehend him. Isn't that right?"

George nodded. "It makes sense."

She turned to Silver. "And if we manage to identify him without him realizing we're doing it, we may be able follow him back to Trask."

"And what if Trask decides not to use Dickens? What if he's out there with his little dish all set to burn you to a crisp?"

"Then it's up to you to make sure he doesn't. I can't do everything." She turned and strode down the hall toward the kitchen. "But I can make myself coffee and some toast, and that's what I'm going to do right now. You argue with George about it, if it makes you feel better. But you know I'm right."

She heard him mutter a curse behind her, but she ignored it. She had no desire to argue with Silver right now. She was having to exert all her effort to shake off this sense of . . . what? Fear, anxiety, foreboding? Maybe a little of all those emotions.

Or maybe her imagination was just working overtime. She had a right to a case of nerves after what had happened at the warehouse.

She had the coffee brewed and was on her second cup when Silver came into the kitchen. "It took you long enough. I thought George was more persuasive than that."

"I didn't waste my time. I knew you had your mind made up." He poured himself a cup of coffee and sat down across from her. "I just talked to him and Ledbruk and set up your surveillance. If you're determined to do it, I want to make sure the security is iron-tight." He took a sip of coffee. "But understand this. I go with you every trip. I'm with you every minute."

"I've no objection."

"And one trip a day. Never at the same time. Never going to the same place."

"That makes sense." She met his gaze across the table. "Now admit I'm right. This way we have a chance at Dickens."

"Okay, you're right." He scowled. "Satisfied?"

"My, that hurt." She smiled. "Jesus, you're a surly bastard. I don't know how I managed to get past that sulkiness to realize you weren't a complete asshole."

His scowl disappeared. "Shall I tell you?" He leaned across the table and took her hand. "Sex is always the bridge." His thumb slowly rubbed her palm. "I may be an asshole, but I'm damn good. Now you admit I'm right."

Dammit, he knew how sensitive her palms and wrists were to touch. He knew everything about her body. He only had to touch her to cause her to be ready. She drew a shaky breath and pulled her hand away. "No big deal. Stop bragging. It's not as if you didn't start with a gigantic advantage over most men." She looked him in the eye. "And I'm not talking physiology."

He frowned and then started to laugh. "My God, Kerry. You really know how to deflate a guy. I hope you'll concede the physiology is adequate?"

She smiled. "Quite adequate."

"Then let's go back upstairs and test it out."

Her smile faded. He wasn't joking. "You can't be serious. We just got out of bed an hour ago."

"I didn't get enough. I don't know if I'll ever get enough. I told you, we're pretty extraordinary together."

She wasn't sure that she would ever get enough either. She had never believed she could be addicted to sex, but now she wasn't sure. And that uncertainty was enough to make her very wary. "That doesn't mean we should spend all our time in the sack."

"Well, we could get up occasionally." He sat back, studying her expression. "No?"

She shook her head. "It's not a good idea."

"But not because you don't want to. You're just afraid that you're liking it too much. That you're liking me too much."

"You're too demanding. You even warned me that you—" She drew a deep breath. "And you're getting sidetracked. What about Trask?"

"I haven't forgotten him. But since we have only one trip a day . . . that leaves all that other time to play." He smiled. "And we *will* play, Kerry. You know it as well as I do. Life's too short to skip the good things."

Yes, she knew it. If they were together, there would be sex, and in the present circumstances there was no walking away from him. But it was important that he not get all his own way. "Not now." She got to her feet. "I'm going to the hospital to visit Carmela. Why don't you make yourself useful and see what you can do about arranging to get her sister out of her mother's house?"

"Yes, ma'am." He rose to his feet. "But I can do that by phone on the way to the hospital. I'm going with you." He headed for the door. "Remember? I go with you every trip. I'm with you every minute."

Y ou're not really a social worker, are you?" Carmela glared at Kerry as she walked into the hospital room. "Who the hell are you?"

Kerry gazed at her warily. "Why do you think I lied to you?"

"I asked the nurse and she said she didn't know anything about you. And the hospital has its own social workers." Her gaze bored into Kerry's. "So are you a reporter?"

"No."

"Or maybe from the police?" She didn't wait for an answer. "I'm not going back to my mother. You can forget it."

"I'm not with the police. Actually, I work as an arson investigator for the fire department."

"I didn't set the fire."

"I know you didn't."

"I didn't see who set it."

"I know that too."

"Then why the hell don't you get out of here?" Carmela's eyes were glittering with tears. "I don't want to talk to you. You lied to me. The owner of the warehouse isn't going to give me any money, is he? I'm not going to be able to get Rosa away from that bastard."

"We're working on it. It would help if you'd admit that Harvey raped you."

"Yeah, sure." She turned her face to the wall. "And the police would arrest my mother too. I know how it works. I went to the library and looked it up before I left home. It's called child endangerment."

"I know you don't want to hurt your mother, but you have to admit that Rosa is in danger."

"I don't have to admit anything to you. I've told Rosa to go on the run if Harvey comes near her. It may not happen. He's going to be careful after I went to Mom about him. Besides, I'll take care of Rosa as soon as I get out of here."

"Okay, but that may be a few days. I believe we'll have to find a way to get Rosa out of that house right away." She held up her hand as Carmela looked at her in alarm. "Without involving your mother with the police."

Carmela stared at her for a moment. "Why would you do that?"

"For heaven's sake, Carmela. Maybe I don't like the idea of a young girl being victimized. Is that so hard to believe?"

"How do I know? I don't know you. And I don't think the fire department goes in for this kind of charity work."

Lord, she was suspicious, Kerry thought. Well, why not? She hadn't had much opportunity to develop trust, and the one person closest to her had betrayed her. Tell the kid the truth. "No, it doesn't. We help where we can, but you're an unusual case. And it's a personal issue with me." She paused. "The person who started the fire wanted you to die in that blaze."

"You're crazy. No one knew I was in that warehouse."

"Trask knew it. He called me and told me your name. He even described you."

"Trask? That's his name?"

"James Trask."

"But why would he want to kill me?"

"It wasn't about you. It was about me. He has a sort of . . . fixation about me. He knew I'd hate the idea of a young girl dying in a fire, and he wanted me to get to know you so that your death would mean more to me." She added gently, "He succeeded. I began to feel very close to you while we were searching for that warehouse."

She didn't speak for a moment. "Really?"

"Really."

"But I still don't see why he'd try to kill me. I didn't do anything to him."

She could see why Carmela was having difficulty accepting Trask's motivation, when Kerry herself found it totally incomprehensible. "I told you, he wanted to get at me through you. I'm the one he wanted to hurt."

"Well, he hurt me too. He's got to be one nutty son of a bitch." She hesitated. "Is he still going to try to—"

"I don't think so. But we have a guard on you just in case."

"Nutty." She shook her head in disgust. "Do you run into people like him a lot?"

"No, not like him." She had told Carmela enough, and she wasn't about to go into details that might frighten her. "But you can see why I'm concerned about you. You may not have known about it, but we have a connection."

"Yeah, that nut who has it in for both of us." Carmela's lips tightened. "If you're telling me the truth."

Lord, the kid was tough. "You have to trust someone sometime, Carmela."

"Why? It's lots safer not to—"

"Here he is." A young candy striper was half pulled into the room by Sam. "The kids in pediatrics loved him." She made a face as she handed the leash to Kerry. "I didn't think you'd be able to convince the head nurse to let a dog in the ward."

"I had to have her call the hospital in Atlanta and get a recommendation." She patted Sam's head. "But I knew once Sam started strutting his stuff that no one was going to kick him out."

"He's adorable." The candy striper smiled as she headed for the door. "And amazingly well behaved once he saw the kids."

"That's because he knows his job. Thanks for bringing him up here."

"My pleasure." She waved as she left the room.

"It probably wasn't a total pleasure." Kerry smiled as she turned back to Carmela. "He's not the best-behaved dog on the planet."

Carmela's gaze was fixed on Sam. "He's . . . beautiful. Why did you bring him here?"

"I thought you might want to meet him. And I knew he'd help the kids." She unsnapped the leash. "Do you want to pet him? Just call his name."

"Sam?"

Sam bounded across the room toward the bed and planted his forepaws on the mattress.

Kerry chuckled. "He doesn't take much urging."

Carmela tentatively reached out and stroked his head. "He feels . . . silky."

"Did you have a dog?"

She shook her head. "Mom said they were too much trouble."

Sam rubbed his head on her hand and gave a soft woo-woo.

Carmela smiled. "He likes this." She looked up at Kerry. "I've heard about arson dogs. Is Sam one?"

She nodded. "He's very famous."

Carmela frowned in puzzlement. "But you told that nurse he knew his job when he was with the kids. That's not his job."

"Sure it is. Actually, he's far more suited to help those kids than he is to fight fires." That was certainly the truth. "Sam has one outstanding gift. He gives love and keeps on giving."

"That doesn't seem to be much of a gift."

"It's the greatest gift. Unconditional love? Not many creatures are capable of that kind of affection. He warms the heart and keeps loneliness away. Why, Sam's a blooming miracle." She smiled ruefully. "He's a rambunctious rascal, but I've never seen him be anything but gentle with any of those kids. He seems to sense when he has to take care."

"He doesn't seem—" She broke off as Sam licked her hand. "He . . . likes me."

Kerry could almost see the wall around Carmela melting. Thank you, Sam. "Yes, he does. And as long as he senses you're not in top shape, he won't jump in bed and lick you to death."

"I wouldn't mind." She laid her cheek on Sam's head. "He's so soft."

"Do you want me to bring him back with me?"

She didn't speak for a moment and then straightened. But her hand remained on Sam's head. "Maybe."

"Will you let me come back? Do you believe what I told you about Trask?"

"It seems weird."

"It's true."

Carmela was silent again and then said, "I think I saw him once." She went still. "What?"

"That day of the fire. Some guy was following me."

"What did he look like?"

"A little heavy, reddish hair. Was that him?"

Dickens.

"No, but he probably worked for him."

"That kook has people working for him? What is he? Some kind of mobster?"

"Not exactly."

"You're not going to tell me." She shrugged. "I don't care. It doesn't matter, as long as you keep him away from me and Rosa." She paused. "Are you really going to go get Rosa?"

"I wouldn't lie to you. My friend, Silver, is downstairs in the parking lot on the phone now trying to arrange a way to get her away from your mother."

"Where are you going to put her? One of those DFACS houses?"

"No, we'll find a safe place for her. Don't worry."

"What a stupid thing to say." Carmela gave her a withering look even as she continued to stroke Sam. "Of course I'm going to worry. She's my sister. I have to take care of her."

Kerry chuckled. "You're right. It was stupid. Worry all you please, but I won't, because I know she's going to be okay." Her smile faded. "And so will you, Carmela. Things are going to work out for you. I promise." She came toward the bed and put the leash on Sam. "Now I'll go and let you rest."

"I don't do anything else in this place." Her hand reluctantly left Sam after a final pat. "Did they tell you when they're going to let me leave here?"

"In a few days. You're still running a fever." She started for the door. "Has your mother contacted you yet?"

"She called me last night." She defiantly lifted her chin. "It's just like I told you, she couldn't get off work. It's not as if she doesn't care about me. She just has . . . problems."

"Well, maybe we can rid her of a few of those problems." Kerry opened the door. "I'll come and see you tomorrow, Carmela."

"You don't have to do that."

"I know I don't." She smiled. "But I know you'll want to hear what progress we're having with your sister."

"You're really gonna help her?"

"I lied to you once. I won't do it again."

"I hope you don't." Her hands clenched on the sheet. "I won't take charity. It sticks in my throat. But if you'll do this for me, I'll owe you big time. And I'll pay you back. I promise."

She could see that the girl was deadly serious, and Kerry wouldn't insult her by refusing. "I'll take you up on that. See you tomorrow, Carmela."

"Wait." When Kerry looked back at her, Carmela said awkwardly, "I wouldn't mind if you brought that pooch back. He's probably good for those sick kids."

"You're right." She nodded solemnly. "Okay, if you really don't mind.

"Good job, Sam," she murmured as she left the room.

His tail wagged as he pulled Kerry down the hall, all gentleness and decorum forgotten. Kerry didn't care. He'd given Carmela affection and softened her pain in a way she could accept.

Poor kid, Kerry thought as she waited at the elevator. Life had not treated her well, and she had all the prickly barriers to prove it. But it was a wonder she wasn't even more defensive and that she'd somehow managed to develop a code.

Silver was waiting in the lobby when she got off the elevator. "How is she?"

"Smart, vulnerable, wary. Sam helped a lot."

"I was wondering why you wanted to take him."

"Sam's great with kids. She needed him. But she found out that we're not social workers."

"Busted. What did you tell her?"

"The truth. I decided she could take it." She started down the corridor toward the parking lot. "I like her, Silver. She's tough, but I think she . . . Oh, I don't know. She reminds me of someone. . . ." She frowned, trying to think who it was, but it didn't come to her. "I *like* her."

"Well, that's clear." He fell into step with her. "I'll have to take your word for it. I'm still too bruised and exasperated from trying to get her to jump off that roof to be objective."

"She was scared."

"And you're being defensive."

"Someone has to defend her. She's not had much help from her mother." She glanced at him. "And speaking of her mother, did you make any progress?"

He nodded. "I contacted Travis and told him to have some strings pulled with DFACS in Louisville. He's going to send a caseworker to put some subtle pressure on Carmela's mother to release Rosa into their care."

"How subtle?"

"Maybe not all that subtle. A velvet-gloved threat that I hope will scare her into cooperating."

"And after DFACS takes Rosa away from her mother?"

"Then we'll make sure there's a grade-A foster home ready to receive her until Carmela is out of the hospital."

"When will we know?"

He shrugged. "Tonight. Maybe tomorrow. I told Travis it was urgent."

"Good. I want something encouraging to tell Carmela tomorrow." She motioned for Sam to jump in the back of the SUV before getting in herself. "It wasn't pleasant telling her about Trask, but she took it well."

"Like you said, tough."

"And prickly as the devil. She wanted to—" Kerry suddenly started to laugh. "Lord, I just figured out who she reminded me of."

"Who?"

"You."

He glanced at her as he started the car. "I beg your pardon?"

"Prickly and surly and not letting anyone near."

He smiled faintly. "I'll accept the description since you said you couldn't help but like her. But you should really examine that response. You obviously have a weakness for difficult people like us."

Her smile faded. She didn't want to examine the warmth she felt for Silver. That softness was even more dangerous than the sexual pleasure she experienced with him. She glanced hurriedly out the window. "Do you think we were followed?"

"If we were, then it was definitely done by an expert." He stopped at the parking-lot booth and handed the clerk the ticket and money. "And I contacted Ledbruk, and his agent didn't think we were being watched."

She frowned. "Then was I wrong? I thought it was a reasonable assumption that—"

"It was reasonable. Maybe Trask just hasn't gotten his shit together yet. There's still a good chance that Dickens will show."

He was probably right. What did she expect? It wasn't likely they'd be able to grab Dickens the first day. But telling herself that didn't stop the uneasiness she felt. Trask wouldn't be spinning his wheels after he learned he'd failed to kill Carmela. He'd want to make a move to show Kerry that she hadn't really won anything of importance.

And if that move didn't involve having her followed by Dickens, what other action was he planning?

"Stop fretting," Silver said. "I learned a long time ago that if you can't do anything about a problem, it's better to relax and gather strength for the moment when you can."

"It must be nice to be so patronizing. I'm not some psychic superman like you. I'm not good at this and I don't have your experience. I *can't* relax."

He gave a low whistle at the sharpness of her tone. "Sorry. I didn't mean to sound patronizing. And you're getting better and stronger all the time. You can block me, and that last time I felt a definite nudge when you made the attempt at a push."

"Nudge? That's not going to do me any good when I come up against Trask."

"I told you that I couldn't gauge how strong that push would translate with someone else."

"That gives me a hell of a lot of confidence."

"Easy. I can't furnish you with confidence, but you know I'll keep on working with you until you—"

"I know. I know." Her lips tightened. "Christ, I'm sick of it all. I never wanted to have to learn anything like this. After we get

Trask, I'm going to take Sam and go back to doing what I do well. I'm going to block these weeks out of my mind and never think of them again."

He didn't speak for a moment. "Or me?"

"What do you want me to say? One goes with the other. Don't tell me you won't be glad to be rid of me too."

"I wouldn't think of telling you that." He looked away from her. "I'm just saying it may be hard to do."

She knew he was right, but there was no way she would admit it. Difficult or not, she was going to break this link between them. She leaned her head back on the seat rest and closed her eyes. "You're wrong. After what I've gone through, it will be a piece of cake."

"Nothing like being sure." His face was expressionless. "We'll see . . ."

———

I may have found a lead to our mysterious Helen," George said when they came in the front door. "I talked to a few of my friends at the FBI, and they wouldn't tell me anything but they pointed discreetly."

"Where?" Silver asked.

"At the CIA." He smiled. "So I'm trying to tap a few sources there."

"Good God, you have as many contacts as a Fox News reporter," Kerry said. "I'm not even going to ask how you got them. When will you know?"

"Soon. Possibly tonight or tomorrow. I believe I've found someone who might have information."

"Let me know as soon as you hear." She started up the stairs. "I could use some good news."

Yes, she could, Silver thought, as he watched her reach the

top of the steps. She was scared and worried and wanted only to bury her head beneath the proverbial covers and hide away from everyone.

Hide away from him, dammit.

You're gritting your teeth," George said. "May I tell you that your dentist would advise you that could seriously contribute to TMJ?"

"No, you may not." Silver turned on his heel. "Shut up, George."

George gave a low whistle. "Nasty." He headed for the library. "Where will you be if I get a sudden breakthrough on Helen?"

"I'm going for a walk." He jerked open the front door. "A long, long walk."

"Excellent idea. Exercise is always a good release. Perhaps you'll come back in better temp—"

The door slammed behind Silver before George could finish.

Fire.

She had to get help for Mama.

She slipped on the icy steps and fell to the street.

There was a man across the street, standing beneath the street lamp.

She picked herself up and ran toward him. "Help. The fire. Mama . . ."

He was turning and walking away. He must not have heard her.

She ran after him. "Please. Mama said I had to—" He turned and she looked up into his face.

She screamed.

"Shh, it's too late. You can't help her." He raised his arm and she

saw metal glittering in his hand as he started to bring the gun down—

Darkness. Yes, darkness . . .

"Stop it!" She was yanked out of that welcoming darkness, back to the horror of that night. "You don't get away with that, Kerry. You're not going to black out now. Look at him, dammit."

Silver!

It was Silver talking, she realized in confusion. Silver beside her, standing beneath the lamppost.

But it couldn't be Silver. He didn't belong here.

But he was here, and the entire nightmare sequence was frozen. The burning building, the lamppost, the man with his hand raised to strike her down.

"Look at him," Silver repeated. "Look at his face."

Panic soared through her. "No, I can't see. It's too dark."

"Look at him."

"Shut up. Get out of here."

"The hell I will. I'm staying until you stop being a martyr and look at that bastard."

"I won't do it." She closed her eyes tightly. "Go away."

"What are you afraid of?"

"He's going to hurt me."

"That's not why you're afraid. Tell me."

"Go away."

"Look at him."

She found herself opening her eyes and looking up at that shadowy face above her. "No! I won't do it. I won't." She frantically pulled away and shut her eyes again. "Go away. Let me alone."

"Dammit, stop pushing me away. I'm trying to—"

"No!"

She woke to see Silver bending over her. "Damn you." She shoved him away and sat up in bed. "What the devil did you think you were doing?"

"I don't have to think, I know I was scaring the bejesus out of you." He swung his feet to the floor and got to his feet. "Come on, let's get you in the shower. You've broken out in a cold sweat."

Yes, she had, and she was shaking so badly that she could barely talk. "And you had nothing to do with it, I suppose. Those nightmares are bad enough without you sticking in your two cents worth."

"Then get rid of them." He pulled her out of bed and wrapped her in a sheet. "Shower. You can spit at me later."

"I want to spit at you now." But she let him lead her toward the bathroom. She was in no shape to fight a battle right now. "You had no right to—"

"Hush." He pushed her under the warm spray of the shower and then got in with her. "You're absolutely correct. I intruded, I violated your privacy, I even broke my own code." He grimaced as he handed her the sponge. "Such as it is. I constantly seem to be bending the rules."

"You shouldn't have done—" She stopped as he began kneading her neck. God, that felt good. The tension was flowing out of her. "I'm not going to forgive you. How can I trust—"

"Shh, think about it later."

Yes, think about it later. The heat of the water was banishing the chill, and his touch was soothing away her tension. She closed her eyes and let herself drift.

"Good." Minutes passed and then he was bundling her out of the shower and toweling her off. "Now let's get you back to bed and I'll let you vent."

She didn't want to vent, she realized. Any attack she made would lead to a confrontation, and she was afraid Silver would—

"You bet I will." He wrapped her in a blanket and tucked her in bed before crawling in beside her. "But you've been through enough tonight. I'll let you off."

"Don't expect me to thank you. And are you still spying on me? Get the hell out."

"I got out. But you know I can't keep from picking up on an odd thought or two when you scream it at me." His arms enfolded her and he cuddled close, spoon fashion. "Go to sleep. You're done with dreaming for tonight." He brushed her temple with his lips. "If you wander too close, I'll jerk you back."

"Or jump in where you don't belong."

"I belong."

"The hell you do." She was silent a moment before she asked, "Why did you do it, Silver?"

"You were in pain. I couldn't stand it."

"It was my pain, my memories. My right to handle them."

"You're not handling them. You're hiding, and as long as you do that, they're going to torment you."

"So you tried to force me to come out of hiding?"

"You'd know it if I used force. I was just nudging a little."

"You kept telling me to look at his face. That was stupid. It was too dark for me to see anything."

"Was it? He was under the streetlight."

"Not when he turned on me. I ran after him. He was in the shadow."

"So he was a total blank page."

"Yes, of course he was." She stiffened. "Why don't you believe me?"

"Because you don't believe it yourself."

"I do. I *do*."

"Easy. I'm not pushing you right now." He pulled her closer. "Go to sleep."

"I can't go to sleep. How do you expect me to sleep when you keep saying things to stir me up? Just stay away from—"

"I can't." His voice was low. "I won't."

"Why not?"

"Because if you decide to walk away from me, you're going to take something with you. This is something I can give you. Something no one else will ever be able to give you."

She was silent. "You mean, you're doing this to give me a kind of ... present?"

"You might call it that. Or you might say my ego won't let me be forgotten. It's my way of assuring my immortality in your eyes. Either way, you have something broken and I'm going to fix it."

"Even if I don't want you to do it."

"Then fight me. You managed to push me out this time. You're getting stronger all the time. You might be able to send me on my way."

"I will." She closed her eyes. "You're *right*. You get in my way and I'll send you packing." It was strange to think of rejecting him in any way when she was lying close like this. He always managed to make her feel wonderfully treasured. Dear God, she would miss it when they were no longer together. "And now I'd appreciate it if you'd stop talking so that I can rest."

"I'll be quiet as a mouse."

"I don't like mice. They scamper."

"Well, I don't scamper. I stride like a lion."

She yawned. "Too many metaphors."

"I agree. So I'll just shut up."

"That was what I asked in the beginning." She tried to relax. Close out the world. Close out the dream. Close out Silver. No, she couldn't close out Silver. He was always with her now. But that was okay because he was like a part of her, comfortable and familiar. . . .

She was just drifting from waking to sleep when Silver whispered in her ear, "What did you see, Kerry?"

What was he talking about? she thought hazily.

"What did you see when you looked up at him? Tell me."

"Can't..."

"Yes, you can. Just tell me and then you can go to sleep. Reach deep. What did you see?"

Reach deep...

Darkness. Fire outlining his tall body and casting his face in shadow.

"Blue eyes," she whispered. "Blue eyes..."

14

Dickens's hands tightened on the steering wheel as he hit a rut and almost skidded off the road.

"Son of a bitch!" The curse was followed by a string of other obscenities. He'd be lucky if he got back to town without a flat tire. That's all he needed. He'd have to change it himself, because he was under Trask's orders not to attract undue attention. As if he'd be that stupid. But Trask thought everybody but himself was an idiot and treated them that way.

Just a few miles more and he could turn around and get out of here. Check it out and then he'd be able to call Trask and give him his report. He hoped to hell it was going to be what the bastard wanted. This was the eighth trip he'd had to take, and he was sick of it.

He drove around the bend and there it was.

He gave a low whistle.

He parked the car on the side of the road before glancing down at the photo on the seat beside him.

Maybe. Just maybe . . .

———

Blue eyes.

It was the first thought that came to Kerry's mind when she woke the next morning. One moment she was deep in slumber and the next wide awake, her heart pounding as if she'd been running. She sat upright in bed. What the hell?

And where was Silver?

She swung her legs to the floor and jumped out of bed.

Five minutes later she was dressed and running down the stairs.

"Good morning," George said as he came in the front door. "You look a bit edgy."

"You might say that. Where's Silver?"

"Right behind me. We were checking over the grounds. He wanted to make sure that the guards weren't missing any signs of intruders. A suspicious man is our Brad."

"Your Brad. I'm not claiming him at the moment."

His brows lifted. "Indeed? Then maybe he had reason to get away from the house for a while." He turned as Silver came in the door. "You're in her bad books." He moved toward the library. "And I'm out of here. I think I should be hearing from the CIA any time now on the identity of our mysterious Helen, and I need to be available." He cast a glance at Kerry over his shoulder. "Try not to damage him too badly. I still haven't had my rematch with him."

"He may have waited too long," Kerry said grimly as the door shut behind George. "Now he'll have to stand in line. What did you do to me?"

"I thought we'd discussed that last night."

"Don't give me that. I mean right before I went to sleep. Did you give me some sort of posthypnotic suggestion to jog my memory?"

He was silent a moment. "Maybe."

"And it wasn't just coincidence I had that dream last night."

He shrugged. "There aren't many true coincidences in this world."

She hadn't known until this moment how desperately she'd wanted to be wrong. "Damn you. It was bad enough that you barged in where you had no business. You actually manipulated me. You said you wouldn't do that. You *promised* me. Why the hell did you break your word?"

"I couldn't think of any other way to do it. You were resisting me tooth and nail. I had to catch you when you were relaxed and your defenses were down."

"And it didn't occur to you that you'd destroy any trust I had in you?"

"It occurred to me. I decided it was worth the chance. He was the monster who haunted you all your life. You needed to face him instead of hiding."

"In your judgment."

"In my judgment."

"You arrogant son of a bitch."

"Yes, I certainly am. I never denied that I'm a selfish bastard and that I probably ran the risk for my benefit too." He added simply, "I couldn't stand you hurting. Every time I touched that part of you, it made me . . . ache. It had to end, Kerry."

"And just what do you think you gained?"

"If you'd let yourself look beyond the anger, you might find out."

"I don't know what you're talking about."

"Blue eyes," he said softly. "He had blue eyes. Why didn't you want to remember that, Kerry?"

"Maybe I didn't remember. Maybe you planted that thought when you were—"

"You don't believe that," he interrupted. "Cut through the bullshit and tell me why you blocked out of your memory the man who killed your mother."

"I didn't. I was in a coma, and when I woke I couldn't remember."

"But you remembered last night. You remembered blue eyes. If I'd probed a little deeper, would you have been able to describe him?"

"No!"

"I think you would."

"You're wrong." Her hands clenched into fists. "You're completely wrong."

"Why did the sight of his face drive you into shock?"

"I was scared."

"Yes, you were." He paused. "Who do you know with blue eyes?"

"That's an idiotic question. I know dozens of people with blue eyes." She whirled on her heel and threw open the door. "I'm not going to listen to you anymore. Just stay away from me."

"I will," he said quietly, as he followed her down the steps. "You need to be alone to sort things out. If I can help, I'll be here for you."

"I've had enough of your help." She started down the driveway toward the trees bordering the gates. "And I have no intention of trying to sort anything out. I just don't want to be around you."

"Intentional or not, you're not one who can bury her head in the sand." He sat down on the steps. "You'll start asking yourself questions in spite of yourself. It's not going to be easy, but you have the courage to face it. When you stop running away, come back and we'll talk."

"I don't want to talk." She could feel his gaze on her back as she stalked into the trees. And she wasn't running away, dammit. She was angry and wanted to be alone. It was a natural reaction when someone you trusted betrayed you. And she wasn't burying her head in the sand. Perhaps he had been able to stir memories that the police and psychoanalysts had never been able to bring to the forefront. That didn't mean she'd intentionally hidden them from—

Blue eyes.

She skittered quickly away from the thought. She wouldn't think about it. She wouldn't think of anything Silver had said. He was wrong. There was nothing that—

Running away.

If she was too panic-stricken to think about his words, then there might be truth in what he said.

God, she didn't want there to be truth. She didn't want him to be right.

She could ignore it. She could ignore him.

The hell she could. It wasn't honest, and she always tried to be honest with herself.

Or maybe she hadn't been.

She stopped in the shadow of one of the giant oaks as the thought occurred to her. Maybe the honesty was only on the surface. Maybe she hadn't had the guts to delve deep.

But Silver had said she would have the courage, and he knew her better than anyone.

She leaned her cheek against the rough bark of the tree and closed her eyes.

Blue eyes . . .

The sun was going down when Kerry came back to the house. Silver was still sitting on the top step where she had left him hours before.

She braced herself. She'd hoped to have a little more time before she faced him. "Don't you have anything better to do than hang around here?"

"No." He smiled. "Well, there were a few earth-shattering matters that might have required my attention, but I figured you were more important. When you turn up the heat, it's only right that you stick around to make sure the subject doesn't boil over."

"I'm not one of your 'subjects.'"

His smile faded. "Sorry. That was a stupid thing to say. But I believe you know that I don't regard you that impersonally. What's between us is definitely on a personal level."

Yes, it was. So personal that sometimes she couldn't bear the intimacy. "And I wasn't about to shatter into pieces because you behaved like an asshole and broke your promise." She sat down on the step beside him. "Though I'll never forgive you for doing it."

He looked away from her. "I knew that was a possibility."

"Of course you did. But you couldn't resist diving in and trying to fix things to suit yourself."

"It's what I do." He didn't speak for a moment. "And since you're not spitting fire and brimstone at me, I must have started you thinking."

"I'm too tired to be angry right now. That may come later."

"Soul-searching can be an exhausting process."

"Don't be pretentious. I wasn't searching my soul. My soul is fine and dandy." She paused. "But just maybe you were right about me hiding from what happened that night."

His glance shifted back to her. "Hallelujah," he said softly. "Breakthrough."

"I said maybe." She moistened her lips. "I can't think of any other reason why I didn't— If it was right there in my memory, why didn't it come to the surface in all these years?"

"You tell me."

Her linked hands clenched together. "Blue eyes."

He didn't speak.

"Dammit, don't just sit there like some kind of all-knowing sphinx."

"What do you want me to say? Do you want me to ask the question again? Okay, who do you know with blue eyes?"

"I told you that—" She drew a deep breath. "My entire family has blue eyes. I have blue eyes. My aunt Marguerite had blue eyes. My brother, Jason, has blue eyes."

"And?"

She couldn't speak for a moment. "My father has blue eyes," she said jerkily. "There. Are you satisfied?"

"Are you?"

"Stop acting like a shrink. Answering a question with a question." But she had to get it out. So just say it. "My father and mother were getting a divorce. I remember . . . ugliness. The fights were very bitter. They were fighting about everything. Me, Jason, the house we lived in. The brownstone was my father's family home, but my mother wanted it. When my father took Jason away on that trip to Canada, I was almost glad he wasn't there anymore."

"A natural reaction."

"I felt guilty about it." Strange that she could remember that day her father left the house now when she hadn't all these years. The memory of watching Jason and him get in the yellow taxi that had pulled up in front of the brownstone and feeling only relief. "But I was hurt that he was taking Jason and not me. I thought he didn't love me anymore. I knew he didn't love my mother anymore. Why should he love me?"

"A child is different."

"He took Jason. He never asked me to go. When my father and mother argued, it was always about whether he was going to get Jason. Mother said that Jason and I should stay together, but he wanted his son."

"I believe I'm beginning to develop a dislike for both your parents. You shouldn't have been witness to any of those battles."

She shrugged. "When there's so much hate, it spills over and feeds on itself."

"Like a fire."

She met his gaze. "Like that fire."

"You think your father set the fire that killed your mother."

"I don't know. All afternoon I've been trying to fight my way through the resentment and bewilderment I felt toward him. He hated her. He didn't love me. He didn't want her to have the house. So what happened? The house burned down. My mother died. I ended up in a hospital for two years."

"But you were a witness. He could have found an opportunity to kill you while you were lying helpless during that period."

"But it would have been taking a chance. Who knows? I was in a coma. I could have slipped away at any time. And after I woke up, I didn't remember anything, so he would have been safe. It wasn't necessary to get rid of me."

"Then you do think he did it?"

"I must have thought it was him. I didn't want to believe he was a murderer. If I did, I wouldn't have blocked that memory."

"A man with blue eyes. Not good enough evidence. What else do you remember?"

She shook her head. "Nothing. You pulled that out of me by sheer brute force."

"But you fought me. You didn't let me dig deeper."

"I saw his eyes. The rest of his face was in shadow."

"The eyes were only your first impression. You thought you recognized him and it sent you into shock. I can help you remember his other features."

"It was too dark," she said quickly.

"It wasn't too dark for you to realize he had blue eyes."

"I must have seen the glint from the reflection of the fire."

"Or it could be that it happened in a split second and you only received a quick impression. If I freeze that moment, you'll have time to look at separate features."

"And now you're stopping time? It boggles the mind. My, my, what next?"

"You never can tell. I'm a man of infinite possibilities." His gaze searched her face. "You're scared, aren't you?"

"I'm not—" She stopped. "Maybe. It's too new. I never realized I suspected my father of being a murderer."

"*Suspect* is the key word. Don't you want to know?"

She wasn't sure she did. Every time she thought about it she felt a rising panic. "It's . . . difficult. I could be wrong. It could be a complete stranger."

"And you don't want it to be your father. There's a basic instinct that makes us want to believe in the goodness of our parents. You recognized it in Carmela. That's probably why you were in denial all these years."

"You have it all figured out. It's not that easy."

"I never said it was easy." He paused. "You're not ready yet, are you? You won't let me help you."

"I believe I've had enough of your help."

"No, you haven't. But that's okay. You need time to absorb the shock and become accustomed to the idea that you can't hide any longer."

"I'm glad you think it's okay." Her voice was laden with sarcasm as she got to her feet. "I'd hate not to have your approval. Now, if you'll excuse me, I'm going to find George and see if he's found out anything more about that woman friend of Trask's."

He nodded. "You do that." He stood up. "And, as I'm sure you'd prefer I stay out of your way for a while, I'll tend to a few of those earthshaking matters I mentioned."

"What?"

He smiled. "I got a phone call from Travis. Rosa's arriving at the airport in a couple hours."

"Louisville DFACS has released her?"

"Into Ledbruk's custody. It took some high-level arm-twisting to ignore all the red tape connected with kids removed from the parental home, but they finally did it."

Relief rushed through her. "Why didn't you tell me?"

"You were a little preoccupied. I'm going to pick her up and take her to the safe house Ledbruk's arranged for her."

"Why not bring her here?"

"You promised Carmela that Rosa would be safe. Do you really think we'd provide the safest haven for her? You're a prime target, and Trask would get the greatest enjoyment out of taking me out."

He was right. The greater distance Rosa was from either of them, the safer she'd be. Kerry just didn't like the idea of a child not having anyone but Secret Service agents around her. "She's only twelve."

"I'm sure Ledbruk will arrange to have a female agent stay with her. And I'll get a phone number from Ledbruk where you can call her."

She guessed that was as good as it was going to get. "Explain everything to her. Tell her Carmela will be—"

"Oh, for God's sake, I'm not going to just throw her out of the car and into the arms of the law," he said sharply. "I do have some sensitivity. Hell, I like kids." He started down the steps. "I'll see you when I get back."

He was angry again, and she could almost feel the sting of the barbs in his voice. Well, she couldn't help it. She wasn't about to try to soothe him right now when she was being jabbed by a few thorns of her own.

A few? That was an understatement. She felt torn and bruised and, yes, scared. Silver had ripped aside the dark curtain of lies she'd been telling herself for years, leaving her naked and vulnerable. She wanted that curtain back. It had hidden a horror she didn't want to face yet.

But when would she want to face it? She couldn't go back. Silver, with his usual brutal efficiency, had made sure she wouldn't be able to deceive herself again.

What was she thinking? Fear was one thing, self-deceit was another, and she'd had her fill of it. She wasn't prepared to delve deep into that memory right now, but she'd have to confront it soon.

"Good." Silver was looking at her over his shoulder as he paused before getting in the car. "That's what I hoped when I—"

"I don't care what you hoped," she said coldly. "And stay the hell out of my mind. You've worn out any welcome you might ever have had."

He shrugged. "It was only a matter of time before that happened. It's not as if I wasn't expecting it." He opened the car door. "I'll see you later."

She had hurt him. She could sense the rawness of his pain as if it were her own. Jesus, she couldn't let him do this to her. She pushed him away, blocking him. That was better. She was stronger than she had thought. She had learned a great deal from him in the past days. Soon she might be entirely free of him. No closeness. No togetherness.

Wrenching pain. Terrible loneliness.

She'd get over it. This addictive intimacy was unhealthy, and Silver had proved he couldn't be trusted not to try to control her. Just because he'd done it because he thought it was in her best interests was no real excuse. He was in a position of power, and he'd misused that power.

She watched him back up and then head down the driveway. It was the first time in days that he'd left the estate without her. Was Trask out there waiting?

Trask would love to get rid of me too.

Why was she worrying when she'd determined she had to fight her way out of this bizarre relationship? Ledbruk's agents would follow Silver and guard him. Dammit, she would *not* watch him drive toward the gates. Block him out. Get on with life. Find a way to locate Trask.

She turned and went into the house to search for George.

———

George was on the telephone when Kerry went into the library, but he hung up almost immediately. "Yes?"

"What did you find out about Trask's Helen?"

His brows lifted. "It took you long enough to come and ask me about her."

"I'm asking now. I was a little preoccupied with something else."

"That was obvious. I hoped to take the heat off Brad, but evidently you weren't to be distracted."

"No, but you can distract me now. What did you find out?"

"I believe the lady's full name was Helen Saduz." George went through the pages in front of him on the desk. "Here it is." He handed her a dossier. "Though there's every possibility that it was an assumed identity and she was in this country illegally."

"Is that why no one could tell us who she was?"

He shook his head. "No one told us because no one wanted anyone to know what happened to her."

She frowned. "What do you mean?"

"Do you remember that the report stated that Trask's lab was blown up by orders from the White House?"

She nodded.

"Well, she was in the lab."

Kerry's eyes widened. "What?"

George gestured. "Boom. The lab went up and so did Helen Saduz."

"How did that happen?"

"We think that Trask sent her to the lab to retrieve something he'd left behind."

"What?"

He shrugged. "Papers, maybe a prototype of some kind... Anyway, she had the bad luck to be there when they blew the building."

"But surely they'd have searched for anyone on the premises?"

"The building was sealed. There wasn't supposed to be anyone there. Any search would have been minimal."

"How would she have even gotten in if the building was sealed?"

"Trask must have told her how to do it. He evidently had to have had a way of getting past security when he was stealing components and information from the other people on his team before he took off."

She looked down at the photo on the sheet he'd given her. The woman was brunette, in her twenties with classic features. "She's beautiful."

He nodded. "Absolutely. And memorable. Which was a break for us. Because there wasn't much to identify when they found her in the ashes. They could tell the age and sex by the skeleton, but the rest was guesswork. Or should I say legwork? None of his coworkers had seen Trask with her, but that wasn't unusual. He was a loner and didn't hobnob with any of them. The Service sent agents to backtrack to all Trask's favorite restaurants and found a few waiters who remembered her. They had an artist render a likeness from their descriptions and then sent it to the database. It came up with Helen Saduz."

"Greek?" Kerry was reading the dossier. She stiffened. "And her father is Iranian?"

"Right. Trask was probably negotiating with Iran before the project was even completed. They sent Helen Saduz to clinch the deal. She was smart, well educated, and very accomplished at persuading men to do what she wanted. As you can see by her background, she was an agent who used sex to lure at least four scientists to come over to Iran's camp."

She lifted her gaze from the page. "She succeeded in fooling Trask. He loved her. Maybe he thinks he has reason to go after everyone connected with blowing that lab."

"Remember, he sent her there. He might not have known they were going to blow it up, but he knew he was putting her in danger."

"That's true. But maybe she persuaded him to let her do it. It would be a way of drawing him closer to her."

"Possibly. And of getting her hands on valuable information that could be photographed before it was turned over to Trask."

"But why didn't the government want anyone to know she'd been killed in that building?"

"The CIA stepped in when they found out who she was. They're trying to link the Iranian government with the espionage. She was well known to them, and they smelled an opportunity. They didn't want anyone to know she was dead and persuaded the President to let them pull the records and take over her part of the investigation. They've been sending messages to her contact in Iran in hope of getting something concrete against the government." He made a face. "That's why all the records about her were erased. No leaks."

"Another 'need to know' case? Good God, don't these agencies tell each other anything?"

"As little as possible. Even Homeland Security hasn't broken through all the bureaucratic bull."

"But Trask isn't dealing with Iran now. You said he was negotiating with North Korea. Why?"

He shook his head. "Since you're on such good terms, why don't you ask him? He hasn't contacted you again?"

"No." But she knew it was only a matter of time. She could feel him . . . hovering. "There hasn't been any sign of Dickens either?"

"You'd have been the first to know if Ledbruk had sighted him. No sign of anyone suspicious at Carmela's hospital. No one following you when you leave here every day."

Then what was happening with Trask? Her every instinct told her he wouldn't have taken that defeat at the warehouse without retaliating.

"You're quite safe," George said as he read her expression. "I made sure Ledbruk has assigned top-notch surveillance people to you. They're not going to slip up and let you get killed."

"Like they did with Joyce Fairchild?"

He made a face. "Touché. But they're smart enough to learn from their mistakes."

"I hope so." She turned away. "Silver is on his way to pick up Rosa Ruiz."

"Yes, he told me."

"Did he? Well, I don't want anything to happen to her." She started to turn away. "And I don't want anything to happen to Silver."

"Even though you're pissed at him?"

"That doesn't matter."

He sat back and his eyes narrowed on her face. "No, it wouldn't. You have a very strong relationship."

There was something in his tone that made her turn back to face him. "What's that supposed to mean?"

He gazed at her innocently. "Why, did I strike a nerve?"

"If you did, it's because you meant to do it."

"Discretion forbids me to suggest I could have merely been referring to the fact that you've been sleeping together."

The bluntness of his words surprised her. She'd assumed he was aware that she and Silver were lovers, but he'd never mentioned it.

Why do it now, out of the blue? "That remark wasn't in the least discreet." She studied him. "And out of character. Could it be that you wanted to throw a red herring into the mix?"

He chuckled. "Absolutely. I was quite enjoying my subtle innuendos, but I should have known you'd see through me and call my bluff."

"Then show me your hand."

He was still smiling as he leaned back in his chair. "I paid a visit to Georgetown University while you were in Marionville. It's an open secret on campus that the hydrostatics lab isn't what it seems. There are all kinds of rumors about the people who come and go from that building. Even a few interesting ones about CIA connections. So I came back and called my buddies at the CIA who owe me favors."

"And?"

"It seems the CIA also owes Brad Silver a few favors for some rather unusual contributions. One might even say weird contributions." He tilted his head. "And I asked myself, if Brad is some kind of psychic guru, what are you, Kerry?"

"I'm sure you came up with an answer?"

"Oh, I did. And I found it fascinating. Life is always providing us with new ways to make our existence entertaining."

"Believable ways?"

He nodded. "Do you mean, do I think you and Brad are wacko? I wouldn't risk my neck on something you 'sensed,' but I have an open mind. I've been in enough bizarre situations to know that there's usually a hell of a lot more under the surface than we can see."

"Then what are you going to do about it?"

"Not a thing. Why should I? I merely yielded to temptation to let you know that I was no longer in the dark. My ego required it. As for the extent of your talent, I'm really not interested as long as it doesn't affect me. You can't read my mind or anything, can you?"

"No."

"Brad?"

She hesitated. "It's the last thing he wants to do."

"You didn't answer me." He grimaced. "Or maybe you did. Perhaps I'm not as comfortable with the situation as I thought. I believe we'd better concentrate on getting Trask right away, in case I decide to bail."

He was uneasy. It was only to be expected. It was the response she'd tried to avoid since that day in the hospital when Travis had explained her talent. But for some reason it bothered her that even George would have that reaction. Dammit, she *liked* him. She tried to smile. "We haven't been concentrating on anything other than getting Trask."

"But I've been letting you two carry the load. I may have to step in and escalate matters." He picked up his phone again. "I'll have to think about it. Is there anything else I can help you with?"

It was a dismissal. There was a subtle change in his manner. That hint of mocking subservience was no longer audible. "No, I got what I came for. Another piece to the puzzle." She turned away. "Helen Saduz."

"Kerry."

She glanced at him over her shoulder.

He smiled. "I'm not thinking of you as a freak. But I'm a private person and I have to protect myself from Brad. I have too many secrets."

"Don't we all." This time her smile was genuine. "I know how you feel. But I think you can trust him."

"Do you trust him?"

Her smile faded. "Hell, no. But our relationship is . . . different. You don't have to get very close to him to have a problem."

He threw back his head and laughed. "Christ, I hope not. I'm really not tempted to go to bed with him."

"That's good." She opened the door. "The situation is complicated enough."

15

Silver called her at nine that night. "Rosa Ruiz is safe. She's settled in a nice little house in a nice little subdivision close to the hospital. Agent Jane Dorbin is taking care of her."

"Is she the only agent on duty?"

"No, there are several guards in a house next door, but I thought you'd be concerned for her emotional well-being."

"I am." She paused. "Is she scared?"

"Yes. But not enough to go home. She wants to stay with her sister. Carmela is being released tomorrow, and I'll pick her up and bring her to the safe house."

"Never mind. I want to pick her up."

"And make sure that she's going to be secure." He paused. "I think you can trust my judgment there, don't you?"

She didn't answer directly. "I just want to see them together and safe."

Silver muttered a curse. "For God's sake, you can't stop trusting me on every level." When she didn't reply, he added bitterly, "Or maybe you can. I'll take you to the hospital tomorrow at ten. We'll both pick her up." He hung up.

Jesus, you've been driving around in circles." Carmela gazed suspiciously at Silver. "Are you really taking me to see Rosa?"

"Yes. Didn't you talk to her last night?"

She nodded. "But that doesn't mean she couldn't have been fooled. She's just a kid." She turned to Kerry. "It's legit? You're not going to send us back to my mom?"

"It's legit," Kerry said. "We only want to keep you safe. Silver was afraid we might have been followed from the hospital."

"Were we?"

Silver shook his head. "I don't believe so."

"Don't tell me that," Carmela said fiercely. "I want you to be sure. I don't want anything happening to Rosa."

"Nothing's going to happen to Rosa," Kerry said. "You can trust Silver, Carmela."

"Can I?"

"Yes, can she?" Silver murmured. "What an astonishing statement for you to make. I'm touched."

She ignored him. "He won't let anything happen to you or Rosa." She added, "And neither will I. We just have to be very careful."

"Because of that nutcase," Carmela said. She was silent a moment. "I do trust you—most of the time. It's just . . . hard. This Trask doesn't seem real to me."

"I can understand that," Kerry said. "Sometimes I find him pretty unbelievable too. I wish he was only a figment of my—" She stopped as Silver pulled into the driveway of a small brick house. "This is it?"

Silver nodded as he turned off the car and opened the driver's door. "Stay here. I'll go in and talk to Agent Dorbin and make sure she knows you're no threat. She'll believe me." He strode toward the front door. "Even though you both appear to have your doubts about me."

"I didn't really think he was selling me down the river," Carmela said haltingly to Kerry. "It's . . . Rosa. I don't have the right to— I *do* trust him."

"He was joking. He understands."

"I hope so." She made a face. "You know, I feel . . . It's weird, but I don't want him to . . . I feel like I've known him all my life. No, that's not right. It's not—" She stopped, puzzled. "What the hell. I don't know how to say it."

Togetherness. Linked.

Kerry supposed she should have expected this after Silver had been joined to Carmela on that rooftop. Evidently he had left a little something behind when he'd left her. "Close to him?"

"Yeah, I guess so." She shrugged. "Something like that. You too?"

"You could say that. At any rate, I don't think you should worry about—"

"There she is!" Carmela jumped out of the car as a small, dark-haired girl appeared in the doorway. "Rosa!"

Kerry slowly got out of the car as she watched Carmela run toward the door. Carmela's expression was radiant and full of eagerness. In this moment she looked even younger than her fifteen years. This is how she should look, Kerry thought. This is how all children should look. Full of life. No suspicion. No worry.

Carmela skidded to a stop before her sister. "You okay?"

Rosa nodded. "You?"

"Fine." She took a step closer and gave her an awkward hug. "It's going to be . . . okay. I promise, Rosa."

"Then stop being mushy." Rosa stepped back. "You're making me feel funny."

Kerry smothered a smile at the typical adolescent reaction. The affection between the two sisters was clear, but she could see that neither child was overly demonstrative. Well, what teenagers were? Most of them would be mortified to admit how much they cared about their siblings.

"Nice, huh?" Silver was coming down the path toward her. "Enough to warm the cockles of your heart."

"Don't be sarcastic." She watched the door close behind Carmela and Rosa. "It does warm me."

"I wasn't being sarcastic." His smile faded. "And you know me well enough to know that. I'm glad we managed to get them together. Do you want to go in and meet Rosa? She's a neat kid."

She shook her head. "Soon. I want them to have a few minutes alone together." She met his eyes. "Providing Carmela will ever be alone again. Why didn't you tell me that you're still linked?"

"She knows it?" He frowned. "It's not that strong. Only a tendril or two. It will probably fade away."

"You didn't leave it there on purpose?"

"For God's sake, do you think I like being linked to just anyone? If there's one thing I've learned from our experience together, it's that I never want it to happen again."

Christ, she was actually feeling hurt. Not that she had a right. It was exactly what she had been telling herself all along. "Ditto." She turned away. "I'm going in to meet Rosa. Are you coming?"

"Not now. I'm going to call George and check in." He headed back toward the car. "By the way, I've set up a foster home for Carmela and Rosa when this is all over and it's safe to get them settled."

"Where?"

"Near Georgetown University. It's a nice residential area, and I know some pretty good people who will take care of them."

"Normal people?"

"Yes." He added solemnly, "I do know some normal people, Kerry. Though I admit I have a definite preference for freaks like you."

"Dammit, I'm not—" He was joking. If she hadn't been so tense, she would never have risen to the bait. "I just didn't want them to think the whole world was comprised of people like— They've had enough problems without having to question their view of reality and—"

"I know." He smiled. "Stop trying to explain. You never have to do that with me."

That was the problem, she thought in despair. Even though she was angry and resentful, there was always that comforting feeling of being totally understood and accepted. It was almost as seductive as the sex they had shared.

"Not bloody likely," he muttered as he opened the door of the car. "Don't fool yourself. Not for either one of us, Kerry."

She could feel the heat flood her cheeks as she started up the walk. She should have known that the one thought she'd wanted to keep from him would be the one he'd pick up on. "Let me know if George has learned anything."

"I don't think it will be urgent enough to break into your visit." He got out his phone. "Or he would have called us. But you can be sure I won't close *you* out."

She was aware of the slight emphasis on the pronoun. "Good God, after everything you've done, are you actually trying to give me a guilt trip?"

"Just stating a fact."

She gazed at him in frustration before she jabbed the doorbell. "Damn you, Silver."

————

Anything new?" Kerry asked as she opened the car door an hour later.

"George says everything is quiet on his front. Not a glimpse of anyone suspicious buzzing around any of the people Ledbruk has under surveillance."

"Then where is Trask?" She shook her head wearily as she settled back on the passenger seat. "And what the devil is he doing?"

Silver backed out of the driveway. "At least you know Carmela and Rosa are safe. You should feel better about that."

"I do." She nibbled at her lower lip. "You're sure we weren't followed here?"

"I don't think so, but I can't be certain. There are so many high-tech long-range devices on the market that Dickens or Trask could be out of sight and still tailing us."

"That's a comforting thought."

"It's an honest answer. You don't want comfort, you want the truth."

He was right. Facing the truth was the only way they might be able to survive. "I guess I was hoping for reassurance that maybe Trask had crossed Carmela off his hit list."

"It could happen. But you might ask who'd be his prime target if he decided to do that."

"I'm the logical—" She stopped as her phone rang and she reached into her handbag.

"How is our lovely Carmela? Fully recovered, I trust."

Trask.

She drew a deep breath. "She's fine, Trask. And fully protected. You can't touch her."

Silver muttered a curse and pulled over to the curb.

"I can touch her. Anyone can be reached. It just takes planning and the proper resources."

"Does that mean you're going to try?"

"Perhaps. She's unfinished business, and I detest untidiness. She's definitely high priority since Firestorm was unable to complete its mission. I have to decide how high."

"You're wasting my time. Why are you calling me, Trask?"

"I thought it time. I've missed personal contact with you, but I've been very patient. I've wanted to call you for days, but I had plans to make."

"What kind of plans?"

"Why, I have to show you that you didn't best either me or Firestorm when you saved our little Hispanic charmer. That was only the opening battle."

"Answer me. Are you going after her again?"

"Possibly. Mysteries are so intriguing. I believe I'll let you stay in the dark about that. That's really why I phoned you. I want to think about you worrying, on edge, perhaps even a little frantic. I find that a satisfying picture."

"I'm not frantic, and I'll leave the worrying to the authorities."

He chuckled. "I don't believe you. It's your nature to want to shape events to suit yourself. Like me."

"I'm nothing like you."

"You'll see. When you stand and watch Firestorm at work."

"I've seen it. It sickens me."

"You're lying to yourself. When you saw the warehouse burning, wasn't there a little excitement mixed with the horror you were feeling?" He didn't wait for an answer. "Never mind, you wouldn't tell me the truth. But I'll be able to see it in your face next time. I'm looking forward to it. I'll be in touch." He hung up.

Her finger was trembling as it pressed disconnect. "The son of a bitch."

"Without question. Did he leak anything?"

"No, he just wanted to touch base." Her lips twisted. "He missed me."

"He mentioned Carmela?"

"He knew she'd left the hospital. He said she was a high priority." She drew a shaky breath. "Call back and talk to Agent Dorbin and make sure she knows we've gone to code red."

He reached for his phone. "He may not know where they are. He could have just checked with the hospital to find out she was discharged today."

"And he could have followed us. You said it was possible."

"He told you that he was going after her?"

She shook her head. "The bastard likes to inflict his little torments. Hell, he likes big torment. He did say that anyone could be reached if you had the right resources." Her teeth sank into her lower lip. "Christ, we have to keep her safe, Silver."

He nodded as he dialed. "I'm not arguing. I'll call Agent Dorbin and then Ledbruk."

While he made the calls she leaned back in the seat, staring out at the small, neat homes lining the street. This pretty subdivision was like a hundred others in a hundred other cities. It seemed impossible that a monster like Trask could be operating here.

It wasn't impossible. Nothing was impossible for Trask. He was completely unpredictable.

No, he wasn't unpredictable. Not if she concentrated on what she knew about him. She just had to suppress the panic and try to get one step ahead of him.

"Done." Silver hung up. "Carmela's protection will be doubled. Though Ledbruk said he doubted if it was necessary. He was satisfied with the number of agents he'd assigned to her."

"Maybe. If Trask was working alone. He mentioned 'enough' resources."

"Dickens?"

She shrugged helplessly. "I don't know. It doesn't seem as if . . . We'll have to see."

He started the car. "That's for sure. But I'm not pleased about having to wait and—"

"Turn around."

He glanced at her. "Why?"

"I want you to take me back to the safe house. I'm going to stay there with Carmela and Rosa."

He muttered a curse. "The hell you are."

"Why not? If it's safe for them, it's safe for me."

"That doesn't mean you should mount guard over them yourself."

"Yes, it does." She met his gaze. "Because I'm the only one who may be able to know if Trask is stalking them. I may be able to stop him before he attacks. You know that's true."

His lips tightened. "Then I'll stay too."

"No."

"What if he does have help? What if he sends someone else in to get Carmela? You'd be blind to anyone but Trask. You need me."

But she didn't need to practically live on top of him in that tiny house. It was bad enough occupying a room in his multiroom mansion. "I'm not worried about anyone but Trask. Ledbruk's agents can handle anyone else."

"Well, I'm worried, and I—"

"No, Silver." She looked away from him. "I don't want you. Now, will you take me back to the safe house or shall I walk?"

He gazed at her in frustration before his foot stomped down on the accelerator. "I'll take you, dammit."

———

Dickens had done well.

The farmhouse was almost perfect.

Trask gazed at the two-story cedar house with the wide front porch with satisfaction and a hint of nostalgia. He'd known that if he found the right place it would bring him this wonderful sense of déjà vu. There was no question this was the right place. It would be the ideal environment for Kerry and him to share Firestorm.

He checked his watch. Five to six. Almost time.

The front door opened and a stocky, graying man came out on the porch and then down the steps. Lon Mackey, on his way to feed the cattle in the barn down the road.

"Be sure you hurry," Lon's wife, Janet, called after him. "They've got those college kids on *Wheel of Fortune* tonight."

He chuckled. "I've got almost an hour. Am I supposed to let the stock starve because Pat and Vanna are on?" He didn't wait for an answer as he strolled leisurely down the path.

Trask waited until Mackey had reached the barn before he left the shelter of the trees and followed him. The only drawback to this place was that it was occupied. But that was an obstacle that could be easily overcome by Firestorm.

Then the farmhouse would be completely perfect.

What are you looking at?"

Kerry glanced over her shoulder to see Carmela standing in the bedroom doorway. "Nothing." She turned away from the window. "Some kids playing basketball in the driveway across the street."

Carmela moved across the room to stand beside her and glanced out the window. "Rosa plays basketball. She's pretty good."

"Well, make sure she doesn't decide to go out and ask to play with those boys."

Carmela made a face. "It's hard to keep Rosa from doing anything she wants to do."

"I mean it, Carmela."

"I said it was hard, not impossible. I won't let her do anything stupid." She added awkwardly, "I know you wouldn't have come back last night if you weren't scared."

"I'm not scared."

"The hell you're not."

She smiled. "You're right. I'm scared. But maybe that's good. When you're scared, you're extra careful."

"He's close?"

Kerry shook her head. "But there's a possibility he may try to get closer."

"So you're going to protect us."

"Me and Agent Dorbin and all those agents in the house next door."

"I'd rather rely on you and Mr. Silver."

"That's why I'm here." She glanced at the basketball players again. It was Saturday, and there was no sign the kids would be going inside soon. The game might prove too alluring for Rosa to resist. "Let's go and get Rosa and see if we can find something decent on TV."

"They've got cable. That means we can watch *Buffy* reruns."

"In the morning?"

"Oh, I'll bet you can always watch *Buffy* reruns."

She smiled. "Thrilling."

"You've got to watch *Buffy*," Carmela said firmly. "But it may be a little confusing if you don't know the characters. I'll fill you in and explain as we go—"

Kerry's phone rang.

She stiffened and then crossed to the table where she had placed the phone.

"Kerry?"

Not Trask. Silver. Her breath escaped in a sigh of relief. "Yes."

"I'm on my way to pick you up."

"I'm not going anywhere. I told you—"

"Ivan Raztov is dead."

She went rigid. "How?"

"Car bomb in his Jeep. Blown to bits. He'd just driven into the parking deck at his apartment."

"How could that happen? Ledbruk's men were watching him."

"How the hell do I know? All I heard was the message from Ledbruk that he was dead. We'll find out more when we get there."

"When did it happen?"

"Forty minutes ago. I thought you'd want to examine the site and see if you could pick up anything. You said you could sometimes get vibes after a fire."

Forty minutes. While she was watching those kids across the street and trying to concentrate on sensing any threat from Trask, he'd been striking at Raztov.

Blown to bits.

"Kerry?"

"Yes, I want to go. I'll make sure they're on the alert here and meet you in the driveway."

———

Blown to bits.

The metal of Ivan Raztov's Jeep had been twisted and blown to the far corners of the parking garage, and the fire that had enveloped it had spread to the other cars in the garage, melting paint and tires.

Jesus.

Kerry took a deep breath before going around the police tape cordoning off the area and walking toward Ledbruk. "Where is he?"

"That's a good question," Ledbruk said. "The forensics team is trying to scrape enough of him together to get a definite ID. It's a good thing it went off here. The concrete walls took most of the hit. Trask must have used enough plastic to blow up the apartment building."

"How could this happen? Wasn't his car watched?"

"Hell, yes. We think that the bomb may have been planted at the parking lot of the lab where he's working now. The agent who was doing the surveillance said a Buick rear-ended a Cadillac and his vision of the car was blocked for a few minutes."

"And he wasn't suspicious?"

"Of course. But the woman had two kids with her, and the accident seemed legitimate. His view of the Jeep was only blocked for a few minutes and the woman waited to file an accident report."

"Then you should have a record to help ID her," Silver said.

"We're working on it. We think her driver's license and insurance card were phony," Ledbruk said curtly as he turned away. "Don't tell me my job, Silver."

"I wouldn't think of it." Silver nudged Kerry toward the forensics team. "Kerry wants to examine the crime scene. We'll be careful not to compromise it."

"There's not much to compromise. Between the fire and the sprinkler system it triggered, it's going to be hell to find any credible evidence." He turned away. "Just don't get in my way."

"A woman..." Kerry murmured as they moved across the garage. "And two kids?"

"It appears Trask may be recruiting new talent."

"It doesn't—it feels wrong." She shook her head to clear it. "Something's not right."

"What?"

"I don't know." She moistened her lips. "Find me a piece of the metal of Raztov's Jeep."

"That shouldn't be hard. It's all over the garage." He nodded at a length of twisted steel that might have once been a safety bar. "That do?"

"Maybe. I hope so." She moved toward the metal bar. "God, I hope so." She knelt and reached out and touched the bar.

Nothing.

Her hand closed around it.

Hurry. Fasten the plastic to the pipe and get out from under the Jeep. Two minutes.

Got it!

Roll out and under the car beside the Jeep. Keep low . . .

"Something?"

She glanced up at Silver. "Trask didn't plant it. The man was black, about forty, and very experienced with explosives. He's done this before."

"Name?"

She shook her head.

"Are you going to be able to find out anything more?"

"I doubt it. I've never been able to see more than a few impressions and the moment of the act itself." She grasped the metal again, held it for a moment, and then released it. "No, it's gone." Panic was suddenly soaring through her. She jumped to her feet. "Let's get out of here."

"Can you give a description to Ledbruk?"

"Not now." *Wrong. All wrong. Not Trask.* "What would I tell him?" She was almost running toward the crime tape. "Let's *go.*"

He caught up with her as she reached the street. "What the hell is the matter with you?"

"It wasn't Trask." She got into the car. "It should have been Trask but it wasn't."

"So it was someone he paid to do it. The result is the same."

"But he always does it himself. And he always uses Firestorm. It's his child, his weapon of choice. We know Raztov was on his hit list. Why didn't he use Firestorm this time?"

His gaze narrowed on her face. "And do you know?"

She was working it out as she spoke. "Because Raztov wasn't as important as another target he'd chosen. He wanted him dead, but he was willing to give up the pleasure of killing him if it meant using his death."

"Using it for what?"

"A distraction." She was starting to shake. "He wanted to focus attention on Raztov and—" She reached for her phone. "Oh, God. Carmela. He's going after Carmela. What's the telephone number at that safe house?"

"I'll do it." He dialed the number on his phone. "It's ringing. Kerry, it will—" He spoke into the phone. "Agent Dorbin? Silver. Is everything okay there?" He nodded reassuringly at Kerry and she went limp with relief. "No, we just wanted to check." He hung up. "No problem. It would be almost impossible for him to get through the protection we've set up for Carmela and Rosa."

"Almost. Not completely." Her relief was ebbing by the second. "I'm not wrong, Silver. Raztov was a distraction, and Trask specifically mentioned Carmela on the phone. That's why—"

"Son of a *bitch*." He was dialing the phone again. "A goddamn red herring."

"What?"

"He wants to hurt you. He wants to get his own back. He doesn't have to use Carmela. She was just the person in the forefront of your mind. By calling you he made damn sure that's where she'd stay."

"What are you saying?"

"I'm saying he could hit closer to home." He spoke into the phone. "George, check with the agents in Macon and make sure Jason Murphy is okay. No, don't call me back. I'll wait."

Shock knifed through her. "Jason? You said he was well protected. You promised me."

"He is, dammit. He and his wife had double the protection Ledbruk assigned Carmela. I don't see how Trask could touch him."

But she could tell he was afraid that Trask had managed to do it. "Resources," she said dully. "He said anyone could be reached if you had enough resources." She reached up and rubbed her temple. "Not Jason. Dear God, I hope you're wrong."

"So do I," he said grimly. "I hope to hell that—" He broke off, listening. "Jesus." He hung up the phone. "Jason left his hotel four hours ago. The agent following him lost him almost immediately, and Jason's not answering his cell phone." He paused. "Agent Fillmore thinks your brother was deliberately trying to lose him."

"That's crazy. Why would he do that?" Her hands clenched into fists. "He's making excuses. They've got to find him, Silver."

"George says they're doing their best. Fillmore called Jason's wife and then the number of every friend and business acquaintance she gave him." He started the car. "He was about to contact Ledbruk and give him a report when George got through to him."

She moistened her lips again. Four hours. "Jason may be dead already."

"I won't tell you there's not a chance he might be. But from what you've told me I'd think Trask would want you there to bear witness. He did with Carmela at the warehouse."

Hope soared. "You're right. I should have thought of that."

"You're working on automatic and thinking with your emotions."

She glared at him. "Of course I am. He's my brother, dammit."

He smiled. "That's better. Nothing like being pissed to start the adrenaline flowing. Now, what would make your brother try to lose the agent who was trying to protect him?"

"He wouldn't do—" But if Jason had done it, there had to be a reason. She tried to think through the haze of fear smothering her. "Trask might have got to him. Maybe he used something or someone to force him to do what he wanted."

"It would have had to be a pretty powerful tool for him to run that kind of risk."

"Laura," she said suddenly. "He'd do it if he thought Laura was in danger. He'd do anything to help her."

He shook his head. "George said Jason's wife was safe and accounted for."

"Thank God."

"Anyone else?"

"Me. If Trask could convince him that I was in danger."

"But he would have phoned you and verified."

That was true. Then there was only one other possibility. "My father. Jason loves my father. And he wasn't under any protective surveillance."

"Do you have your father's cell-phone number?"

She nodded. "In my phone book." She searched in her purse and pulled out the dog-eared leather book. A moment later she was dialing her father's number. After six rings she got his voice mail. She hung up and dialed again. Same voice mail. "He's not answering."

"Any other numbers you can call?"

She shook her head. "He has an apartment in Boston, but he's seldom there. He moves around a lot on assignment but tries to stay in the South so he can be near Jason. He's a reporter, dammit. He should be answering his cell phone."

"I'll get George to keep on calling him." He started to dial. "Though I somehow doubt he's going to answer."

No, he wouldn't answer if Trask had him. Fear iced through her. And, if Trask had her father, he also had Jason. "I'll talk to George. You head for the airport. We have to get to Macon. Trask is a wanted man. He wouldn't risk taking Jason very far from where he captured him."

"I agree." He pulled out into traffic. "I think that's where we have our best chance to find Trask."

"We're not going to have to look very hard. He took Jason," she said unevenly. "He'll want me to find him so that I can watch my brother die. We just have to wait for him to call me and tell me where and when."

Silver's lips tightened. "You're not going to play the martyr and walk into a trap. No way."

"I don't know what I'm going to do." She looked him directly in the eye. "Except I'm not going to let Jason die. That's not an option."

"I won't let your brother die, but I can't—" He broke off with a curse. "I'm not getting through to you. Listen, you have me and you have the whole damn Secret Service to help find Trask. You're not alone."

"And if I call on Ledbruk for help, Trask might decide the game he's playing with me isn't worth the trouble and kill Jason."

"And if you die, Trask wins and it still won't save Jason. Use your head."

Her head wasn't working too well at the moment. She was too scared. "I'm not going to let him die," she repeated.

He was silent a moment. "Okay. We try not to involve Ledbruk, but you're not closing me out."

"I had no intention of closing you out. I may need you."

"How gratifying. And I'm telling George to beat it to the airport and meet us there. We may need him." He shook his head as she opened her lips to protest. "He won't talk to Ledbruk if I tell him it's a condition for letting him in on the action. He wants Trask."

She thought about it and then nodded. They might need all the help they could get, and George could be trusted if he gave his word. "So do we all. But not at the risk of getting Jason killed. Make him understand that." She drew a deep breath. "Now get us to that airport."

16

George took the key from the clerk at the rental-car desk at the airport in Macon. "I'll run out and bring the car around to the front entrance like the obliging bloke I am."

"I hope you've been discreet as well as obliging," Kerry said.

"Certainly." He picked up his duffel bag. "My training forbids any other course of action." He smiled. "Don't worry, Kerry. I haven't been talking to anyone. I wouldn't do anything to hurt you."

She believed him. "What the devil is in that duffel? It took you forever to get through security."

"Oh, just a few necessary items. I was caught off guard, but I managed to grab a few things." He enumerated. "A machete, an M-16, and an H&K 94 SG-1. Oh, and a garrote."

Kerry blinked. "And they weren't confiscated?"

"I also had my old Secret Service ID and a special letter from Homeland Security. But you notice they did make me check it through anyway. I approve. It's exactly what they should have done." He smiled. "Give me five minutes." He strode out of the terminal.

She felt a surge of warmth as she stared after him. There was something very comforting about having George working with them.

"It probably won't take five minutes," Silver said as he took her elbow. "This is a tiny-ass airport. We could probably have saved time by going with him. Is your cell phone on?"

He was thinking that Trask might be calling her. Lord, she hoped he was right. She felt blind and helpless. "I turned it on right after the plane landed. I had two missed calls."

"No message?"

"That's not Trask's style. He'd want to hear how scared I am. He'll wait until—"

Her phone rang.

She hurriedly pressed the button.

"I do hate wasted effort, Kerry," Trask said. "Your father's phone kept ringing and ringing, but he couldn't answer."

Her hand tightened on the phone. "Where's my brother, Trask?"

Silver's gaze narrowed on her face.

"With his father," Trask said. "Such a wonderful bond between them. It's enough to warm the heart."

"I want to talk to him."

"Not your father?"

"I want to talk to my brother," she repeated.

"I'm sure you do, but that's my decision. I believe I'll leave that as a special treat. Here's your father."

"Do whatever he says, Kerry," Ron Murphy said. "Jason's life depends on it."

"I want to talk to him."

"Jesus, I know you don't trust me, but do you think I'd lie to you about Jason?" he asked roughly. "You're the one responsible for this mess. Now, get Jason out of it before this bastard kills him."

"Did you call Jason and tell him that Trask had you?"

"No, Trask called him, and he went to my motel room and found a note Trask left for him. I could never have been forced to put Jason in danger."

"But you'd do it to me."

There was a silence on the other end. "What do you want me to say? I can't let him kill Jason. Neither can you."

"No," she said wearily. "I can't let him kill Jason. Put Trask back on the line."

"You'll cooperate?"

"Put Trask back on."

Another silence and then Trask came on the line. "I told you that the bond between them is something at which to marvel. But I can see why you wouldn't feel equally warm toward your father. He didn't even ask why I wanted you here. Do you suppose he could guess?"

"I want to talk to Jason."

"Tonight. I'm going to send Dickens to escort you. I have to warn you that he's very good at knowing if he's being followed. If he notices any sign of that, he'll call me and that will mean an early and disappointing conclusion to this business. The same result if you and he don't show up in a reasonable time from the moment he picks you up. I'm not having Dickens pressured by the Secret Service into giving out information. And when you arrive here, you'll find that I have ample protection to guard your father and brother. Not that anyone is going to interfere with us once we come together. I've already told the guards that all I'd have to do is press one button and Firestorm would turn the house into a bonfire. Now, if you're a good girl and follow instructions, hopefully you can talk to your brother on the way here."

"Where is here?"

"I believe you'll know it the minute you see it. I hope so anyway. I chose this place very carefully. Such a homey little house."

"I'm not coming until I know my brother is alive."

"Your father told you he was alive. Well, not in so many words, but do you think he'd lure you here if there wasn't a chance to save him?"

"Then why can't I talk to him?"

He sighed. "Unfortunately, your brother refused to add his plea to that of your father. He decided to sacrifice himself for you."

She moistened her lips. "And you killed him?"

"Kerry, you know me better than that," he chided. "It would spoil everything if I couldn't watch your face when Firestorm kills him. He's quite safe right now."

Right now.

"What do you want me to do?"

"Are you in Macon yet?"

"I just arrived."

"Very good. You didn't waste any time. I knew you'd come running once you found out about brother Jason. Where are you staying?"

"The Hyatt."

"Dickens will call you when he's near the hotel and tell you where to meet him tonight."

"What time?"

"Nine." He paused. "I hope you know how important you've become to me. I had to think long and hard before I decided to give up the satisfaction I'd feel to rid myself of Raztov in the way he deserved. But I had to throw a few red herrings out to keep you from thinking about your brother."

"Carmela wasn't enough?"

"She probably would have sufficed, but it took me a while to set up our little meeting tonight. Everything had to be just right, and I was afraid you might become suspicious at the delay and start thinking about other possibilities. So, since I'd made a deal with my honored patron anyway, I decided to let him dispose of Raztov a little early to cloud the waters."

"Who killed Raztov? Dickens?"

"God, no. Dickens can be lethal, but he has no skill. I had to make a deal with my future patron to hire an expert. He was very expensive."

"But you had the 'resources.'"

"Exactly. At least, Ki Yong had and he was willing to cooperate. But he struck a hard bargain, so I'm determined to make sure that our time together is worth it."

"What kind of bargain?"

"I'm going to let him take care of Senator Kimble and Handel right away so that my business here is completed. He's very tired of waiting. But in return I have to turn over Firestorm to him immediately after I finish here tonight."

"You'll never turn over Firestorm."

He chuckled. "How clever of you to realize that. But Ki Yong isn't that smart, even though he thinks he is. He knows he needs me for the initial testing period. And I'll be able to dangle the carrot for quite a while before I decide to skip away from him."

"Like you skipped away from our government? And killed Helen Saduz while you were doing it."

"I didn't kill her. She killed herself." His tone was sad. "I truly loved her. She would have completed me."

"But you didn't feel guilty sending her into danger."

"How could I feel guilty? She wanted to take Firestorm away from me. I knew from the moment she offered to go get those rather unimportant documents I'd left behind that she was going to betray me. I was profoundly grateful when the lab blew and I wasn't forced to deal with her myself."

"So grateful you immediately started negotiating with someone else for Firestorm."

"I couldn't bear doing business with anyone connected with Helen. It hurt too much."

"You're incredible."

"Yes, I am. And so are you. That's why tonight is going to be such a fascinating experience." He hung up.

Silver was studying her face as she pressed disconnect. "Okay?"

She nodded jerkily. "He has my father and I think he has my brother. But he wouldn't let me talk to Jason. Dickens is going to pick me up tonight and take me to Trask."

"What time?"

"Nine."

"Shit." He looked at his watch. "Three hours. We don't have much time."

Three hours. Fear jolted through her. "You and George are out of this. He said that Dickens would know if he was followed."

"He won't know." He opened the front entrance. "Trust me."

"I can't trust you. Jason is too—" She stopped, trying to gain control. She had to trust someone. "What can you do?"

"I'll be waiting near the place where you're to meet Dickens. I doubt if he'll be closed to me. I'll go in and he won't even know I'm there."

"What if he is closed to you?"

"Don't borrow trouble. Trask is the exception. I'll get through. If Dickens is difficult, I'll bulldoze him like a tank."

The words were confident, cold, and totally brutal. "Bulldoze? You said you had to be careful. You were worried about Carmela. Would Dickens's mind survive that kind of treatment?"

"No, but his body's not going to survive long either, so it doesn't matter." He looked at her. "He's a dead man, Kerry. I don't know if he helped Trask kill Cam, but I'm not taking any chances. Sorry if you're feeling qualms."

She wasn't feeling sorry for Dickens. It was shock at the ruthless transformation she was seeing in Silver that was causing her to question him. She hadn't seen this side of Silver since those first days she'd known him. "I'm not arguing. I don't know if he was an accomplice to your brother's murder, but I know he helped Trask set up Carmela to burn to death." She started toward the car George had pulled up to the curb. "Do what you have to do."

"Oh, I will," he murmured as he opened the car door for her. "And it won't be letting you go dancing into that booby trap alone."

She looked up at him as she got in the car. "In the end I'm going to have to go in alone. He mentioned a house where he's keeping Jason and my father. If you rush that house, he'll press his little button and everything will go up in flames."

"With him in it?"

"I'm not taking a chance with that crazy bastard when Jason's life is at stake."

"Then you'll have to get us a target," George said. "Can you get him to stand in front of a window or door where we can pick him off?"

"Maybe."

"And maybe not," Silver said. "You don't know yourself if you'll be able to push him to do what you want."

"You will *not* rush that house. You don't run any risk that might endanger Jason."

He lifted his shoulders and slammed the door. "Okay, we don't rush the house."

But he hadn't addressed her last, more comprehensive demand, she realized.

Well, she couldn't argue with him right now. The full impact of Trask's call was hitting home. She had to garner her strength and try to rid herself of this cold, paralyzing terror.

The call came from Dickens promptly at nine that night.

"Walk two blocks east to the Baptist church. I'll be there in ten minutes. If there's anyone with you, I take off and I won't be back."

"I'll come alone." She hung up the phone and turned to Silver. "Ten minutes. The Baptist church two blocks east."

"We're on our way." He headed for the door. "Come on, George."

"Action, at last," George said as he stood up and grabbed the duffel at his feet. "Let's go."

"Wait," Kerry said. "How long will it take you to get into Dickens's mind?"

"Not long. It depends on the subject. Five. Ten minutes."

"And how will I know whether or not he's blind to you?"

"You'll know. I won't let you go two blocks with the bastard if I can't do it."

"The hell you won't. I'm not going to forgive you if you do something to make Trask—"

"What have I got to lose?" There was a touch of recklessness in his tone. "You're not big on forgiveness where I'm concerned, anyway. If it comes down to you or your brother, guess which one I'm going to choose?"

"Out, Brad," George said quickly. "Haven't you ever heard honesty is overrated in a situation like this?" He opened the door and pushed him out. "It seems Brad's barbaric instincts are at the forefront, Kerry. I'll make sure you see us tailing you, since Brad says he'll make Dickens blind to us. I don't quite believe him, but it's a most interesting situation."

Interesting? It was terrifying, she thought. "You listen to me." She stared Silver directly in the eyes. "You've broken your promise to me before, but you can't break this one. You promise me right now that you'll wait until I give you a safe target to take out Trask."

"And what if you find you can't push him? I'm supposed to sit around and watch him burn you all to kingdom come?"

"Then you'll have to trust me to find some other way to lure him to expose himself."

He just looked at her.

"Promise me, Silver."

He was silent a moment. "I promise you I'll give you your chance." The door closed behind him.

It wasn't the answer she'd wanted, but it was all she was going to get. It was bad enough that she wasn't sure she could influence Trask. Silver had become an unknown quantity.

She checked her watch. Only a few minutes had passed, but it was time she left. How did she know what Dickens would do if she wasn't there on time? He was another unknown quantity. Her life seemed to be full of them.

The blue Ford made three passes around the block where Kerry stood before it pulled over to the curb.

"Get in." Dickens leaned over and opened the passenger door. He took her purse, rifled through it, and then ran his hand over her breasts and arms.

She pulled away. "What are you doing?"

"Checking for weapons and to see if you're wearing a wire." He gave a nervous glance at the Baptist church and then down the street. "Let's get out of here. I want to get this over with."

"No more than I do." She slammed the car door. "Where are you taking me?"

He dialed his phone. "I've got her. No, there's no one around. I made sure before I picked her up. I know my business, Trask."

"I want to talk to him."

He shrugged and handed her the phone.

"You said I could talk to my brother, Trask."

"Ah, yes. I was a little worried he'd be reluctant, but I believe he has something to say to you."

Jason came on the line. "Kerry, don't come. Find a way to get away."

He was *alive*. She hadn't realized until this moment how frightened she'd been that Trask had already killed him. "Are you okay?"

"Don't come," Jason said desperately. "My life isn't worth—"

Trask came on the line. "He must care a great deal for you. He's a smart man, and I don't believe he has any doubt that his own life is on the line. Now, you be good and don't give Dickens any trouble. He's nervous and he can be quite lethal. I don't want anything to happen to you." He hung up.

She handed Dickens the phone. "He said you're nervous. That must mean you don't like doing this. Wouldn't it be smarter to help me save my brother and bring Trask down?"

"Shut up." He pulled away from the curb. "I'm not nervous. Everything's fine. This is all going to be over tonight."

Where was Silver? He'd said five or ten minutes, and yet Dickens showed no sign that— Hell, what did she expect? She didn't know whether she'd even be able to tell any difference in Dickens's behavior if Silver had managed to get into his mind. "They'll catch you, Dickens."

"No, they won't. I'm through here the minute Trask gets on that plane with Ki Yong." He turned the corner and headed for the edge of town. "I'll disappear into the sunset with a bag full of money."

"If Trask doesn't decide you'd be perfect for one of his experiments with Firestorm." With seeming casualness, she shifted her gaze to the side mirror. Her heart sank as she saw the street behind them was empty. No one was following.

Dear God. Had something happened? Don't think about it. If she had to cope, she'd do it. "Trask is capable of any deceit. You must know what he did to Fairchild. What's to keep him from—"

A brown Lexus had turned the corner with George at the wheel.

Get closer," Silver said curtly. "You can't lose him."

"No?" George raised his brows. "You'll excuse me from being ignorant of the process, but wouldn't you be able to find out where he's going?"

"I don't want to waste the effort," he said curtly. "I'm having to dig down beneath layers of slime to find out what I need to know about the guards surrounding the farmhouse."

"Farmhouse?"

"That's where he's taking her. A farmhouse. Dickens had to scout it out for Trask."

"Then maybe you should find out where it is so that we can go ahead and wait for—"

"For Christ's sake, it doesn't work that way. I don't know this asshole's mind. I have to pick up what I can until I get control."

"Okay," he said soothingly. "Just a suggestion. You're right, I don't how this works. Who the hell does?"

"Sorry." Silver's gaze never left the car ahead of them. "Just get closer and don't lose him."

"You're sure he won't see us?"

"No, I'm not sure, but I don't think he will. I believe I've already got that much control."

"Then it's a chance."

"Hell, yes."

Wʜat is it?" Dickens was staring suspiciously at Kerry's face.

Shit. "Nothing." She looked hurriedly away from the mirror and tried to distract him. "Trask's not stable, you know. Anyone's a target."

It didn't work. Dickens's gaze had followed hers to the mirror.

She tensed. Jesus, George had moved to only a few car lengths behind them and wasn't even trying to avoid being seen.

Dickens shrugged and glanced away. "Shut up and stop trying to spook me. I'm not buying it."

And he clearly wasn't seeing the brown Lexus behind them.

Silver had gotten in.

She let out a deep sigh of relief. "I was just trying to save you from making a mistake. I won't waste my breath." She forced herself not to look at the mirror again. "Where are you taking me?"

"Into the country."

"Where?"

He scowled. "I can't tell you. Trask wants it to be a big surprise. Stupid..."

Sʜe smelled the smoke first. Harsh, acrid, evoking a hundred nightmare memories.

Her heart leapt. Had that bastard already turned Firestorm loose on Jason?

"Get Trask on the phone, Dickens."

Dickens shook his head. "The place is right around the bend up there."

"Then hurry up, dammit."

"Don't give me orders." He glared at her. "I'm tired of everyone telling me what to do."

She barely heard him. They were already going around the curve in the road and she saw the fire.

A large barn down the road, burning, blazing, devoured, and devouring.

Anguish tore through her. *Jason.* "Let me out."

"Do what you please." Dickens had pulled up in front of a farmhouse. "I've done my part."

She threw open the door and jumped out of the car. The intense heat struck her as she started at a run for the barn.

"He's not there, Kerry."

She whirled to face the man who'd spoken behind her.

Trask had come out of the house and was standing on the front porch. There was no mistaking him. The childlike blue eyes staring at her were the same as the ones she'd seen in his photo. The reflection of the fire lit his amused smile as he started down the steps. "You keep thinking I'd cheat myself by being too impatient. After waiting all this time I want to enjoy every nuance."

She ignored everything but that first sentence. "Jason's not in that barn?"

"No. I even turned the livestock out of their cozy home. I merely wanted to light a beacon to welcome you."

And scare the hell out of her, she thought bitterly. "Where is he?"

He jerked his head toward the house. "In a room upstairs with his father. They're so affectionate I knew they'd want to be together."

"I'm going now," Dickens said as his foot pressed on the accelerator. "I'm supposed to meet Ki Yong down the road to get my final payment."

"By all means." Trask didn't look away from Kerry as Dickens drove away. "Though he may have a surprise," he murmured. "I doubt if Ki Yong is going to be prepared to pay him off. He'll probably prefer to rid himself of a potential witness in a more lethal manner."

"Good. I don't care about Dickens. I want to see Jason."

"You will." His gaze returned to the burning barn. "But I want you to look at my fire first. I've gone to a great deal of trouble, and I want to savor it with you."

Her gaze followed his to the flames. "I'm supposed to appreciate this destruction?"

"Maybe not. All you see is a shell with no true meaning." He smiled. "But it's not as empty as you think."

She went rigid. "You told me Jason wasn't in there. You said he was upstairs. And that you let the livestock out."

"Oh, I certainly did. But I couldn't insult Firestorm by not providing the fuel it deserves."

"What did you do, you son of a bitch? Who's in there?"

He chuckled. "The owner of this farm and his wife. But don't worry, they felt no pain tonight. I was forced to dispose of them last night. I couldn't chance them causing me any problems." He shook his head. "Too bad. The effect would have been much more powerful on you if I'd been able to provide you with a little serving of hors d'oeuvres before the feast."

Horror chilled her. She closed her eyes. Fight it. Fight him. She wouldn't have a hope of controlling him if she was this frightened.

She opened her eyes. "I don't want to see you cremate those poor people. That idea is as sick as you are. Take me to see Jason."

He frowned. "You're disappointing me." Then his expression cleared. "But I shouldn't be surprised. I expected a battle. Do you recognize this house?"

"Why should I? I've never seen it before."

"True. But the Bartlett pear trees? The river?"

She had not even noticed the river in back of the barn. Something stirred in her memory. "What are trying to tell me?"

"I gave Dickens an old newspaper photo of the Krazky house and told him to find one similar."

"Why?"

"Because that was probably the most thrilling kill I've ever made. The first time is always special, isn't it? And it means even more to me since that moment when I watched you looking at the ruins of that prick's house and suddenly realized how close we were." He took a step closer and she could see the tenseness of his muscles, the excitement glittering in his eyes. "Look at the fire again and let yourself open to it. Doesn't it excite you?"

"No. Take me to Jason."

He hesitated. "Very well." He turned away. "End of Act One, and no applause. But it's early yet. I'll do better." He started up the porch steps. "Come along. We'll reunite you with your family."

She dared a quick glance down the road as she climbed the steps. She'd seen no sign of the Lexus since a mile or so before she'd smelled the smoke of the burning barn.

Don't panic. Naturally Silver and George wouldn't let any of the guards watching the place see them.

But, God, she felt alone.

There he goes," George murmured as Dickens's car drove past the stand of trees where they'd parked. "Should we take him out now?"

"No. He's on his way to get his payoff. We may need to use him to get to Ki Yong."

"Wouldn't it be better to put him out of action? We don't know how long this business is going to take."

"No." Silver was quickly drawing lines on the pages of his notebook. "He's already out of action."

George looked at him. "I beg your pardon?"

"I had to damage him to get the information I needed," he said absently as he put four crosses on his page. "He's brain-dead."

George shook his head. "He's driving that car."

"No, *I'm* driving that car. And I'd better park it so that I can concentrate on something besides Dickens."

"Christ."

Silver glanced at him. "You don't believe me?"

"I do believe you. That's what's scary. Did the CIA know you could do stuff like this?"

"No. Do you think I'm an idiot? I gave them what I wanted to give them. Information is one thing, mind control is another. They'd either try to use me as a tool or consider me a threat they couldn't handle. Probably the latter. I'd have a sanction on me within a few months."

"So when you park his car and withdraw from Dickens, he dies?"

"Not right now. I'll leave a few tendrils to keep his vital signs going. We may need him later."

"I don't believe I like the idea of using a"—George searched for a word—"zombie. I'd rather trust myself. If you don't mind, I'll take care of whatever you'd planned for Dickens."

"Suit yourself."

"I will." He looked down at the page on which Silver was writing. "Tell me about the crosses."

"One guard on the riverbank behind the barn to keep an

eye out for boats." He pointed to another cross. "A sniper with a Springfield behind the shed at the rear of the house." He pointed to the third cross. "This sentry is a half mile ahead, guarding the road to the farmhouse."

"And the last one?"

"Ki Yong and his driver. He's waiting ten miles from here for Trask to finish his party so that he can whisk him off to the airport to board his plane to Pyongyang."

"You found out all that from Dickens?"

He shrugged. "It wasn't easy. Otherwise I might not have had to damage him." His lips tightened. "But I probably would have done it anyway." He looked down at the map. "We have to move. Which target do you want to take first? The one guarding the road?"

George nodded as he opened the car door and got out. "And the one on the riverbank. You get the sniper. Then we both go for Trask."

"Not until Kerry presents us with a target." Silver fell into step with him. "We'll stay outside and wait until we can get a clear shot at him. I promised her."

George's lips lifted sardonically. "And how long will you keep that promise if you see Trask become a threat to her?" He lifted his hand. "Never mind. Don't answer that. I don't want you to get angry and 'damage' me."

"I wouldn't do that."

He glanced at him. "No, I don't think you would. Do me a favor and wait until I join you before you try to take a shot at Trask. I don't want to insult you, but I have a better chance at making the score."

"If you get there fast enough."

"Oh, the pressure." His pace quickened. "It should take us no more than five minutes to take out that first guard. Then the road to the farmhouse will be clear."

———————

Where are they?" Kerry glanced around the shabby living room as she entered the house. The windows were wide open and a faint haze of smoke was sweeping into the room, giving the room a surreal, otherworldly look. "Where's Jason?"

"Upstairs." Trask was already climbing the staircase and motioned her to follow him. "I'm sure they'll be very glad to see you. Particularly your father. He seems quite desperate, ready to clutch at any straw on the chance of saving your brother. Not really very intelligent behavior. But then, that's what you're doing too. Emotion makes reason fly out the door, doesn't it?" He opened the door at the top of the steps. "I gave them the master bedroom. Nothing is too good for the people you care about, Kerry." He stepped aside. "Go on."

She hesitated.

"You think I may have an unpleasant surprise for you? Perhaps two cadavers like our farmer and his wife?" Trask smiled. "You won't know until you go in and see for yourself."

She forced herself to enter the room.

No cadavers. Dear God, they were *alive*.

Her father was lying on the bed, tied to the bedpost, and Jason was roped to a chair by the window.

"You shouldn't have come, Kerry." Jason's voice was hoarse, his face pale and strained. "I told you not to do it."

"She was right to come, Jason," Ron Murphy said. "This is her responsibility." He looked at Trask. "You've got her, you've got me, why not let Jason go?"

"Jesus." Jason gazed at him in horror. "Do you think I'd walk out of here without the two of you? If there's a chance for you to get out of here, do it, Kerry."

"Save your breath. Trask has no intention of letting anyone out of here alive." Kerry's gaze shifted to Trask. "Isn't that right?"

"Regretfully." Trask smiled. "Even though I feel you're a true soul mate and I'm hoping for a breakthrough, it would require time I don't have to test you enough to be sure of you. Unfortunately, Ki Yong isn't giving me any leeway." He glanced at his watch. "I'm allowing myself your company while Firestorm takes your father and brother, but you'll have to join them before I leave here tonight."

That telltale glance Trask had given his watch scared her. Time might be running out.

Stall. Give Silver and George time to get here.

"Then may I spend a few minutes alone with them?"

He hesitated and then shrugged. "Why not? It might make the experience more poignant." He headed for the door. "I'll give you fifteen minutes."

Immediately after the door closed behind him, she ran to the nightstand and opened the drawer. No scissors, dammit. Nothing sharp enough to cut the ropes.

"What are you doing?" her father asked.

"Looking for something to get you free."

If she broke the window, Trask would hear it before she could get the shards . . . She went to the bureau and started going through the top drawer.

Nothing.

"Try to make a deal with Trask," Ron Murphy said. "You didn't even try to persuade the son of a bitch. He's your brother. Save him."

"Shut up, Dad." Jason said to Kerry, "If you can find a way to get out of this, do it. Don't think about me."

"Don't be stupid. I love you. I'm going to get you out of this."

"I don't deserve you giving up your life to save mine."

"The hell you don't." She added unevenly as she started

quickly going through another drawer, "Besides, Laura would kill me if I let anything happen to you. I'm not about to—"

"I thought you wouldn't waste time on sentiment when you had an opportunity to take action." Trask had opened the door. "See how well I know you? Move away from that chest and come downstairs with me." He pulled a small remote device out of his pocket. "I really don't want to set Firestorm loose just yet unless you force me. I cherish my time with you."

She stiffened, her gaze on the remote. Then she moved slowly toward him. "And where is Firestorm?"

"Set up outside in the van."

"Then why would you press the button? You'd be incinerated like the rest of us."

"I know which areas it's going to strike first. I'd be able to get out in time." He gestured to the door. "After you, Kerry. We're going to sit down in the living room and talk, and I'm going to look at you and anticipate." He looked down at the remote. "I imagine you'll be doing a little anticipating as well."

17

oftly.

Quietly.

Don't spook him.

Silver moved closer to the guard behind the shed. He was a tall, lanky man and he was definitely jumpy. He was pacing restlessly back and forth, his watchful gaze on the house.

Could he get in his mind?

He probed.

He'd probably be able to do it, but the guard wouldn't be easy and it might take too long. He didn't know how much time he had left.

He didn't know how much time Kerry had left.

Screw it. Forget about getting in. Go for it.

Be quick and silent. Get behind him and break the bastard's neck before he could raise that rifle.

Sit down." Trask gestured to the couch. "Make yourself comfortable."

"Is that supposed to be a joke?"

"A little one," Trask said. "But I would like you to be as much at ease as possible."

She coughed. "Then why don't you close those windows? How can you stand that smoke?"

"I like it." He sat down in the chair opposite her. "You'll get used to it. The fire's too far away for it to be dangerous."

"How comforting."

"I've no desire for you to be afraid. I've won and I hope I'm a generous victor."

"If you were generous, you'd let Jason and my father go." She couldn't wait any longer. No matter how much she dreaded what she had to do. Concentrate. Dive into that horror he called a brain and meld with him. She drew a deep breath and made the effort.

Ugliness. Darkness. Fire. Scorched flesh.

She scurried away from that slime. Oh, God, she couldn't do it.

"My generosity doesn't extend that far," Trask said. "I've been looking forward to this for too long. I hate being bested. Almost as much as I hate being humiliated."

"Stupid nerd." Tim Krazky straddled him, sneering, "Crybaby." He got off him and glanced around the crowd of kids watching them before he turned back to Trask. "Go home to Mama, asshole."

Get even. Get even. Get even.

Flesh melting into bone. Screams. Heat.

Joy.

"You're not answering," Trask said. "Don't you believe me?"

Talk. If she didn't reply he might get impatient and she'd lose the time she needed.

Smell of roasting flesh.

Talk? She was so lost in his visions she could barely function. Death and hate and burning flesh were so much a part of his memory and motivations that she couldn't get near his mind without being overwhelmed by them. She wanted to run away.

Stay there until you become accustomed to his mind. Then look for a path. That's what Silver had told her to do. Stop being a coward. Force yourself to do it. Find that damn path.

But she had to keep Trask talking while she was concentrating. She wildly searched for a subject. Of course: the element that dominated his life. "I don't imagine many people have had the courage to humiliate you. But you were only a child when you set the Krazky home on fire. I'd think you'd choose a simpler way to punish him."

"There's nothing simpler than fire." He leaned back in his chair. "Nothing cleaner. Nothing more beautiful."

A little girl pounding on the window, trying to get out.

Block out his memory. Move behind the ugliness. Try to find the right path. If there is one . . .

"Why do you think that most people name a fireplace as one of the most desirable features in the home?" Trask asked. "Everyone is fascinated by the flames and by the idea that they can control them. Foolish. The flames only lie in wait for a careless moment and then they get their own back." He looked down at the remote in his hand. "I'm the only one who can control it."

That path went nowhere. Try another. Keep him talking. "Firestorm. But do you control Firestorm or does it control you?"

"It's my creation." He frowned. "Of course I control it."

"I don't think so."

She'd found a new path! Deeper, more convoluted. Move fast. Jesus, let this be the one.

"Think what you like." His frown faded. "And I can see why you'd think Firestorm was all-powerful. That's how I intended it to be. From that first moment when I decided that to control fire was to be close to Godlike. It's not often a man has a chance to be God."

She'd gone deeper in his mind than ever before. This might be the right one. Move faster. Pray that she didn't run into a barrier. "How?"

"Power. Doesn't the Bible say the world is going to be destroyed by fire?" He snapped his fingers. "I can do that."

She was there! Now settle in. Then start to push. What had Trask said? "Firestorm isn't that powerful."

"Not yet. Give me another five years and I'll have it ready. The ultimate power. You'd be impressed. Too bad you're not going to be around to see it."

She braced herself. Could she do it? Only one way to find out. *Push!*

He didn't seem to notice. "I can't tell you how I regret not letting you—"

Suggest, not demand, Silver had said.

Push. Smoke. Dizzy.

Trask shook his head as if to clear it. "That smoke coming in the window must be pretty thick."

Thank you, God. "I didn't notice."

Smoke. Lungs tight. Eyes stinging. "Usually I don't notice either. I . . . like it."

Lungs hot, hurting. Push. Push. Push.

"I'll get a glass of water. That will probably make me feel better." He rose to his feet and went to the sideboard and poured water from a pitcher into a glass. "Drinking is the only good use for water, you know. I detest it in principle."

Throat tightening. Choking.

He started hacking. "Christ. I can't even . . . swallow. I guess I'll have to close it. Too bad." He moved toward the window across the room.

Throat tighter. Lungs burning.

"Christ, I can't...breathe." He shoved the remote into his pocket as he fumbled at the window.

Keep it going. Searing pain in the lungs.

Was he framed against the window? What if he got the window down and moved away? Christ, what if Silver didn't have enough time?

Push.

"Shit." Trask jerked his hands away from the window. "It's hot, dammit."

"What do you expect when you spend your life setting fires? You're bound to get burned sometime." Keep his hands busy and away from that remote. "Try again."

"Are you crazy?" He moved away from the window. "I can't touch that sill without something to protect me. Maybe we should go outside. The smoke's probably less in front."

And it would be harder for Silver to get his shot with a moving target, dammit.

"Come on." He moved toward the front door. "Get going."

―――――

I almost had him." George started to curse as Trask disappeared from view. "Two seconds more and I would have had him in my sights."

"Keep a bead on the window," Silver said. "He'll be back."

"It's your call. But I wish I was that sure," George said. "Sometimes you only get one chance."

He wasn't sure, Silver thought. If Kerry had lost control, then she might not be able to get it back. Every instinct told him to rush into that house and forget this damn waiting game.

Give her more time. Trust her.

God, he hoped he wasn't making a mistake.

———

What are you waiting for?" Trask looked over his shoulder at Kerry as he reached the front door. "I told you we're getting out of here."

"I'm coming." She slowly rose to her feet. She had to keep him inside. If he went out on the front porch she couldn't be sure what he'd do. Hell, maybe he'd decide to activate Firestorm from his van. Keep control. Stop panicking. She could do this.

"Going outside is probably a good idea." She moved toward him. "I can't breathe either. Do you think the smoke will be less there?"

"It can't be—" He broke off, coughing. *Push. Lungs throbbing as he reached the front door. Eyes stinging, tearing.*

He stopped. "Maybe not. It seems heavier here by the door."

"Then what are you going to do?"

Push. The window. The window.

"What I should have done before. Close that damn window." He jerked a doily from the chair and strode toward the open window. "I'll just use this to protect my hands."

"Yes, you do need protection."

"What?" He looked over his shoulder but he reached out for the window, framed again in the lighted opening. "Why are you smiling?"

"Am I smiling?" If she was smiling, then it was with savage satisfaction. "I wonder why? Maybe it's because you're not going to be God after all."

"Why do you—"

The impact of the bullet drowned out his words.

"No!" He jerked as the bullet struck him in the chest. "Shit."

He was falling, but even as his knees buckled he was reaching for the remote in his pocket. "I won't let you—"

She was across the room in a heartbeat. She knocked his hand away and grabbed the remote. "No way, you bastard."

"Bitch," he whispered. "You won't win. Won't let you—"

"I've already won. You're a dead man, Trask."

The hatred in his mind was overwhelming. Even in this final moment there was no fear of death. Only fire and darkness and a thirst for revenge.

Swirling.

Poison.

Fire.

"Get out." It was Silver's voice, Silver standing beside her. "What the hell are you still doing in his mind? Get out!"

She couldn't get out. She was chained, held by the sheer power of evil in the center of Trask's being.

"Let him go!" Silver said.

Trask's eyes were glazing over, but she sensed somewhere, somehow, he suddenly *knew*. He smiled. "You're...caught.... Told you I'd win. Coming...with me."

"The hell she is." Silver was there between them. "Hold on, Kerry."

She screamed in agony as she was torn free and spiraled wildly into darkness.

———

It's okay, Kerry. Wake up, dammit."

She opened her eyes to see Silver's face over her. "I'm... awake." She sat up, her gaze on Trask. His eyes were still open, but his face was twisted in the final death rictus. "Gone?"

"Dead as a doornail." He stood up and helped her to her feet. "May he burn in hell."

Her knees felt weak, and she held on to him for a moment before she could stand alone. "No fire and . . . brimstone. He'd . . . like that too much."

"Sit down." His gaze narrowed on her face. "You're still not good."

"Better than if you hadn't pulled me out of that bastard." She sank down in the easy chair. "Where's George?"

"After he took his shot at Trask, he bolted and went after Ki Yong." He hesitated. "I should go see if I can help him."

"Then do it. I'll rest for a few minutes and then go release Jason and my father. They're tied up in a bedroom upstairs. Don't worry, I'll be fine."

His gaze raked her face. "Yes, you will." He turned and headed for the door. "This shouldn't take long. I probably won't get there in time to be of use to George. He moves pretty fast."

She leaned back and closed her eyes after he left the room. Lord, she felt weak.

She took another couple minutes to gather her strength. She was drained. It seemed impossible that it was over, that the evil that was Trask had vanished from the earth.

But Jason didn't know he was safe, and it wasn't fair to leave him in ignorance.

She slowly got to her feet and moved sluggishly toward the kitchen. Find a knife to cut the ropes and then go upstairs and free them. Where was the cutlery drawer? The smoke seemed heavier in here. She opened three drawers before she found a butcher knife.

She heard it as her hand closed on the hilt of the knife.

Crackling.

Above her, through the ceiling of the kitchen.

Where the bedrooms were located on the second floor.

She stiffened. "No!"

She whirled and ran out of the kitchen and up the stairs. Smoke, everywhere. Not from the barn. Here in the house!

You still won't win, Trask had said. The bastard had set a timer to go off automatically on Firestorm if he didn't press the remote.

Flames licking the banisters of the staircase just as they had in Jason's house in Macon.

No, it was more like the fire in the brownstone all those years ago.

Mama, where are you?

Right behind you. Get help, Kerry.

I don't want to leave you.

Why was she remembering that night now? She wasn't a little girl anymore. She wasn't helpless. She could save Jason.

She tore toward the bedroom door that was outlined in fire.

Smoke. So much smoke. Cover her face.

No time. She threw open the door and ran into the room. The curtains and carpet near the window were blazing.

Jason was slumped forward against the ropes but he was still conscious, coughing. "Get out of here, Kerry!"

"Don't talk, breathe shallow." She sawed at the ropes.

The fire jumped from the curtain to the bed, and the bedspread caught fire.

"Get . . . Dad," Jason gasped.

She glanced at her father.

A man standing under the light post.

Blue eyes.

"After I get you free."

"That whole bed will be blazing in seconds. Get him."

"I'll have you loose . . . in a minute." The ropes gave way at last and she tore them off him.

He grabbed the knife from her and leaped to his feet. The next moment he was standing beside his father and cutting him free. Kerry ran forward and helped him tear the ropes away. Then Jason was picking him up and carrying him toward the door, lurching, coughing.

Kerry grabbed a throw from a rocking chair and covered her mouth and nose as she ran after him. The first floor was now ablaze.

God, the smoke was so heavy she couldn't see Jason anymore. Where was he?

Then she saw him.

And she screamed.

Jason was on fire, his entire body blazing. Yet he still was clinging desperately to his father.

"Drop him, Jason. Get down on the floor." She pulled her father out of Jason's arms, threw the blanket over Jason, and tried to beat out the flames.

"No." His voice was choked. "Too late. Save . . . him." He stumbled back toward the burning railing. "Have to save . . . him. Have to make—" The rail gave way and he fell backward into the flames below.

"Jason!" His name was a cry of agony.

Try to get to him. It seemed hopeless, but maybe there was a chance. . . .

She started toward the stairs and then stopped short.

Save him. Have to save Dad, Jason had said.

But she didn't have to save him. Not when there was the slightest chance of saving Jason instead.

Yes, she did.

She picked her father up in a fireman's lift and struggled down the stairs.

Smoke. Darkness. Blazing patches of intense flame in the living room below.

And Jason was in the center of one of those hellish patches of fire.

She'd been lying to herself. There was no possible chance. No one could live through those flames. He was probably already dead.

"I'll take him." Silver was beside her, lifting her father from her shoulder. "Get the hell out of here."

She looked back and knew she had to make a try. She started back toward the fire. "Jason. I can't leave him. I have to—" She stopped as she watched the staircase buckle and fall toward her.

Or was it the butt of a gun coming down?

Man by the lamppost.

Yes, that was it. Fire.

Mama.

Mama, who could never be saved.

Try! Run.

But the path to the lamppost across the street was like an unending tunnel.

It's too late.

The gun coming down.

Blue eyes . . .

Yellow walls. White linen sheets. A plump nurse moving quietly, adjusting the oxygen in the tank beside her bed.

Hospital.

"Where . . ." She sounded like a frog.

The nurse turned and smiled. "Hi, I'm Patti. I bet your throat could use a little water?" She put a straw to Kerry's lips and held it while she sipped it. "You're at Macon General, and you're doing fine. A few first-degree burns and smoke damage to your lungs. You were lucky. Evidently that was quite a fire."

Jason ablaze as he fell into the flames below. She closed her eyes for a moment as waves of pain assaulted her. "Yes."

The nurse's smile faded. "Well, maybe not so lucky, but you still have people who care about you. Mr. Silver hasn't left the waiting room since they brought you in. Would you like me to check with the doctor and find out if you can see him? He's making his rounds now."

"Not yet. What about . . . my brother?"

She didn't answer. "I think I'd better let you talk to the doctor."

Because the nurse didn't want to tell her that Jason was dead. "Is my father in this hospital?"

She nodded. "Two rooms down. He's doing fine. They'll be releasing him later today."

"Would you ask him to come in and see me?"

"Now?"

"Please."

"I think that would be a good idea." She moved toward the door. "I'll check with the doctor."

Jason.

She closed her eyes as the tears welled up and ran down her cheeks.

"You want to talk to me?"

She opened her eyes to see her father standing in the doorway. He didn't look as fine as the nurse had led her to believe. He looked tired and pale and . . . broken.

"Jason is dead?"

His lips twitched. "Yes. You made a mistake. You should have saved him and not me."

"I tried. He wouldn't have it. He's the one who carried you out of that room."

He flinched. "No one told me that."

"No one but me knew it. The last thing he said was that you had to be saved." She paused. "He loved you very much."

"I loved him."

"I know." She paused. "You loved him so much that you protected him all his life."

He stiffened. "I don't know what you mean."

313

"He was the one who set the fire the night my mother died. It was Jason who was standing underneath that light post watching the house burn."

"You're crazy."

She shook her head. "It was Jason."

He stared at her. "You remembered?"

"Tonight." Her lips twisted. "I hoped it was you. But it wasn't. It was Jason who set the fire, Jason who hit me. All I want to know from you is why? Why would he do that?"

"He didn't mean to hurt you. He loved you. He was just a mixed-up kid." His lips tightened. "It was my fault. Mine and that bitch Myra's. We tore him apart. You were just a kid, but he was an adolescent and he knew what was going on. He was always a sensitive boy, and all that quarreling... It nearly destroyed him."

"So he killed his own mother?"

"He didn't mean to kill her. I'd told him you and your mother were going to leave for Macon to visit your aunt. I thought it would be easier for him to leave Myra and come with me to Canada."

"If you were both in Canada, how did he get back to Boston?"

"I got called away on assignment when we were at a lodge outside Toronto. The story was only supposed to take a couple days, but that was the window of opportunity for him. He told me later that he'd been planning on torching the brownstone before we even left Boston. He'd been hiding gasoline in the alley behind the house. After he dropped me off at the airport, he took my rental car and drove back to Boston." His lips twisted bitterly. "Anyone can get back from Canada to the U.S. if they want to avoid the border checks. Jason was always very clever."

"Yes, very clever," she said dully.

"Stop *blaming* him," he said fiercely. "He didn't mean to hurt anyone. I tell you, he thought the house would be empty. He knew I didn't want her to have it. He knew how much it meant to me. He did it for me."

"But it wasn't empty. He knew that when I ran up to him in the street. He might have saved our mother."

"It was probably too late then."

"He could have tried."

"He panicked. He was in shock." As she continued to stare at him, he said harshly, "It's easy for you to judge. I tell you, I did this to him. Myra and I. Do you know how tortured he was for years later? While you were in that coma in the hospital, I was having to get psychiatric help for Jason. He wanted to go to the police and confess. He wanted to be punished. I wouldn't let him. They would have locked him up for something I'd caused."

"So you got him to agree to keep it secret?"

"He deserved a good life. It wasn't his fault."

"Not in your eyes. I don't think he ever got over the guilt. When he was trying to save your life, he wouldn't give up. I don't think he could bear the idea of another death laid at his door. He said something . . .

I have to make—

"He didn't get to finish, but I think he was trying to say he had to make amends."

"He was a good boy." She could see the tears glinting in her father's eyes. "And he didn't want to hurt you. Over and over he said that he should be the one in that coma, not you."

"What did he hit me with? I thought it was a gun."

He shook his head. "A piece of lead pipe he found in the alley where he stored the gasoline. He didn't even know why he picked it up. I guess he was scared to death about what he was going to do." He drew a shaky breath. "When you woke up from the coma, he did his damnedest to be the best brother he could to you. You can't deny that."

"No, he was a good brother. No one could have been kinder or more loving."

"See? He couldn't help— It was my fault." He turned away.

"And his death is my fault too. He'd never have walked into Trask's hands if it hadn't been for me." He suddenly turned back to her. "You think that I wasn't a good father to you. That it was all Jason." He defiantly lifted his chin. "Well, maybe it was. I had a duty to him. I'm sorry, but there wasn't room for you."

She stared at him without answering.

He muttered, "The funeral is the day after tomorrow." He turned and left the room.

She closed her eyes as the tears came again. She wasn't sure if she was crying for her mother or Jason or maybe for the father she'd never really had. Maybe for all of them.

Christ, it hurt.

She finally fell asleep near dawn.

Silver was in the chair beside her bed, holding her hand, when she woke a few hours later.

"Don't tell me to go away," he said harshly. "It's not going to happen. I won't bother you. I'm just going to...I want to be with you."

He was with her in that most intimate sense, and she didn't want to shut him out yet. She needed the comfort of that closeness. "You know about...Jason?"

"How could I help it? Since the moment you found out that house was on fire your mind was screaming. That's why I turned around and came back." His lips tightened. "And you never stopped screaming. Only, after you woke up here, it was more like a child sobbing. Do you think I could stay out when you were hurting?"

She tried to smile. "Well, at least you didn't try to fix me."

"I was tempted. But that would keep you from healing. You have to deal with the pain."

"Yes, I do. I . . . loved Jason, Silver."

"I know you did. I guess we know why you didn't want to remember who torched the brownstone. You couldn't stand the idea that the one person you loved was responsible."

"I still can't stand it." Jesus, don't cry now. She changed the subject. "Ki Yong?"

"George took care of him and his driver. Very efficiently, very lethally. I called Travis and told him to get a team down here to get rid of the body so that we wouldn't have a diplomatic incident."

"Firestorm?"

"Destroyed. We're still searching for Trask's pad so that we can gather any documents. There were a few gas receipts in his van that might yield some answers. If not, they'll just keep looking."

"They have to find everything. Someone else might . . . Armageddon. Dangerous . . ."

"They'll find it. Don't worry. Just go back to sleep."

"I will. I don't want to stay awake. Sad . . ."

"I know." His hand tightened. "It will get better."

"I hope so." She said unevenly, "I'm going back to Atlanta right after the funeral. Will you have someone bring Sam down to my house in Atlanta as soon as possible? I need to work."

He nodded. "I'll do it myself."

She shook her head.

He shrugged. "I thought I'd try. That's okay. I'll give you some space." He paused. "How long?"

"I can't . . . I don't know. Maybe it would be better if we went our own ways."

"Hell, no. That's not acceptable. How long?"

"Stop pushing me."

"Why not?" His lips twisted. "I'm so good at it. It's the one facet of my personality you found valuable." He stood up. "But you're not fair game right now. I'll let you have your period of mourning."

She glanced away from him. "And I want you to try to break the link."

He stiffened. "Bullshit."

"It's time we were both free."

"Then break it yourself. I like it fine just the way it is."

"Why? You told me yourself you hated to be tied to anyone."

"You know why." He leaned forward, grasped her chin, and turned her face to look in her eyes. "If you'll admit it to yourself. Tell me, how long do I want to be tied to you? How many years? How many ways?"

She couldn't tear her eyes away from his. For the first time he'd left himself totally open to her. Open, vulnerable, and lonely. Dear God, how lonely.

The moment seemed to go on into eternity. It was Silver who broke it by turning away from her. "I'll stay apart from you as long as I can stand it." He walked out of the room.

Christ, she was crying again. It made no sense. He was everything that was prickly and rude and dominating, and life with him would never have the normalcy she'd craved all these years. She'd been right to attempt a total break with him. It was the smart, practical path to take.

And this feeling of desolation would go away soon.

————

The long trail of cars was winding its way out of the cemetery as Kerry moved toward the limousine where Laura was talking to her father.

Don't look back at that tent that sheltered the coffin. Keep your eyes on Laura. You can get through this.

Laura turned as Kerry approached. Her eyes were red from weeping, and she looked haggard and . . . old. "It was a nice service, wasn't it? So many people loved him. . . ." Laura's voice broke and she had to stop. She drew a breath before she continued. "Ron was telling me how brave he was. He was a real hero."

Kerry's gaze shifted to her father. He looked almost as broken as Laura. "Yes."

"But then, I always knew what a wonderful man Jason was." She shook Ron Murphy's hand. "Thank you for being so kind to me. I know it wasn't easy for you to talk about it, but it means a lot to know the details of that night."

"Call on me if there's anything I can do for you. Jason would want me to take care of you." He glanced at Kerry and said jerkily, "Good-bye, Kerry." He walked quickly toward his car, parked behind the limousine.

Kerry turned to Laura. "Do you want me to go back to the hotel with you?"

Laura shook her head. "I'm going to my mother's house. I thought maybe I'd try to work in her garden. I need to keep busy, and there's so much life and rebirth in a garden." She tried to smile. "It's funny how we go back to the womb when something tragic happens, isn't it? We haven't progressed very far from the time we lived in caves."

"I think that's a great plan." Kerry hugged her and then stepped back. "I'll call you in a few days."

Laura nodded. "Yes, do that." She got into the limousine. "But not now. Later . . ."

Kerry stood watching as the limousine pulled away from the curb. Life and rebirth. Even in her despair, Laura was reaching out to try to find some sense, some continuity to the meaning of life. She wished she was that far along in the grieving process.

"Kerry?"

She whirled to see Carmela standing a few feet away. "What on earth are you doing here?"

Carmela didn't answer, her eyes on the green awning over the grave. "What a bummer. I'm so sorry, Kerry."

"Thank you. It's very kind of you to come."

She shifted uncomfortably. "Well, I didn't exactly come to tell you that. I kind of hate funerals."

"Me too. So, why did you come?"

"To take care of you."

"What?"

"Mr. Silver said you needed someone to take care of you. He said you were pretty much alone right now and that sucked. He said that Rosa and I had the job." She rushed ahead as Kerry started to speak. "I told you I owed you. I don't want a free ride. I can do all kinds of things. I'm good at cleaning and cooking. I'll get my driver's license soon and then I can do the grocery shopping. I'm going back to school, but Rosa can help out."

Kerry shook her head in bewilderment. "Silver sent you?"

She nodded. "He picked us up last night and drove us down here. He said he'd originally had another place in mind for me to go, but this was better. He knew I wouldn't want to go to strangers. I don't trust many people." She moistened her lips. "So I said sure, I'd take care of you. Rosa and I packed our bags and Mr. Silver dropped us off here."

"And where's Rosa?"

Carmela nodded down the road. "I told her to wait for us by your SUV with Sam. Now, can we get out of here? Rosa doesn't like cemeteries."

Rosa or Carmela? "Cemeteries are sad, not scary."

"Whatever. Can we go?"

Silver had no right to do this to her, dammit. He was trying to run her life, trying to "fix" her.

"It's okay. Don't feel bad." Carmela's gaze was on Kerry's face. "Mr. Silver was wrong, wasn't he? You don't want us."

"I didn't say that."

"Because you feel sorry for us." She lifted her chin. "Well, you don't have to do that. We'll get along just fine."

Pride, fear, and resilience were all there in her expression.

And the dawning of life and rebirth.

"Silver wasn't wrong." She took Carmela's arm and started toward the car. "I do need you. I'm a lousy housekeeper and I'll work you to the bone. And Sam will drive you crazy. You have no idea how messy he can be." Her pace quickened as she saw Rosa. "And I have a yard that I've neglected terribly. I want to plant something wonderful. How are you and Rosa at gardening?"

EPILOGUE

OAKBROOK

ELEVEN MONTHS LATER

It's about time you got here." George's face lit with a smile as he opened wide the front door. "I was about to bail. Brad's been as mean as a lion with a thorn in his paw."

"So what's new?" She stood there smiling at him. "Brace yourself. I'm going to do something that will offend your sensibilities." She took a step closer and gave him a quick hug.

He sighed. "Some people never learn to strike the correct balance."

"I didn't say good-bye. So I said hello. That's the correct balance. I wasn't sure you'd still be here, George."

"Why not? I never leave a job unfinished. It's terribly untidy."

"I thought you considered this job finished."

He shook his head. "But I think it may be heading in that direction. How is our Carmela?"

"Fine. She and Rosa are both in school and doing well. I don't know what I would have done without them. There's nothing like teenagers to keep you from dwelling on the past. They always live in the present."

"That's what Silver intended when he sent them to you."

"I know." She looked past him at the library door.

He was there. She could *feel* him.

And soon she would see him, touch him.

"I believe I'm de trop," George said. "Did you bring luggage?"

"Just Sam." She was already on her way down the hall. "Would you get him out of the car?"

"My pleasure. I haven't been trampled or slurped in months."

She paused outside the library door. Stupid to be this scared. She knew what waited for her in that room.

She opened the door.

"Good God, it took you long enough." Silver scowled as he turned away from the window. "If I wasn't as patient as Job, you'd be in big trouble."

She started to laugh. "Patient? You? Are you trying to tell me that you haven't been nudging me for the last three weeks?"

He was silent a moment. "Maybe a little. But you could have shut me out anytime."

"Yes, I could. And I should have done it. You've got to learn to let me make my own decisions. You're lucky I'd made up my mind before that."

He went still. "About what?"

"That I shouldn't let you intimidate me, that I can hold my own with you, and that there's no reason why I shouldn't take what I want."

"And what do you want?"

She smiled at him. "You tell me." She started across the room toward him. Jesus, she loved him. She loved every rough edge, every protective barrier, and that vulnerability he'd never show to anyone but her. "Come in and see for yourself."

He looked at her, and a slow smile lit his face. "Don't mind if I do."

Linked.